SNOW WITCHING WHITE

A Glass Slipper Adventure Book 6

Allie Burton

Allie Burton

Snow Witching White

A Glass Slipper Adventure

CONTENTS

INTRODUCTION

Join my newsletter and receive a free book!

Details at: www.allieburton.com

Stay in touch with Allie:

allie@allieburton.com

www.facebook.com/AllieBurtonAuthor

www.instagram.com/allieburtonauthor

"Mark my words, there's trouble a-brewing'." - Grumpy

Chapter One

*"**I**f you want to lift the curse of the Wicked End Prophecy, you must discover your heritage by returning to the Inferis Coven."*

The words punched my gut and soothed my soul. I'd recently learned I was part witch, and a coven would have the resources to teach me about my witch powers. Powers that surprised me and were uncontrollable at times. And if I was a witch from this coven, I might have distant family members living there. Temptation had me standing on edge.

"Are you going to go, Destiny?" Stone clasped my arm in a death grip, still protective and possessive at the same time.

He flung his head back and his long blond hair swung behind his back. Lips, that I just kissed, flattened in a disapproving line. His Adam's apple bobbed on his thick neck. The movement led down to his broad chest on display in the open deep V on the black leather tunic he wore. Black leather breeches encasing his muscular legs took a defensive stance.

I loved how he protected me, especially after what I'd been through with the banshees. But I'd also learned I could protect myself. I had powers. Strange, unusual powers. More than banshee powers, it must be the witch magic.

The message I received continued to pound in my head. The request—no threat—in the message swirled in an unstable pattern. My heart weighed heavily. "Do I have a choice?"

I never had a choice. Forced into a hermit existence by my grandfather—although I'd learned it was to keep me safe. Imprisoned and forced to work for the evil Regent Theobald. Kidnapped by banshees, lied to, and almost forced into marriage. "I might have family in the coven. They might know more about my unusual magic."

My powers scared and enthralled me, showing up at unexpected times. I didn't know when or why or even how. Before my adventures started, I'd had no abilities. I wasn't special at all. Now, I was a powerful banshee and witch, and I was enticed into learning what I was capable of.

Scanning the early morning scene, I took in the banshees celebrating their new leader. The females were especially loud, dancing and singing around what used to be known as the Proving Sphere. A campfire roared. The brownies celebrated their freedom in their small group, hugging and jumping. My friends stood nearby watching the party. Overseeing the activities was a large dragon, Drago.

The coven might know more about the prophecy.

Doom settled in my lungs. The Wicked End prophecy was never far from my thoughts because I was somehow part of it. No one I'd met fully understood the meaning of the prophecy, but with that name it couldn't be good.

"What if the witches treat you the same way the banshees did?" Stone gestured to the group of banshees celebrating and discussing how they planned to move forward.

My shoulders dipped. I'd thought the banshees would become family. That they respected me and my grandfather. Instead the sinister Grand Lord Justicar had planned to use me and my powers to advance his plans with the evil regent. I'd put a stop to his machinations. In doing so I'd freed the banshees, especially the females. And the brownie slaves. Now, I'd allocated a new leader in my stead.

An almost seventeen-year old shouldn't have such great responsibility, shouldn't be alone in the world without family. I heaved a deep breath. I wasn't alone. I had my friends and I had Stone.

His strength in body and character emanated beside me. His perseverance and loyalty had him searching for me, not giving up. He was gorgeous inside and out with green eyes melting me from inside out. I wasn't alone.

The thought helped me shake off the dread weighing me down. I whipped my hand on the shula skirt. "If the witches mistreat me, you'll be by my side to help stop them."

Stone glanced down and then up at the sky. His lips twisted together in an uncomfortable position. He wasn't telling me something. We'd stepped away from our group of friends and now I wished they were closer for moral support.

Holding in the frisson of nerves, I took his hand in mine and tried to get him to look at me. "What?"

Lifting his gaze, his mouth dropped open. Then he scanned Prince—no King—Zacharye, and Princess Ellery.

The newly anointed king stood with his arm draped around the shoulders of the beautiful fairy princess. They'd met without knowing either of them was royalty and fallen in love. Their tale was a romance with adventure, betrayal, and deceit.

Even though the king and princess were engaged, she had some hold on Stone. "What."

His sheepish expression told me he held a secret. "I agreed to be an advisor to King Zacharye."

My heart dropped and my lungs constricted. He'd made plans without me. "Living in the palace?"

"Yes." His clipped tone and pinched expression didn't tell me much.

"Oh."

"With you." He lifted my hand to his lips and kissed my white knuckles. "Living in the palace *with you*."

The kiss and his words ricocheted tingles of pleasure inside of me. Living together at the palace would be how we'd imagined it as kids. When Stone had just been Vi, not a double agent or a lord. And I'd been me—a kid banshee without unusual powers.

The coven's invitation, or threat, stood between what I needed and what I wanted.

"I mean, not living-living together." He backpedaled on his claim causing my tingles to fizzle. "We'll have our own rooms at the palace. We'll be together, seeing each other every day, and someday..." He bit his lower lip and stared down. "Someday...there will be more."

"Oh." The fizzling squashed. He wasn't ready to commit.

"Your inflection says so much without even a word." He dropped my hand and placed it on his hip. "What're you thinking?"

I didn't know what I was thinking. My brain rattled. He'd accepted a great position without any thought to what I wanted. He'd committed to work for the king in a tenuous time in the kingdom. I understood the king needed Stone by his side. But I wanted him to be beside me.

If I was half witch, shouldn't I find out about the witch part of my heritage? Wasn't it time to discover me? Professor Nilsen had said something similar. How I needed to find myself. Doubts and insecurities swirled inside causing an internal storm. I'd taken control of the banshee clan, and yet I still didn't know who I was. Getting my childhood memories back had opened more questions than answers. Answers I needed to know.

Biting my lip, I needed to do what I thought was best for me. "I'm thinking...I need...to visit the coven."

The second those words spewed out the air swirled around me, lifting my shoulder length hair, ruffling my cloak, and rattling the beads around my neck. Waves rippled in lustrous concentric circles in front of me. A popping filled the atmosphere. The circles firmed and became an oval shape larger than me. I could see my friends Cassia and Lukas on the other side, although not clearly. Cassia rubbed Drago's snout. The dragon's body shimmered through what resembled a filmy glass.

My gaze widened watching the atmosphere change in front of me. What was happening?

The popping grew louder, and the billowing winds stopped. A sucking sensation tugged at my skin, pulling me toward the strange luminescent oval wanting to swallow me whole. My stomach tightened and my muscles tensed.

Stone yanked me back and wrapped an arm around me.

"Oh my stars!" Cassia rushed to our side, the cloak she wore flapping open. She never took off the cloak because she didn't want to reveal the shula skirt and bikini top underneath that the banshees had forced her to wear. "It's a witch's portal."

"Don't get close, Cassia. It almost sucked in Destiny." Stone protected everyone. He'd do a great job working for King Zacharye.

"It won't hurt her." Cassia approached the portal with caution. "Destiny, did you agree to go to Inferis Coven?"

Her question caught me off guard. I hadn't really made a definite decision. Apprehension squirmed in my gut. "I said, *I think* I need to go."

"You did agree." She jumped up and down, clapping her hands. "That's why the portal appeared. Although I've never seen this one."

I'd never seen one, ever. My nerves spiked. "I thought I'd visit." I wanted to make it clear.

Stone's sharp emerald orbs went wide. His gaze darted between me, Cassia, and the portal which wavered like a vertical pond. Was he shocked about the portal or that I wouldn't fall into his plans to go to the palace?

Learning about my magic tempted. I was tired of various powers show-ing up and surprising me. I thought the banshees could teach me. I'd been wrong. They didn't even have banshee magic anymore. I needed to know what I could do and how to control it before a major incident happened. Cassia had begun the training while pretending to be a banshee, but she'd said several times I needed someone with more experience.

"That's a start." She clapped again and tugged Lukas closer, wrapping her arms around him to celebrate. She quickly dropped her arms and blushed. "You have so much more to learn."

Lukas stiffened before tugging at his shirt collar. I thought the werewolf and the witch would make a cute couple.

"Will Destiny be safe at this coven?" Stone's expression went hard and distrusting.

I softened my earlier assessment about him not wanting to commit. I knew he cared for me. Doubt ticked in my assuredness.

"She's a witch and it's my coven." Cassia's cheeks blushed red. "Of course she'll be safe with other witches."

"That's what I thought about being with the banshees." My sarcasm tasted sour, reminding me of my recent loss.

The banshee leader had killed my grandfather with the help of his crooked son and the healer. My ribs squeezed, pressing against my bruised heart. They'd used him to get to me.

Svante, the new ruler, stood on the leader's chair. His long dark hair flowed in the wind as he consulted with several warriors, and his sister. He'd be a good and strong leader. He'd treat every banshee fairly and build up the clan's reputation. He'd be on King Zacharye's side. I'd never planned to stay and lead, or get married.

The banshee glanced in my direction. His eyes widened at the portal and he jumped off the chair and hurried over. His wary expression and the way his hand reached for the ceremonial halberd told me he would fight for me. "What's this? Are you okay?"

I'd left the banshee clan in good hands. "A witch portal." Studying the portal, something about the shape and outer design seemed familiar.

"It's not dangerous or a threat." Cassia took a step away from Lukas. "Destiny accepted an invitation from the Inferis Coven—"

"To visit." Repeating myself, I regarded Stone. I wanted to discuss the whole living at the palace thing privately.

"Mistress Lita from my coven sent transport." Cassia's enthusiasm raised her voice. She must be ready to go home.

"Just her?" Stone snarled and his gaze narrowed.

"No. It will take whoever Destiny wants to go with her."

Uncertainty beat through my bloodstream. I glanced at Stone and quickly looked away. He needed to make this decision on his own, not based on the desperation in my gaze.

My friends gathered closer around us. Cassia with her green and black hair, excited at the prospect of going home even though she'd been tattooed with the mark of a banshee. Lukas, a werewolf who'd become my first friend in prison. Helartha, the grumpy yet loyal female elf. Pith, a brownie who'd also been captured by the banshees and almost enslaved. Gnit, a goblin, who was street smart, not book smart. Trolgar, the troll, who was no longer mean or sleepy as he'd been in the cell. And now Svante, the banshee I thought was my enemy but became my friend. He couldn't go to the coven because he needed to lead the banshee clan.

"Is this the coven Violet was taken to?" Lukas crossed his arms and wore a skeptical expression.

Violet had fought by our side against the prison guards. She'd been hit by bullets and frozen by her own magic. She'd sacrificed herself to save us and was in a hibernation state. Worrying about her added to my stress.

"Yes, although we didn't get into the coven." Gnit's silly voice sang. "They have a perimeter ward."

"We met at the outskirts of the coven and discussed Violet with the person Cassia told us to." Helartha's elf ears twitched. "The witch took Violet in and promised to work with the fairies to heal and unfreeze her."

"Jinx. She's my older sister and an apprentice with the witch doctor."

Lukas jutted his hip toward Cassia. "Are there any male witches?"

She slapped his arm. "Of course, they're called warlocks."

My friends laughed. The laughter had an edge of wariness. They'd thought this would be the end of our adventure. I wasn't so sure.

"Well?" Stone raised a blond brow.

Thoughts whirled in my head while nerves tangled in my stomach. I needed to learn everything I could about my powers and myself. I had to control my magic so I wouldn't injure anyone else. I needed to finish the path of discovery to who I really was.

I nodded. "I'd love for all of you to come and continue our adventure together. But I understand," pausing I peered at Stone, "if you have other commitments."

Pivoting away, I let them discuss amongst themselves. I didn't want to influence or intrude on their decisions. Each one of them needed to do what was right for them, just as I needed to do what was right for me.

I hugged Svante. "I know I'm leaving the banshee clan in good hands."

"You're welcome to come back anytime." He bowed to me. "We would welcome you."

Heat rushed my cheeks. "Thank you."

When we separated, his sister ran up and threw her strong arms around me. The young teen would become a great banshee warrior. "You can't leave. You've changed my entire future for the better."

"You don't need me to succeed." I hugged Reitha back. She'd saved my life in the final seconds of the fight. "You will succeed on your own and become the first female banshee warrior."

"You were the first female banshee warrior."

"I didn't earn it." I'd been granted the title because of my name and my powers. "You will. Good luck."

She hugged me one more time and I returned to my friends and their decisions.

Glancing at Stone, my eyes stung. At least we'd get to say goodbye this time. "Well, um, good luck at the palace."

"I'm coming with you."

My spirits leapt, but I tamped down on my instant joy. "You can't. You promised you'd work with the king."

"I will, after I see what trouble you're getting yourself into." His attempted tease insulted me.

"I can protect myself. I'm a banshee and a witch."

"Which is why the second you were out of my sight you were kidnapped by banshees." Stone pointed out the harsh truth.

"They drugged me." My voice rose at the unfair observation.

"Never take food from strangers." His lips twitched with the tease. "Besides, I'm your...we're a...I'm responsible for you." Scowling, he pushed back a lock of blond hair.

I watched as he stumbled and blushed. Did he believe he needed to keep me safe or did he want to be with me? He took his commitments seriously, to me and the king and princess. I didn't want him to go if the reason he was coming was his duty to protect me. "Do you want to go to the coven?"

His lips flattened into a firm line. "Doesn't matter what I want, I'm coming."

The answer didn't make me happy. No thrills shot down my spine. I didn't want him to come with me because I was an obligation or he thought he needed to protect me. I wanted him to come because he wanted to be with me, because he didn't want to be separated. We'd spent so much time apart.

My group of friends stared, watching the exchange. I couldn't display doubt or any rancor between us. We were a team.

"The portal won't last much longer." Cassia quivered with nerves. She was ready to leave.

The portal shimmered about to fade.

"Why won't the portal last longer?" I wasn't ready to leave. "I thought the witch leader was all powerful?"

"If you leave a portal open too long someone unwanted might sneak through." Cassia held out her hand in front of the shimmering image. "We should hold hands when we walk through so we don't get lost."

My jitters jangled. It was a portal to a specific place. How could we get lost?

"Lost?" Stone asked the question I'd thought.

Cassia shook her hand, urging someone to take hold. "The portal is mostly a straight line, but there are refractions and magical telekinetic waves."

Stone gripped my hand. "I'm definitely going now."

Disappointment seeped into my veins. His statement meant he wasn't positive about going with me before. I hated that he felt the need to watch me like a child.

"If you don't want to come, then don't come." I couldn't stop my peevishness.

"Coming." He nodded at Cassia.

"Okay everyone," She took Lukas' hand and Stone's other hand.

Lukas held Helartha's hand, who held Pith's, who held Gnit's, who held Trolgar's.

My chest filled and overwhelmed with emotion. My friends were coming with me, they wanted to stay by my side and help me on my journey. I squeezed Stone's hand. He returned the squeeze understanding my thoughts.

With Cassia leading the way, we stepped into the shimmering substance of the portal as one. The sucking sensation intensified. My skin puckered and tugged, wanting to pull away from my bones. It didn't hurt, yet the power of the portal made its presence known.

A scream shattered the strange silence.

Stone's distorted face showed pain. His mouth was sealed shut. His body appeared misshapen. Fear shot up my spine, paralyzing my thoughts. Had this been some type of trick? Cassia had seemed so sure.

Peering down the line at her, I noted she was relaxed and normal. No stress or strain in her expression. Lukas resembled a werewolf more than usual. His fangs flashed and his brown hair had gone shaggy. Helartha's red hair streamed behind her as if the strands were being yanked. Her head bobbed back and forth. Pith and Gnit shrunk to half their normal size. Trolgar opened his mouth to a gigantic shape and screamed.

"Ahhhhhhhhh!"

I wanted to cover my ears, but my hand was gripped by Stone. Cassia leaned forward and pulled the line of us with her. I'm glad she knew what she was doing. The sucking sensation tugged me back. She angled forward again and the rest of us whipped through with a final high-pitched sucking noise.

Stepping out of the portal, I was surprised to find nothing stuck to my skin. My entire body relaxed, glad to be free.

Stone's grip loosened and he fell to the ground. My other friends fell, too. Their mouths gaped open. Only Cassia stood beside me.

Panic bulleted through me and I dropped to my knees. "What's wrong, Stone?"

"Can't...breathe..." He gasped and his eyes rounded with the loss of oxygen. He knelt on his knees and clutched his chest.

My own chest constricted as if I couldn't breathe. I surveyed around, helpless. I didn't know what to do or how to help him or anyone else. My friends lay on the ground gasping. "Cassia. What's happening to them?"

"I thought since you were invited and they were our friends it would be okay." Her gaze darted around and she dropped to her knees between Lukas and Pith. "I'm guessing it's a protection curse. In non-witches it manifests in suffocation."

My pulse skyrocketed. They weren't intruders. They were my friends. And because of me they were going to die.

CHAPTER TWO

"What can we do? They're going to die!" I begged Cassia for an answer. Terror raked across my lungs.

She cradled Lukas in her arms. "We have to find Mistress Lita."

Stone's body went limp. My other friends struggled to take in oxygen. Desperation clawed my throat. "We don't have time."

"You can fix this, Destiny." A woman appeared on the plateau where my friends might die. She had long, straight black hair. Prominent apple cheeks, a long-sculpted nose, and grayish-purple eyes. Familiarity ticked my brain. A billowy dress covered her tall frame. Magic crackled off her. She must've apparated like Cassia had done once before.

I shook my head with lightning speed trying to communicate that I hadn't a clue how to fix this. I didn't even fully understand what had gone wrong. "I don't know how to help."

Cassia appeared as confused and desperate as me.

"You're a witch, a powerful witch." The woman, clearly more powerful than me, didn't lift a finger, didn't seem concerned, didn't care.

"I don't know how to use my powers." I screeched as frustration and fear slammed me. "That's the reason I came. Do something."

Another woman apparated. "Don't ever talk to Mistress Lita that way again." A red dress hung on her skeletal frame. Her short, cropped hair stuck out against her copper colored skin. Her expression darkened and her brows drew together like thunder.

A shiver crossed my skin at her fierceness.

The first woman, Mistress Lita, relaxed the muscles in her face and slowly smiled as if forcing herself. "Because she is new to the coven, the child will be forgiven."

"I don't care about forgiveness. I want to save my friends." Agony scraped in my voice. My friends were here because of me. "Please."

Mistress Lita focused on the other woman. They consulted by glances. The communication wasn't clear to me.

"Well?" My nerves twisted and I felt slightly sick.

Mistress Lita stared deep into my eyes. If what was in my gaze was going to make the decision, I'd plead with her. I raised my brow and put my hands together.

She raised her arms and waved them in a smooth motion. "For you, I would do anything. Remember."

Something in her tone raised the hairs on my arm. It was either that or the electricity zapping from her person. Did she expect a favor from me in return?

Her lips whispered a chant, a song, maybe an incantation. Energy whipped around her and I sensed the static charges zip and zing along my spine.

This must be magic. Powerful magic. Magic I was here to learn.

Amazement glittered a prize begging me to take it.

But perusing my suffering friends, I didn't know if I could stay.

Swirls of purple and orange lit the area around us. The swirls circled Stone and my other friends. Small zaps caused their bodies to spasm. Stone shuddered in my arms. Color returned to his strong cheeks.

"Stone!" Studying him, I raised his torso so he could take in air. Relief lightened my load. "Are you okay?"

Others started to cough and move. Lukas shifted in Cassia's arms to face her. Everyone else breathed. I breathed easier too.

Once everyone was back on their feet, we hugged. I checked on each one of them making sure they were really okay.

"Thank you." I veered toward Mistress Lita and the mean red-haired witch. Wishing I could learn to do magic, I knew I couldn't stay. Not if Stone and my other friends weren't allowed. We were a team and a team stuck together. "We should leave now."

"Leave?" The second woman pitched the word into a question. Or was it a wish?

"I can't stay if it hurts my friends." My heart contracted remembering their predicament seconds ago. I never should've come. When I was back at the palace, Professor Nilsen could again help me learn how to use my magic and then I wouldn't put anyone else in danger. Although he'd thought I was a full banshee and had never mentioned witch knowledge.

It didn't matter. My friends mattered.

"Please open the portal so we can leave." I spoke to both women, unsure who was the one in charge.

Cassia held her arms out and crossed her wrists one on top of the other. "Mistress Lita, we meant no harm by bringing friends with us. They've helped us escape Regent Theobald's prison and rescue Destiny and I from the Skjult Banshee Clan. You can trust them."

"What is the hideous mark on your forehead, Cassia?" The second woman arched a red brow.

Cassia bowed her head. "Provost Morgane, it's...it's a tattoo forced upon me," my friend glanced at me with a sorry expression, "by the banshees."

"Those awful creatures." Provost Morgane peered at each one of my friends, assessing the non-witches in the group.

My body tensed waiting for her judgment. Except I was tired of being judged. Did the witches believe they were superior to other majiks? I pulled back my shoulders. "No need to trust my friends. We're leaving with or without your magical portal."

We'd fought our way out of the dungeon and escaped banshees. We could leave this place too.

For the first time I scanned the area where we'd landed. The ground we stood on was made of shifting sand and gray rocks. A harsh wind lifted the sand and tossed it up, pelting small particles against my skin. A tree stood here and there sprouting from the scorched soil. The roar of the wind competed with the roar of water. There must be a river close by.

Whitish-brown cliffs surrounded us. The cliffs came to sharp points as though sand had been drizzled on the top and dried into a hard cone. On the sides of the sheer cliffs, deep gouges had been carved out by Mother Earth over time.

The harshness of the land contrasted with the distant green mountains in the Kingdom of Alandaska. Mountains I was more familiar with. Mountains where the palace and the capital city of Lindenhamn were located. Mountains that felt like home.

"Wait." Mistress Lita held up her hand with long purple fingernails. "If they are your guests, Destiny, of course they are welcome." She snapped her fingers and a man dressed in black apparated carrying a tray of drinks. "This potion will let non-witches breathe in our atmosphere."

I looked at Cassia. How didn't she know this? She shrugged and mouthed, *must be new.*

"Where are we, the moon?" Lukas received a glare for his murmured sarcasm.

The location did have an out of this world impression.

"This is Alandaska. Why can't other majiks breathe?" None of this made sense to me. The small island kingdom was located under a temperature-controlled dome. There were no changes in atmosphere.

"Our coven is situated near an opening to earth's core. Rare particles charge into our air."

"Especially right now," the other woman said.

Mistress Lita held her palm up. "The particles are impossible to see."

The man wearing black passed out the drinks to everyone except me and Cassia.

"Wait." I remembered Stone's comment about not accepting food from strangers. "What if it's poison?"

Mistress Lita gave a rusty chuckle. "Why would we poison them? They are your friends and rescued you. I'm grateful."

My cheeks heated and I didn't enjoy the way she made me the center of attention. I wasn't the only one captured by the banshees. "Cassia and Pith were rescued too."

"Cassia and Pith." Provost Morgane sneered at my smaller friend and ignored him. "Destiny, you are among friends and family."

My pulse leapt. "Family?"

"Cassia's family has missed her terribly." Mistress Lita bestowed a quirk of the lips on the young witch, ignoring my question. So much for being the center of attention. "You poor child. Why did the banshees mark you?"

My friend ducked her head. "They tried to pass me off as one of them."

"You're a witch. The mark will have to go." Provost Morgane tutted and her gaze switched between the two of us. "The witch doctor will take care of it."

I understood why Cassia would hate the banshee mark. She wasn't a banshee.

"Your sister Jinx missed you." Mistress Lita waved her hand in the direction of a small village with a tall building in the far distance resembling a church. The structure had four tall spires topped with round golden pentagons. The wind quieted with the dawn and it became steamy and stifling.

"And my parents?" Cassia sounded hopeful.

"Of course." The mistress held out her hands and the drinks floated from the tray toward each of my friends. "Drink up and we can get settled."

My friends squinted at the glasses in their hands. Lukas sniffed the potion and scrunched his nose. Helartha lifted the glass high and examined the liquid from every side. Pith could barely hold the glass. Stone's skeptical expression cut through me.

I raised my hand. "Don't drink it for me. You can all go home or wherever you're needed."

"Are you staying?" Stone paused in his motion to drink.

Studying Cassia's anxious expression, I knew she wanted to stay and see her family. My lungs hitched. I wanted to meet whatever family I might have and learn how to use my magic. I needed to master my powers to not cause any more accidents. This time, I wouldn't be tricked into staying. It was my decision. "Yes."

"Then I'm staying too." He drank the liquid in one swallow.

A knot formed in my throat as if I'd drunk the potion. He didn't really want to stay.

The others followed, each of them reacting with disgust from the taste.

Mistress Lita spread her hands wide encompassing me and my friends. "Welcome to Inferis Coven. Cassia and Destiny, I'm glad you both have finally returned."

I stiffened, not understanding what the woman meant. All my memories had come back on the precipice, even those I'd had as a small child. I don't remember ever being here.

Flashes from my dream visions came back to me. Mom holding a glowing ball in her hand. Her forehead had been clear when I'd been little. A banshee mark had been added later. Because she wanted to identify as banshee or to hide?

"Thank you, Mistress Lita." Cassia made the same crossed wrist motion. "It's good to finally be home."

The mistress clapped her hands and other men dressed in black apparated. "These are my acolytes. They will take you to your rooms. This way."

Grabbing hold of Stone's hand, I followed Mistress Lita and Provost Morgane. Cassia skipped beside us, excited to see her family. The rest of my friends dragged behind. They acted unsure and a bit sluggish. They must be tired. It had been a long night with no sleep.

We walked through the town and passed large, elegant homes and a small main street housing shops with interesting names: Witch's Brew and Warlock's Brew, Affinity Enchantments, Crystals and Runes, Hellfire Weapons for Witches Only, and Familiar Menagerie.

As we walked through an empty field between the town and the academy, a familiar girl ran toward our group. Her long, green hair streamed behind her. She wore a form-fitting orange dress and tall black boots. "Little sister!"

That explained the similarities in their faces. However, the older sister emanated maturity and flamboyance while Cassia would never wear that outfit based on the cloak she'd used to cover herself the entire time at the banshee encampment.

Cassia's expression lit up and she ran toward her sister with her arms wide open. "Stop it. I'm taller than you."

My shoulders relaxed. Our original arrival had been a mix up. A mistake. The coven hadn't meant to curse my friends and have them almost choke to death. Cassia had said others could sneak through the portals. The witches must've been worried we were intruders with so many showing up at once.

Cassia and her sister hugged. They whispered and Cassia laughed.

My other friends and I watched the happy reunion. Tears burned. I wished I had a sister who loved me the way Cassia's sister obviously did.

Any family. Maybe I'd find someone at the coven who at least remembered my mom.

"Destiny, I want you to meet my sister, Jinx." Cassia tugged her sister toward me. "I've told her all about you."

I glanced at the ground, not sure what she'd said. "In five seconds?"

"My little sister and I communicated after she was freed from the dungeon until she was taken by the banshees." Jinx wrapped an arm around her sister and pulled her in close as if she would never let go. "I was happy she helped find you."

My earlier thought about having a sister, or anyone, morphed to yearning envy in my veins.

"And these are my other friends." Cassia pulled on her sister to introduce her to the others.

"There will be time for introductions at the welcome dinner tonight." Mistress Lita glided forward, her skirt flowing behind her. "I'll show you where you'll be staying, Destiny and Cassia."

"What about my friends?" Concern eddied in my gut and settled like a rock. I wondered if I should've RSVP'd for eight. "You said the acolytes would take all of us to our rooms."

"Of course, we can always make room for unexpected guests." Provost Morgane sounded stiff and unbending.

"May Cassia stay with me, Mistress Lita?" Hope edged Jinx's question. "And our parents, of course."

Mistress Lita considered the request. No emotion expressed on her face.

"I'd love to stay with my family." Cassia clung to her sister's hand.

The green envy surged. I understood she hadn't seen her family in forever and she'd spent a lot of time with me. Still, I felt abandoned. But I tried not to begrudge Cassia. I understood wanting to be with family. It's one of the reasons I was here. Provost Morgane had said something about family earlier. Not that I was desperate enough to immediately bond or share my secrets with someone who espoused they were family. I'd be cautious. More cautious than I'd been with the banshees.

"Very well." Mistress Lita nodded and continued strolling toward a bridge leading to the tallest building. "Destiny, come with me."

Cassia peeled away with her sister, without even saying goodbye.

Dumped, a tremble of sadness wobbled through me. I'd see her at dinner and I had Stone and my other friends by my side.

"The rest of you follow me." A male acolyte indicated a rock-strewn path between two large boulders.

"What? We're not staying together?" My temper rocketed. After our initial treatment, I was tired of being separated from Stone and my friends. I was just plain tired.

"They will be staying near the warlock barracks." Mistress Lita's tone brooked no argument. She pointed at the tall building. "You will stay at the academy."

Not a church, but an academy or school.

The building was the same whitish-brown color as the cliffs behind it and the spires were almost as tall. Dozens of gothic arches clashed with Art Nouveau modernism in the stonework and balustrades. A moat surrounded the entire building similar to a medieval palace.

"I don't mind staying somewhere else. I'd probably be more comfortable." With Stone and my friends.

"You are a witch. You were expected and your room has been prepared." Provost Morgane sauntered forward toward the moat. "Your friends are unwel-unexpected guests."

Everything inside me hardened. "It's a big building. I'm sure there are a few extra rooms." I refused to be separated again. In the dungeon, we'd lived in a single cell. "We don't mind sharing."

Mistress Lita started to shake her head. "There are restrictions—"

"Let them come." Provost Morgane smiled brittlely. "Sometimes people need to see they don't fit in."

My blood boiled. The red-haired woman did not like my non-witch friends. She probably didn't like me either. I didn't care. I'd spend as little time with her as possible.

Stone's mouth flatlined and his brow sported an angry ridge. Lukas fisted his hands. Helartha, Trolgar, Gnit, and Pith watched the exchange with wide eyes. None of them were happy with the situation and they appeared apprehensive about my demands.

Provost Morgane led the way and Mistress Lita shook her head while signaling the acolytes to follow. They were dark and silent ghosts following our little group.

I straightened my shoulders. I'd won this skirmish. I hoped there weren't many more. Squeezing Stone's hand, I needed his comfort.

Provost Morgane pivoted her head and glared, her gaze narrowing as she sized him up. "I know how it is with young people and the banshees. Our coven is a little old fashioned. You cannot stay together."

She must have eyes in the back of her head or some weird sixth sense. My cheeks flamed. I understood what she inferred.

"Yes, ma'am." He dropped my hand and stared at the ground. A slight blush stole over his cheeks.

I was untethered without his touch. I wanted him to declare his feelings for me in front of everyone but I realized we should tell each other first. I was certain how I felt. Was he?

Our group moved forward toward the bridge. The water beneath was dark and sluggish, while a current pulled at the surface. The moat had steep, slick sides, one with the academy building and the other covered in brown moss and mildew.

"I have a fairy friend named Violet who was brought here for treatment." My frozen friend should've been one of my first thoughts instead of concern over where everyone was sleeping. "Do you know anything about her condition?"

The silence had dread dropping in my stomach.

"The fairy is with the medical staff." Mistress Lita's neutral voice told me nothing.

"Do you know anything about her condition?" I needed to know. Violet had sacrificed herself to save us.

"I know the witch doctor is consulting with fairy healers about the best way to heal and unfreeze her." The mistress added information without really telling us anything.

"It's been weeks. Has there been any change?" Stone strode beside me. He sounded tentative. "Why wasn't she sent to the fairies?"

"No change." Provost Morgane barely acknowledged his question.

"It would be difficult to transport the fairy in her current state." Mistress Lita at least gave a reason.

"We want to visit her." I spoke for all my friends.

"In time." Mistress Lita stopped at the step to the drawbridge. "Here we are."

A tingling sensation overtook me. Something about the building called and tugged me forward. I didn't know if it was the magic surrounding it or if I'd been here before.

Provost Morgane tread onto the wooden drawbridge.

"Are you sure this is a good idea?" Mistress Lita hovered near the back of our little entourage with the acolytes.

I held in a huff. She didn't want my friends staying at the academy either. I thought she was more accepting.

"Destiny is used to getting her way." Provost Morgane flipped her cape.

If only she knew, I never got my way. She didn't understand me. I wasn't being selfish in my request. I was standing up for myself and my friends.

"Come on." I grabbed Stone's hand and pulled him toward the bridge. "This will be so much better than the dungeon."

We stepped onto the bridge.

Boom.

Stone's hand yanked out of mine. His body leapt into the sky as if he'd been tossed. He flipped and flopped.

My gaze followed him. He couldn't control his body. My pulse jolted, sending shock through my system. He put out his arms and his mouth dropped open. He went up and over the railing of the drawbridge.

Splash.

Stone had been tossed into the muddy moat.

Chapter Three

My breath sputtered watching Stone. I rushed to the railing and leaned over.

Anxiety pierced my lungs. Stone might've hit his head or sunk to the bottom of the moat. The smoothness of the surface had my heart racing. Green algae floated on top undisturbed.

Where was Stone? I didn't even know if he could swim.

In a spray of water, he surfaced from beneath. Drops streamed down his face highlighting his pinched expression. His blond hair clung to his head, as well as the algae. He spit out a mouthful of dirty water. *"Hvitspyd."* He swung his arms in a half-swim motion while saying the giant curse word.

My racing heart slowed. He hadn't drowned. "Are you okay? Do you know how to swim?"

When he didn't answer and started to sink, I yanked off my sandals ready to dive in.

"Destiny, no!" Mistress Lita's terror stopped me. What was in the moat?

He swiveled and splashed around. "I think something bit me."

"Stone!" Lukas, Helartha, Gnit, Trolgar, and Pith charged onto the drawbridge, pushing each other to get to the railing. They wanted to check on their friend.

Boom. Boom. Boom. Boom. Boom.

My body tensed. Before I could shout a warning, they flew as if a large, invisible hand picked them up. The invisible hand or spell or curse tossed them over the railing and into the water. They didn't even have time to yell.

Splash. Splash. Splash. Splash. Splash.

I gripped the railing, bracing myself to be tossed into the moat too. Nothing happened.

Lukas surfaced and shook his head, droplets flying out of his brown hair. Helartha stroked with one arm and grabbed Pith with the other.

"I can't swim." Gnit raised a hand before sinking beneath the surface.

My muscles locked. It was my fault they were in danger. I lifted my leg, ready to dive in to help with a rescue.

"Got him." Stone dove under the water.

I held my breath until he resurfaced holding the goblin.

Provost Morgane's malicious laughter slapped. She'd known this was going to happen and believed it was funny.

I shot her a disgusted glance. If I didn't need to help my friends out of the water, I might've actually slapped her. For all I knew, the moat could be filled with curses. "I'll figure out how to help you."

"No one listens to me. Not even my own family," Mistress Lita muttered.

I didn't care about her family squabbles with the provost. "What happened? How do I get them out?"

"I did try to warn you about the restrictions." She bent her head and her body jerked. Was she laughing?

I gripped the rail tighter. "Am I going to be thrown in the moat too?"

"No, sweetie." Her warm smile confused me. "You are a witch."

Half witch but I wasn't going to argue.

"There's a ward on the drawbridge to dispose of any non-witch trying to cross." Provost Morgane's glee stoked my fear and anger.

"Can we get some help here?" Lukas raised his hand.

Stone held Gnit and Helartha held Pith. Both struggled to hold their heads above water. The current pulled them downward, which didn't make sense. Green slime clung to the straight walls around the moat. There was no way to climb out. Something slithered in the water behind them.

I gasped. An alligator or something magical and more dangerous? "There's something coming. How do they get out?"

"How else? Magic." Provost Morgane's calm tone contradicted my high-pitched question. "You must know a simple *suspensionis* spell."

"No, I do not." I gritted my teeth. "I hardly know any spells."

The creature slinked closer. Small, squinty eyes and big, sharp teeth. It resembled a black alligator but with teeth twice the normal size.

I didn't know what to do. My pulse darted. I couldn't jump in and save them because there was no way to climb out. I shifted to Mistress Lita, the nicer of the two. "Can you get them out? Please."

"You came to the right place to learn magic." She waved her arm. "You'll be able to do this spell in no time."

Her lips moved yet I couldn't hear what she said. The same tingling of electricity filled the atmosphere. Streams of swirling colors spun around and down, curling around my friends.

They lifted out of the moat. Water streamed from their clothes and hair. They floated upwards. Helartha's jaw dropped. She clung to Pith. Gnit closed his eyes and tucked his head into Stone's chest. Stone appeared tense, not afraid. Lukas growled.

They crossed the railing and passed the drawbridge. landing on the ground with a gentle thud.

My mouth gaped at Mistress Lita. Her magic was impressive. I wished I could be as powerful and controlled as her someday. But why hadn't she stopped this from happening in the first place?

I ran to my friends. Water dripped from their bodies forming puddles at their feet. A piece of seaweed clung to Helartha's red hair. She set

Pith down, who ran around in circles. Lukas shook his entire body like a dog—well a wolf. Stone gave me a grim look. He wasn't pleased with me or the two dry women.

"Now you see what I was talking about. Non-witches are not allowed inside the academy." Provost Morgane used a superior tone to prove her point.

Then again, had she ever not used a superior tone since we'd arrived?

"I'm sorry about your friends." Mistress Lita snapped her fingers and black towels presented in their hands. "We tried to warn you. Simon will show your friends the way to where they will be staying."

"Don't dawdle, Destiny." The provost waved at me with sharp, arrogant movement.

I hung my head. I should've asked more questions before demanding something when I didn't understand the consequences. Consequences that didn't affect me, but my friends. At least Mistress Lita was nice and rescued them. I was glad she was the leader of the coven. My brain went back and forth with the contradictions between these two women. They were night and day.

Stone stepped beside me, keeping far enough away so I didn't get wet. "I don't enjoy being separated from you. How will I know you're safe?"

My knees weakened. He wanted to stay with me. Was it for protection only? Was I a duty or his love?

"This is one of the most protected buildings in the kingdom." Mistress Lita raised her hand to encompass the academy. "Besides the magical moat, there's an enchanted door, and wards throughout the academy."

"Almost too safe." My friends could never visit. Why weren't non-witches allowed inside? What were they hiding? I was no longer an innocent child. I'd lived through many betrayals. I'd grown, changed, become more suspicious.

Stone's eyebrows gathered in a thundercloud. "Between the coven perimeter wards, the protective curses, and an actual enchanted drawbridge, what are you afraid of?"

I tensed. He thought along the same lines. Although he thought they were afraid, I believed they were secretive.

"I take nothing for granted." Provost Morgane stared at Stone and pointed at me. "Neither should you."

Did she mean not to take my safety or me for granted? By Stone promising to work for the king and assuming I'd agree, was he taking me and my decisions for granted?

Mistress Lita pouted puffy red lips in a coaxing expression. "This is the finest witch academy. You'll have complete access to the teachers and the library full of spell books. You are here to learn."

She was right. The better access, the quicker I'd learn.

"You won't be far from your...friends." Her promise soothed my nerves.

"And that mushy stuff." Provost Morgane must be familiar with teens and grossed out by their actions toward each other.

Stone's worried expression warmed, but I also understood what I needed to do, why we came to the coven.

"I'll be fine. As you said, this building is overprotected. I'll get settled and then come visit you and the others." I tried to reassure him.

"You have so much to do before the welcome dinner tonight." Mistress Lita rushed as if I was already behind schedule. "Plus, you must be exhausted."

I raised a brow. "I have nothing to do. I don't even have clothes to unpack."

"Exactly." She appraised my current banshee outfit of a shula skirt, bikini top, and beads strung over my body like a Christmas tree. "You and your friends have appointments at the spa. Haircut, nails, facial, massage, and makeup."

Overwhelmed, and remembering how the banshees gave me the best of everything, suspicion wove through my mind. "Why are you doing this for me?"

Provost Morgane exchanged a look with Mistress Lita. "You're one of us."

"Why are you helping my friends?"

Stone's wet shirt clung to his broad chest. His pants dripped water, causing a mini rainstorm. My friends appeared drowned.

Provost Morgane laughed again, the trill not as mean. "Although they're already clean."

I huffed and glared in her direction.

"Even though we weren't expecting them, we will take care of them at the spa." Mistress Lita was more accommodating. "Grooming, clothes."

Same excuse which made me feel worse for barging in with everyone.

"Say goodbye." Mistress Lita glided across the drawbridge and stopped at Provost Morgane's side, giving us a few seconds of privacy. "Until later."

"I don't like this." Stone gripped my hand.

"Neither do I, but I'm sure it will be safe. And while Provost Morgane isn't warm and fuzzy, Mistress Lita seems okay. They know the best way to teach me." I squeezed his hand back and stood on my tiptoes to reach his lips. "I'll be fine and I'll see you soon."

He snarled before bending his head. My gaze widened. I couldn't believe he'd kiss me in front of the two women. I beamed wanting the kiss, and something heated in his eyes before his lips brushed mine.

"Destiny!" The provost interrupted us.

Separating, I lowered onto flat feet wondering if witches had romantic relationships. Besides the acolytes, I hadn't seen a single warlock. "I should go."

Revolving slowly away, I crossed the wooden drawbridge and through the large double doors. My feet tapped on a dark marble entryway. Dark wood paneling covered the walls. Candelabra with flickering blue flames lined the corridor.

Magical flames.

Similar to the portal, a tugging sensation pulled at me. I couldn't tell if it wanted me to leave or come further inside. I followed the two women through the incredibly high entryway.

Gray curtains fluttered in the first grand room even though there was no breeze. The images on the stained glass windows were indecipherable. Large, heavy, velvet-covered furniture dotted around the room. Near one of the windows sat a group of girls.

"Was that a giant?" a girl with brown hair sat at a window seat overlooking the front of the academy. She must've seen my friends being tossed into the moat.

"It was a werewolf, elf, and other majiks trying to cross the drawbridge," the second girl giggled. She must know about the protections.

Their backs were to us, and they wore identical clothing as if on a sports team. What team, I couldn't figure out.

"Even a troll." A third girl fake shivered.

My lips flattened and I held in my immediate defense. Staring at Mistress Lita and Provost Morgane, I hoped one of them would say something. They paraded forward toward a wavy grand staircase. Maybe they hadn't heard.

The provost halted at the bottom of the stairs. "I need to see to my duties." She turned to me. "I will see you later."

I stiffened. Were her words a threat?

Mistress Lita ascended the stairs with the same easy glide as I chugged behind her. The main staircase curved back and forth. Apparently, the architect had been drunk. Reeling, we walked across a balcony with multiple closed doors. We took a smaller, narrower set of stairs up and then went up a set of spiral stone stairs. The stairs wound tighter and tighter and up and up and up again.

I breathed heavily. If we had magic, why didn't we fly to the top or apparate? "How high up are we going?"

"To the top." She didn't even huff.

She appeared to be around thirty and was in good shape. I was almost seventeen and I had a hard time keeping up.

When we reached the top of the stairs, there were four doors. She opened the door to the left and stepped inside.

The pentagon shaped room had small circular windows on every side. A huge bed with dark curtains took up most of the space. The bed had different shaped pillows and the deep blue comforter made my eyes drift closed. I hadn't slept last night.

"I'll let you get comfortable. Rest for a bit. There is a new nightgown on top of the dresser for you. You'll be more comfortable napping in the nightgown than in your current attire."

I scanned the skimpy banshee outfit and agreed. I was glad she'd brought me to my room instead of the provost.

"Someone will be up to take you to the spa later this morning." She glided to the door and stopped. "Have a good rest. I'm so glad you're here."

Her words wrapped around me in a non-touching hug. I believed she meant it. At least someone was happy I was at the coven.

I twirled around the room taking in smaller aspects. A gothic-styled candelabra hung in the center of the room with the same magical blue flames. A handwoven rug featuring a star pattern covered most of the floor. A desk, shelf filled with books, and a comfy chair were in the corner by a window.

The dresser was a dark brown color with gold handles on the drawers. On top sat a white nightgown suggesting something virginal or sacrificial. I chuckled but it changed into a cough. My imagination was running wild.

Above the dresser hung a large oval-shaped mirror with gold trim. My hollow purplish-gray eyes had dark shadows beneath them and my white skin was paler. I tugged on my black hair and yawned.

Hurriedly, I stripped off the hated banshee shula and bikini top and slipped the soft nightgown over my head. Sitting on the bed, I bounced up and down testing out the softness. It felt just right. I laid down. "I'll nap for a few minutes."

"If her power is not controlled, Destiny will destroy the kingdom." The old woman who named me glared at baby me. "She and the Dark Angel will conspire against me...against the coven and the kingdom."

The scene was familiar as if I'd witnessed this before. All my memories had returned, including those I'd had as a baby. Unusual, but helpful in piecing my life together.

"I won't let that happen." My grandfather picked me up and rocked me with angry jerks.

"You know you won't outlive me, old man." The old witch appeared older than my grandfather and yet she pledged to live longer.

Something about her long-sculpted nose was familiar and her eyes were the same color as mine, except hers were dull with a rheumy film. No way would she outlive my strong grandfather.

I choked back a scream and woke up from the dream. Or was it a memory? The images were already disappearing from my mind. By the heaviness of my body, I guessed I'd been asleep for more than a few minutes. Shaking my head, I tried to piece together the dream. I remembered my grandfather saying he'd outlast the old woman. Tears burned. He'd died, killed by the banshee clan to make my magic more powerful.

The banshees had given me a nice tent and beautiful clothes. They'd wanted me to marry the future banshee leader and let them use and abuse my powers. I wouldn't fall for that trick again.

At least the coven hadn't kidnapped me. They'd welcomed me and, besides the treatment of my friends, I was comfortable here. I couldn't wait to start training and understanding their culture. And when I left with Stone, at least I'd know how to use my magic, even if I didn't fully comprehend our relationship.

Rushing toward one of the windows, I planned to get the lay of the land. I pushed back the heavy curtains and opened the door which led to a small balcony. Stepping out, I inhaled. There was a different smell in the air. Hot and dry, and yet I saw the roaring river from my balcony. I leaned against the stone balustrade.

The river looked more brown than blue. Small whitecaps foamed as it hit debris or one of the sheer cliff walls before making a sharp turn. Short, scrubby vegetation lined the sandy banks of the river on the other side. I didn't understand how anything could grow.

Large black boulders appeared to have been tossed onto the sand. The boulders built together and formed dark shapes between themselves resembling a niche or a cave. The academy building sat next to the large boulders and the small town scattered out in a semicircle.

Right next to the academy was a large field with stands on either side. Low-lying buildings and what seemed to be a stable were located beyond the stadium.

A group of witches and a warlock surrounded a large lump at the edge of the stadium. With their matching uniforms of black and white plaid skirt, matching vests, and black shirts the witches weren't distinguishable from each other. The warlock was taller. He wore black pants and a shirt with a vest in the same pattern.

They pushed and prodded at the lump, laughing and taunting. The lump was a hunched majik, not a witch or warlock. The witches used their magic to lift him.

A troll.

The only troll who would be at the coven was... "Trolgar!"

Anger burst through me, exploding in heated veins and sparking fingers. Without thought, I tossed light toward the group. The ball exploded and the witches and wizard flew backward, hitting the ground with a hard thump. The only one left standing was Trolgar.

He appeared stunned. Standing there, unsure whether it was safe to move. His large goopy gaze watched his torturers lying on the ground.

My heart ached. He was a guest and they treated him poorly.

The warlock braced on his elbow, black streaks on his handsome face. "No way can a troll do such powerful magic."

"Who could?" a witch with raven black hair asked.

Another witch rolled over and her glance zeroed in on me. Her expression changed from surprise to shock to vengeance.

Sweat formed on my body, and not from the burst of light I'd created. I hadn't wanted to hurt anyone. I wanted to scare them into leaving my friend alone. Now, I'd demonstrated to other witches that my magic was completely uncontrolled.

CHAPTER FOUR

"Put the drawbridge down!" I shouted when I'd run down all the stairs, through the foyer, and pushed open the large front doors only to be greeted by the wall of the drawbridge. "Put the drawbridge down!"

Nothing happened.

I'd been hoping with the main door open someone would be nearby, someone who could help lower the drawbridge. I didn't know what spell to say.

Fisting my hands, I pounded them against the wood. I needed to get out of the academy building, make sure both Trolgar and the others were okay, and apologize for my misused magic.

"Let me out!" My raw voice scratched with despair.

"Where do you think you're going?" Provost Morgane apparated beside me. Her cloak was gone and she wore sparkly black pants with a bright red blouse that matched the color of her hair. "Is your elegant room not to your liking?"

"No. I mean, of course. It's beautiful." I shook my head, confused. This wasn't about my accommodation. "I need to get outside."

"We promised your...giant that we'd keep you safe."

"I did something." I bit my lip. How did I explain that I'd injured innocent witches? Well, not so innocent. They'd been mean to my friend.

"I, um, accidently used magic from my window and might've injured someone. Several someones."

She arched her red brow to a fine point.

Tension threaded through me. She was going to be mad. "I'll explain later. Please open the drawbridge."

Provost Morgane spoke a quick incantation I didn't understand and the drawbridge began to lower. Mortification that I'd needed help mixed with my anxiety about Trolgar and the others I'd hurt.

The bridge creaked with each inch it lowered. When the drawbridge finally rumbled to a stop, I dashed across and rounded the academy to the spot I'd last seen my friend.

Acolytes dressed in black, like the ones serving Mistress Lita, surrounded Trolgar. He had chains around his wrists and ankles. The teen witches and the warlock who'd been teasing him stood to the side. Their faces were marked with black soot and their uniforms had rips and tears.

I sucked in a sharp breath. Did I do that? I'd make amends later, first I needed to help my friend.

"Let him go!" I slid to a halt in front of the group. "Trolgar is my friend and a guest of the coven."

Trolgar lifted his chin. His palpable relief had me relaxing. He was okay.

The acolytes said nothing. I glared at the witches standing by watching. They'd harassed my friend and sort of deserved what they got.

"The troll performed magic against us. We have every right to detain him." The warlock flashed a bright white grin even though soot covered his face. His chocolatey brown eyes gleamed. He was used to giving orders and having witches fall under his spell.

I had news for him. I didn't fall for anyone because of their looks or charm.

"Ridiculous. I heard you say trolls don't have that kind of magic. You knew he didn't do it." I'd caught him in his lie.

"Then who did?" One of the witches jutted out her hip. Long bangs fell down to her gray eyes and her painted lips smirked.

"Me. I'm the one who cast the spell, not him." My pulse beat faster. Now, they might arrest me.

"And who are you?" The witch who'd spotted me in the window glared. Her thick hair was parted in the middle and her heart-shaped face hinted that Cupid had drawn the shape himself. "Are you wearing a nightgown?"

I glanced down at the nightwear and hoped the white color wasn't see-through. Standing straighter, I refused to be embarrassed by my clothes. "It was an accident." It shouldn't matter what I wore or who I was. It should matter that Trolgar was innocent. I shifted away from the teens and faced the acolyte dressed in black who gripped the chains holding Trolgar. "Trolls don't have that kind of power. He didn't do it. I did."

At least I knew something about trolls. Clearly, the acolytes didn't if they thought for a second Trolgar was guilty.

The acolytes ignored me and stared at the teen warlock.

"The judge will decide." The handsome warlock smoothed his hand over the shaved hair around his ears and through the curls on top of his head. He believed he was superior too.

I was tired of everyone believing they were better than me and my friends. I might not have control of my magic, but I had integrity. I wouldn't tease an innocent troll. I'd planned to apologize, but now not so much.

Looking behind me, I scanned for the provost but didn't see her coming. I thought she'd follow me to check if I was doing something wrong. I stepped in front of the warlock. "You and your girlfriends were taunting him."

"That's not a crime." His lips twitched. He enjoyed this confrontation. "But using a direct magical attack inside the coven enclave is illegal, especially when it's another majik against a witch."

"I didn't know." I held up my hands, trying not to display my frustration. "I just arrived."

"I bet you don't know much, banshee." The third teen witch pouted her pink lips. Her hair had been twisted into two long, thick ropes. Not something as simple as braids though, the style was more elaborate.

Her remark hit me right in the solar plexus and I lost my breath. She was correct on both counts.

The other girls giggled.

The giggling scraped against the raw wound inside me of not knowing how to control my magic. "Well, you aren't very nice. Majiks should be working together to help King Zacharye."

"Because I'm sure you're his best friend." The same girl's sarcasm sliced.

"Or his girlfriend." The witch with the angel face laughed. She was no angel.

I huffed. "No. He's engaged to Princess Ellery of the fairies. I've met him though and I agree with his policies."

She sneered. "Interesting."

"Ladies." Mistress Lita apparated beside our group. Fine lines etched around her puffy lips as if she'd grown older in a matter of hours. Impossible. It must be anger forming the wrinkles. "I believe you should be headed to class."

Straightening, I was glad the mistress had showed up. She was nicer than the provost and would stick up for me.

"Mistress Lita." The raven-haired witch stuck out her arms and crossed her wrist over the other.

Cassia had made the same motion when greeting the mistress. It must be a sign of respect similar to a bow to royalty. Witches didn't have royalty. They had a council made up of the leaders of the coven. Mistress Lita was at the top of the council.

"Go and get cleaned up." The mistress' sternness would've made me run to do her bidding. "Provost Morgane will not be happy if she hears three of her best students are late."

My shoulders slumped. If they were the best students and mean, how cruel would the other witches be? Frowning, I wondered if the provost had told Mistress Lita about me running out of the building.

The girls sneered as they hastened away. They thought I was in trouble and maybe I was. My hackles rose. I didn't care about being in trouble with Mistress Lita, not really. I cared whether my magic had misfired again. If I couldn't control my power, I'd always be in trouble.

"Trolgar didn't do anything. They were taunting him, and I got upset." I noticed my window in the highest tower. "I didn't mean to injure anyone." I pointed to the warlock who seemed to have taken control of the situation and the acolytes, "Tell him to release Trolgar and arrest me if you want."

"Damien." The guy tipped his head and flashed another smile.

I didn't want to know his name. He needed to release my friend.

"Now, Destiny." Mistress Lita tried a complacent tone that I wasn't buying. "Your friend shouldn't be wandering. He could be a spy."

"A spy for who?" I tried to keep my voice tamped down.

"I was sick and took a walk." Trolgar jangled the chains around his wrist. "I got lost."

My sympathy went to him. I understood. "Are you saying my friends can't leave their guest quarters? If so, I think I'll find them and we'll go right now."

The threat had worked earlier. Anticipation stretched in my muscles. She might toss us out.

Mistress Lita tapped her pointed shoe. "Release the troll and escort him back to where he's staying."

"I'll go with." I wanted to see where my friends were located.

"You'll miss your appointment where you're expected." She softened her smile into one of coaxing. "You don't want to hurt anyone else's feelings."

My mouth opened to protest.

"Cassia will be there, and your other friends will join you in a bit."

My insides warmed. I couldn't wait to talk to Cassia about her reunion with her entire family. We'd become closer since she'd been captive with me in the banshee camp. "Will you be okay, Trolgar?"

"If they take these off." He shook his hands and the chains clanked.

Mistress Lita nodded at Damien.

He tapped his wand against the chains. The chains unlocked and clanged to the ground.

"I'll see you later, Trolgar." I let the mistress lead me away.

I'd already caused an incident and demanded to lower the drawbridge. I didn't want to make another scene. I'd see my friends at the spa. Together, we could discuss if we wanted to stay or go.

Mistress Lita skated, while I half jogged to keep up. With the authority she possessed, I was surprised by her young age even though she appeared older than when we'd first met hours ago.

"I'm still wearing a nightgown." I tugged on the nightgown as we hurried toward the other side of the stadium.

"You'll have new clothes soon enough." She led me to one of the flat buildings. "This is the *medisinsk* spa."

"This is where I'll meet my friends?" Compared to the grand academy building, it resembled a warehouse.

The metal double doors opened automatically knowing we'd arrived. We stepped inside and my opinion changed dramatically. The same whitish-brown stone of the cliffs lined the walls of the reception area. Lighting had been recessed into the stone making the atmosphere relaxing. Comfy chairs floated above the floor.

A quick greeting to the acolyte behind the counter and we were led into a locker room, except nothing so mundane could describe the space.

The walls were lined with black metal lockers with no key or keypad. Attendants stood by holding robes and towels. Clear water flowed from the faucets and a hot tub bubbled. Witches sat in the hot water with drinks, laughing and gossiping. I couldn't hold back a smile.

"This is Doctor Everbleed." Mistress Lita introduced a tall woman with unnaturally blond hair. She wore a pink lab coat, pencil skirt, and high heels. "She will fix you up."

"Thank you." *I think.*

"I want you to look your best at the welcome dinner tonight." The mistress squeezed my upper arm with fondness. "You'll be introduced to everyone."

I was uncomfortable with this strange woman's touch, why was she interested in me? Additionally, never before in my life had I met a lot of people, and yet in the last couple of months I'd met so many. The majiks in the dungeon, the humans in the palace, the banshees at their camp, and now witches and warlocks.

"Come along, Destiny." Dr. Everbleed tapped her heels while she focused on my forehead. She couldn't stop staring at my banshee mark. "We have lots of work to do."

I rearranged my bangs to cover my mark.

"Have fun!" Mistress Lita apparated out.

"First a thorough shower." Dr. Everbleed snapped her fingers and a towel and robe appeared on the bench.

This should be a fun experience, not torture. And once my friends joined me, she'd explain the processes and procedures of the spa. I'd never been to one and didn't want to show my ignorance. I wiggled my shoulders, forcing myself to relax. That's what going to the spa was about.

After I took off the nightgown and put on the robe, the doctor led me into a dark room filled with hissing steam. "Shower."

My midsection constricted in a warning. This was too similar to how the banshees treated me. Forced to get clean, being told what to do. I didn't understand why a doctor was needed to supervise my shower and give me a simple beauty treatment. "When will my friends arrive?"

"I don't know. I'm not in charge of them. I'm in charge of you." Dr. Everbleed wasn't pleased.

No one was in charge of me. But I realized now wasn't the time to argue. This must be standard spa procedure and I did need a shower. Taking off the robe and hanging it on a hook, I stepped in. Steam surrounded me like a serpent.

"Aqua." The second Dr. Everbleed spoke the word, water poured on my head.

I picked up the bar of soap and washed myself. Scents of lavender and patchouli enveloped me.

After the shower, I was led into a small room with a long table. The low light barely divulged the counter and stool. A chanting, ringing caught my ear. Spicier scents filled the room.

"Facial." Dr. Everbleed pulled back the black sheet on the massage table. "Lay down."

She wasn't very talkative. I wasn't sure I wanted her giving me a treatment.

Wearing the black robe, I climbed on the table. My skin wasn't in bad condition. I sighed. After all I'd been through, I deserved a little pampering.

Dr. Everbleed slapped goo on my face and spread it into my skin.

"Um...why is a witch doctor giving me a facial?"

"Because there's much work to do."

The insult cut through whatever ego I possessed. Sure, the girls who'd teased Trolgar were beautiful with smooth skin and silky hair, but beauty came from within and their actions weren't kind. Then again, I shouldn't question the free spa treatment. I'd barely seen Stone since we'd been reunited and usually I was at my worst—in a dungeon cell, during a battle, after a fight against the banshees. It would be nice to look good.

This reminded me of something. "Are you the witch doctor taking care of a fairy named Violet?"

The doctor's fingers paused. "Yes."

"She's my friend. I was with her when she became frozen. How is she?" Urgency drummed through my veins.

The woman's fingers moved, pausing in odd places. "She's the same."

That's what the mistress had said. It couldn't be good.

"Mistress Lita said you've been consulting with fairy healers." I wanted to know everything.

"I am." Dr. Everbleed rubbed harder on my forehead.

The substance rubbed salt in a wound. It burned and scraped my skin.

"What did they say? What's Violet's prognosis? Has she woken up at all?" Could a witch doctor not share information about their patients?

"Much." The doctor pressed against my forehead. "The same." Her strong fingers scraped and tugged. "No."

Not much of a talker. She focused the treatment on my forehead. The abrasive substance chafed against my skin.

A facial should be enjoyable, not torment. "That hurts. What are you using? Acid?"

"There's an idea."

Pain shot from my forehead to my soul. "Stop."

"It will hurt more if we need to use *slipemaskin*." She pressed a hot cloth to my skin.

I grabbed her wrist to stop the motion. "My skin is not bad."

"This is what was asked for." She jerked her hand out of my grip.

"I didn't ask." I refused to go easy or comply with the witches and warlocks of the coven. It hadn't gone well for me with the banshees. I needed to demand what I wanted from this point forward, even if the first time had gone awry with my friends being tossed in the moat.

"I promised I could help." Her harshness sounded determined. "Do you want me to get in trouble?"

Bewildered, I thought about my face. I wasn't terrible looking. Stone liked me and his opinion was the only important one. "Help what?"

"Help extract the monstrosity from your forehead."

My mouth gaped. She wanted to remove the banshee mark. A mark I'd always hated but now understood was part of my identity. Part of me. I refused to not be me. I didn't want to change.

"What? No!" I jerked into a sitting position and knocked away her hands. "The mark is part of who I am."

"The coven won't accept it." She pushed me back down.

Leather straps slithered across my body and held me in place. She'd barely lifted a finger. She was a powerful witch.

Unlike me.

Air whooshed out of my mouth. I shifted and rotated and struggled against the restraints. The leather straps felt like iron. Magic held my body in place.

She came at my forehead with some kind of device. A rough round disc came to a point and spun around on the handheld machine. The tip whirred creating a high pitched squeal.

A squeal I wanted to mimic in a terrified scream.

Chapter Five

My pulse skyrocketed. Panicking, I jerked my head to the side and struggled against the restraints. My veins charged with fear. "I don't care if the coven accepts me."

I was there to learn how to use magic. I didn't care if anyone approved. I'd leave before submitting myself to any other forced treatments or tattoos or marriages.

Been there, done that with the banshees.

"This is what is expected of you." Dr. Everbleed gritted her teeth as she spoke.

The device came closer, whirring and shrieking. The tip was made of a rounded scaly stone. It would remove the skin on my forehead.

My skyrocketing pulse exploded. Power poured through me in an uncontrollable rush. My hands flared and light burst from my fingertips. The straps ripped apart and I fell off the table.

Stumbling to a stand, I stared at the shredded straps. I'd done that. For good reason though. "You will do nothing I don't approve."

Her mouth dropped open. Her round gaze churned with fear. I wasn't sure why she was afraid of me. She clearly had experience with powerful magic. Releasing the straps had been a lucky break for me.

Panting heavily, I stormed toward the door and jerked the handle.

It was locked.

Dread dripped through me. I twisted the handle again and again.

Searching my mind, I knew there was a spell or an incantation to unlock a door. I just didn't know one. I gripped the knob tighter, hoping my earlier fear that ignited my power would do its thing again. I twisted the handle. Nothing.

My body froze. The witch doctor would come at me with the device. She'd use her learned magic to get me back on the table or freeze me in place so she could finish the job.

My shoulders dropped and prickles of fear cruised my skin. I was here to learn, not to change. Not to turn into something I wasn't. Swallowing, I pivoted and pressed myself against the door. "I don't want you to remove my banshee mark. Let me out."

"I can't." The witch doctor stuck out her arm and wiggled her fingers in a come here motion. "I have my orders."

My feet slid on the floor toward her. I scuffled, trying to stop the momentum of her magic. Tingles scraped through me yet my magic didn't surface. Why would my powers work sometimes and not others? I noticed it was when I was angry or emotional. But, I was angry now. "Stop!"

Dr. Everbleed ignored me because I kept sliding forward. I had no traction, a rag doll being controlled by everyone but me.

"Stop." My fingers sparked. Sure, now my magic made another appearance. If it would've shown up seconds ago, I could've left the room with a little dignity. Energy built inside. With the fear and anger, my power grew as if a bubble about to burst. I couldn't control it. "Please, stop."

A plea. Because I didn't know if I'd damage the room, do something to her, me, or both.

One of the bottles from the counter beside her popped and exploded. Red lotion squirted her hair and face, dripping down her pink lab coat. Her mouth gaped and she swiped at the red paste.

Another bottle exploded and another. Purple, orange, green, and pink shot out. None of the colored goop landed on me. It landed on Dr. Everbleed. She used her hands to cover her face. It was no use. Soon she was covered in lotions, salves, and oils in varying colors.

Rolling my shoulders, I watched with horror. My lungs shrank. I hadn't meant to attack, only to stop her.

She shrieked, mimicking my banshee wail. Her lips pursed in an intense frown. She took one of her fingers and brushed at the liquid coating her face. Beneath, her skin turned a sickly shade of green.

I took a step back. I didn't know what the potions cured or caused. "Um...sorry."

Not really though. She'd tried to force me back onto the table. She'd wanted to change me against my will. I was tired of others trying to change me. I wanted to be me.

"Look what you did!" She took another swipe at her cheek. That skin was also green.

I bit my lip. "I didn't mean to...it just happened."

Uncontrollable magic. My biggest issue. Uncontrolled and unknown. I didn't even know everything I could do. What if I killed someone because of anger? My legs started to shake as I realized that even if I hated it at the coven, I needed to stay.

She grabbed a hot towel and wiped the goo off her now-green face. Something popped out on the tip of her nose.

I tapped my nose. "You missed a spot."

Whirling, she faced a mirror sitting on the shelf. "Ahhhhhhh!"

Her scream echoed through the room, through the entire spa.

Covering my ears, I watched her swivel toward me. Her face turned green and warts sprouted on her skin.

My mouth dropped open. "I'm sorry. I didn't know..."

Mistress Lita apparated into the messy room. "What did you do, Destiny?" She sounded disappointed.

I held up my hands in innocence even though I wasn't. "Nothing. I mean, I got angry and squirted some lotions at her." I took a step back. "Is that what the witch doctor was going to do to my skin?"

"Of course not." Mistress Lita waved her hand in front of the doctor's face.

Nothing changed.

"Go take care of yourself." Her frustration exhibited in her tense tone. "I'll take care of Destiny."

My stomach walloped. I'd learned in my travels that taking care of someone often meant killing them. The protection around the academy wasn't to keep others out, it was to keep people in. To keep me in.

The witch doctor apparated from the room.

I wished I could tag along with her. I took a calming breath. Mistress Lita had welcomed me, but so had the banshees. I couldn't trust anyone except my friends.

"You're giving me gray hairs." Sure enough, a few gray strands mixed with her dark hair.

"You're not doing anything to me." I held up shaking hands. Maybe she'd believe I knew what I was doing. "I don't want my banshee mark removed."

"Why ever not?" Her brow furrowed. "It's ugly. And a reminder of your other part."

"Exactly." My spine straightened. "My other half. It's part of me and if you want me to stay, you'll respect my decision."

"You must stay, sweetie." The endearment did nothing to convince me. "There's so much more for you to know."

I scanned the room. Colored lotion clung to the counters and the table. I remembered the witch doctor's ugly face. My uncontrolled magic had done that to her. I nodded. "But not forever. Just to learn."

"Good." Mistress Lita's satisfied grin bothered me. "Let's continue."

I shook my head. "No more facials."

"Fine." Her lips tightened and the fine lines around her mouth deepened. "How about a manicure and pedicure? And we must do something about your hair and clothes."

"Nothing outrageous or too much change. Nothing I don't approve." Tugging at the damp strands, I remembered the female banshee's rules about cutting their hair. "Where are my friends?"

"They've showered and are having their own treatments." Mistress Lita used her magic to open the door and glided out.

"You better not change them." I'd hate it if they did something permanent that my friends didn't want. With the banshees, Cassia had been forcefully marked with a tattoo.

"Just facial, hair, makeup, and clothes." Mistress Lita led the way out of the messy room. "They'll fit in better at dinner tonight."

I didn't want any of the goo getting on me and turning my skin green. I was a big enough mess as it was. I followed her into another section of the spa. A row of seven raised chairs floated in front of a long mirror on the wall. In those chairs sat Stone, Lukas, Pith, Helartha, Gnit, and Trolgar. One was empty for me or Cassia.

Lightness filled my soul and I smiled. The gang was back together again.

Although none of them seemed happy. Trolgar had an ugly black wig stuck on his head. His goopy eyes had rounded. A woman cut Gnit's naturally long and sharp nails. Pith's nails had been painted a bright red. Helartha's beautiful red hair had been unbraided and straightened and a woman wove ribbons in her long strands. Lukas had curlers in his short locks. He sat with his arms crossed and his lips pursed in an angry line.

Stone had a black bib tied around his neck. A woman clipped his long hair. Inches lay on the ground. He was even more handsome with the stylish cut.

"Your hair looks great." I beamed.

"Short hair is not for giants." He whipped off the bib and stood. "I went along with this because they said you were supposed to be here. Where were you?"

I touched the banshee mark on my forehead. He was angry they'd sheared his hair. At least his hair would grow back and it didn't hurt when cut.

"They didn't hurt anyone, did they?" I made sure none of them had been changed permanently. "Trolgar, that hair..."

"It's a wig." He tugged the wig off. "She said it made me appear cuter."

"They cropped my talons." Gnit studied his nails. "Do you know how long it took me to grow these? They're for defense."

I never knew the reason why he kept his nails long.

"And look at this?" Pith waved his fingers. "Iban will hate this color. Any color."

Holding in a smile, I'd wondered about the two of them. He'd met Iban at the banshee encampment. "I'm sure the nail polish can be taken off." I glared at Mistress Lita and she nodded at an old witch.

The witch grabbed a bottle and a cotton swab.

I wished I could do something about Gnit's nails and Stone's hair. "Can you make Stone's hair grow again?"

The old witch tucked her chin in and her gaze widened. "It's illegal to use magic on another majik."

My body deflated. "Oh." I could respect that, especially since I saw how Damien and the three teen witches had treated Trolgar. They must've known what they'd been doing was illegal.

"I don't have to keep these things in?" Lukas ripped at the pink curlers in his short hair. "I look ridiculous."

I bet he was glad Cassia hadn't seen him with curlers. "Where is Cassia?"

"She's visiting with her family." Mistress Lita glanced away to scrutinize my friends. "I'm sure she'll be along soon."

"What about you, Helartha?" I approached where she sat in the raised chair. "Do you like your hair?"

She fingered one of the ribbons. "I love it! I didn't think I would at first. Can they do my makeup too?"

I peered at Mistress Lita again.

"Of course. Whatever your friends want." She tugged at her hair. She'd been right about me giving her gray hairs because she'd had none when I'd arrived. Maybe she needed a haircut and style. Or would magic take care of any signs of aging? "I realize we weren't as welcoming as we should've been. I want to make amends."

"Yippee!" Helartha clapped her hands. "I'd love to get my nails done too."

Smiling, I appreciated her enthusiasm.

"This is Destiny." Mistress Lita shuffled me forward toward a woman wearing the same outfit as the other spa workers. "Give her the works."

"Manicure, pedicure, hair." The woman pulled out the empty chair.

"Works?" I glanced at the mistress.

She huffed. "Keep it simple."

I didn't know what simple meant. "No changing my hair color or anything crazy."

"Correct. Do what Destiny wants." She took my hands and examined them. "Your family color is purple. Will you at least wear purple nail polish?"

No harm in the color and if it honors my family legacy. I'd do it. "Okay."

"Thank you, my child." Her wispy tone had me staring at her. Tears shone in her eyes. "I'll leave you to the experts. I need to check on the witch doctor."

She apparated out of the room.

I wanted to learn how to apparate. I could pop in to see my friends and Stone at any time. My cheeks heated. I could spend time with him and no one else would know. Wasting time on nails and hair was pointless. I wanted to start learning.

Settling into the chair, I'd promised to go along with the treatments. As long as I agreed with everything they did. "What's next on your agenda?"

Stone growled. "Apparently, our clothes aren't good enough for the grand soiree taking place tonight."

"I hope they have something amazing to fit me." Helartha twirled around, her long red hair flinging out around her.

"I hope they have something to fit me." Pith was the grumpy one now. He used to be bashful.

"I don't see why we have to get dressed up." Lukas pulled on his curled strands trying to straighten the tufts.

"It's a dinner party." I let the woman place a heated and lavender scented wrap around my neck. "Stone, you know how it is at Reximus Palace." He'd lived there almost his entire life.

"All of you, this way." The woman who'd cut Stone's hair shooed them out the door.

He glared at her before giving me a wave. "You'll be okay alone?"

"Yes." I wouldn't tell him about what happened with the witch doctor because I didn't want to worry him more. "They'll only do what I want. I will see you at the dinner."

I had to admit I was excited about being dressed nicely in front of Stone and I wanted to make a good impression on the witches. I needed them to help me learn.

Another woman put my feet in a tub of hot water, while a third picked up my hand and filed my nails. This wouldn't take much time if they applied all the treatments at once.

"Destiny, darling!" Cassia strutted into the room.

"Cassia!" My spirits lifted, happy to be with one of my friends. "Darling?"

She waved away the action. "Sorry. My family is rubbing off on me."

"I'm glad you finally joined. You missed everyone else." I wanted to tell her about what happened with the witch doctor since I couldn't tell Stone. Looking around, maybe I should wait and tell her in private.

"Of course, Destiny." Cassia perched on the chair next to me. She'd changed into a tight-fitting orange jumpsuit. The clothing made her appear more mature.

My jaw dropped. "What happened to your banshee tattoo?" Surely, she hadn't been tortured with the machine.

"Oh, the witch doctor zapped it right off." She snapped her fingers.

Remembered pain jolted me. "They tried to scour my banshee mark off with some machine. Didn't it hurt?"

"Yours is a real banshee mark you were born with. Mine was a tattoo. A simple removal spell did the trick." She leaned toward me and stroked the mark on my forehead. "I guess they had no luck taking off yours."

Indignant at the suggestion, I bristled. "I didn't want the mark off."

"Why ever not?" She waved orange painted fingernails.

"I'm a banshee." I shouldn't have to explain to her. "You've already had your hair and nails done." Disappointment sagged my frame. I thought we were going to have a spa day together.

"My sister is a whiz at hair and makeup." She fluttered her hand in front of her face. "Do you like?"

The sophisticated hairstyle must be what made her seem more mature. She sat straighter and was more confident. I smirked. "I'm sure Lukas will."

"The werewolf." She flashed a predatory grin.

"You like him." My smirk beamed. It would be great if they became a couple. The four of us could do things together.

"I don't know." She pressed her painted lips together showing doubt. That was the Cassia I knew. "Does he like me?"

Images of the way he watched her came to mind. "I think he does."

"Oh moons." Her voice dropped lower.

My brow furrowed and I laughed. "That's a new expression."

She gave a throaty giggle. "I'm home with my family and remembering all the little things I used to say and do. You know how it is."

I didn't. I had no family. I wanted to hear about hers though.

A commotion at the door caught my attention. Racks wheeled in by themselves and hanging from them were colorful dresses. A small witch apparated in carrying a full length mirror.

"Oh my stars!" Cassia jumped off the chair. "Check these out."

"What're they for?"

"For you, silly. And me." She draped a bright red dress across her body. "What do you think?"

One of the spa women sprinkled dust on my finger and toenails. The polish dried instantly. Magic or some new hi-tech polish? I'd never had my nails done before so I didn't know. She nodded for me to get out of the chair.

"We get to choose one from all of these?" I stepped to the rack and caressed a silky chiffon.

"We can choose as many as we want." She hugged a sparkly silver sheath. "So much better than a uniform."

I fingered a pink dress with flounced boa sleeves and a full skirt with pink trim. "I like this without the puffy sleeves."

She laughed with a deep inflection. "These are the templates or ideas. We can change anything."

"By tonight?" The dinner was the one thing I needed a dress for.

She laughed again. "We're witches." She snapped her fingers and the silver sheath she'd held was now on her body. "Do you like it?"

The beautiful outfit seemed too flashy for Cassia. "It's a bit attention-grabbing."

"I know." She squealed and spun in a circle in front of the mirror. "What about in gold?" She snapped her fingers and the dress changed color. "Or shimmery purple." The dress changed color again. "You try."

I shook my head. "I don't know how."

"That's why the designer is here." She indicated the small woman who carried the mirror. "Destiny wants to try that on without the ugly sleeves."

A whoosh caught my attention, and suddenly I was wearing the dress minus the sleeves. Once I learned how to do that, I was never getting dressed the old fashioned way again. Standing in front of the mirror, I flattened my hands over my hips.

"Try this." Cassia flicked her fingers and another dress whooshed on me.

I stumbled before standing straight. The white dress had a ruffled neckline taller than my head. The ruffles cascaded down to my sides in a divided train. The white top had a plunging V and a tiny waist. The long, slim white skirt hugged my hips too tightly.

"That's not right." Cassia held up a green dress. "Try this."

A whoosh and I wore a different dress. The one-shouldered creation draped across my body. A thigh-high slit completely displayed one leg. I analyzed myself in the mirror as apprehension gathered in my stomach. I couldn't pull this dress off.

"No." She tapped her chin. "This one."

Whoosh.

A peach bubble dress popped on my body. The strapless top had beaded, glittery, apple shapes. The skirt portion poofed up resembling a balloon.

Before I could say how much I hated it, Cassia spouted, "You need something more regal." She picked a yellow and blue silk dress from the rack. "Try this."

"I don't know." I took a step back thinking the dress would bite. My mind whirled with the changing of clothes and kept stumbling when I remembered the hair and clothes from the banshees. They thought they could buy me with nice things. "I don't want to look too...too..."

"Too beautiful for that handsome giant of yours?" She held the dress closer and winked. "He'll love you in this color."

Whoosh.

The dress fit as if it had been made for me. The silk peplum top was encrusted with diamonds and came to a point at my waist. The top wasn't too low cut and a red jewel nestled between my breasts. The sleeves were yellow and blue tying together the blue top and the wide yellow skirt beneath.

I appeared sophisticated and a little sexy. Thinking of Stone's reaction, my insides melted.

"I love it." Giddiness bubbled inside. I couldn't wait to show Stone. My body thrummed knowing he'd look perfect no matter what he wore.

"We should head to dinner." Cassia grabbed my arm and led me out of the room before I could change my mind about the outfit. I hadn't even gotten a chance to fully assess the dress, make up, and styled hair altogether. I felt glamorous, and yet the same old me was still inside the fancy dress.

Cassia had become sleek and sophisticated. Gone were the sneezes and the down-to-earth attitude. She'd gone full witch persona back in her real home. She'd always been pretty. Now, she was stunning.

A shivery anticipation slid down my spine. How would my other friends be dressed? I already knew how handsome Stone looked in formal attire. And with his new haircut he'd be even more gorgeous, even though he hated the short style.

Cassia and I arrived at the dinner location behind the academy building and I stopped short. A large cave with stalactites and stalagmites hosted the event. Floating bulbs of light danced above a long table groaning with candles, formal place settings including several glasses at each spot, and cloth napkins shaped into flames. The witches knew how to throw a fancy party.

"Isn't it great?" She squealed the question with excitement.

I wasn't a fan of caves. I'd spent too much time in a dungeon. So had she.

Witches in a splendid array of colored outfits stood in groups near the table. Behind them stood warlocks wearing elegant black tuxedos. They laughed and flirted with the witches in attendance.

While I knew I fit in with my new dress and styled hair, inside I was squeamish. I wasn't used to this luxurious world with sophisticated witches and warlocks. What would I say? How would they feel about my banshee mark? Not that I cared. They wouldn't change me. But that didn't mean I wouldn't be self-conscious. Which reminded me of my future plans. How would I fit in at Reximus Palace with the pomp and circumstance? I needed to get used to it here before moving into the palace.

The tinkling laughter and light gossip stopped, replaced by hushed whispers. The hushing waved through the group starting with the witches and warlocks closest to us. Everyone stared.

At Cassia and me.

No, just me.

My squeamishness morphed into outright nausea. My anticipatory smile faltered.

Cassia's grin turned brittle and she took hold of my hand. "Don't pay attention. They're curious."

Good old, Cassia. She understood me and knew how to make me comfortable. I forced a stiff smile. "Or jealous of how good we look."

She laughed loudly, the tinkling almost acting as a signal to the others. They rotated away and continued talking but I noticed the surreptitious glances under downcast eyes.

"Here." She grabbed a tall flute from a passing waiter.

The purple glass warmed in my hand. "What is it?"

"Something to relax you."

I lifted the glass to my nose and sniffed an acidic scent. I pretended to take a sip while thinking about Stone's warning about accepting food and drink from strangers. Except Cassia wasn't a stranger. She was my best friend. I took a sip and choked on the strong taste.

The talking grew louder. A shriek followed a shocked exclamation.

Who could be causing a bigger stir than Cassia and I? Circling toward the commotion at the entrance, I craned my neck and spotted Stone.

With his height, he stood out above the crowd, especially with his now-short blond hair. The black tuxedo jacket fit his broad shoulders and he wore a silver shirt beneath it with a silver bow tie. I melted until I scanned his face. His angry expression proved that he hated being treated like a dress up doll.

Except he'd dressed formally at the human palace. Was it only dressing up in front of witches and warlocks that bothered him?

Helartha wore a long, lavender dress matching the ribbons in her red hair. Gnit and Pith both wore black tuxedo shirts with matching pants. Trolgar wore no shirt, just a tuxedo jacket and pants. And Lukas wore a blue tuxedo with a ruffled shirt.

I didn't understand why their pale faces displayed fear. Until I noticed their arms.

Shackles wrapped around their wrists like fancy bracelets.

My friends weren't guests at the party. They were prisoners.

Chapter Six

Shock rooted me to the ground while mortification swamped me.

My friends might've been treated at the spa, but they were guarded like captives. Besides the shackled wrists, they were escorted by half a dozen acolytes dressed in black uniforms and carrying wands. The warlocks were dressed like a militia.

My legs trembled and anger pushed me into a run. I couldn't believe the coven would treat my friends this way. Fury pulsated and my fingers tingled. I fisted my hands, not wanting untrained magic to escape.

Stone shook his head in warning.

The acolytes pointed their wands at me thinking I was a threat.

I slid to a stop. "What's going on? They're not prisoners." I yanked at an acolyte's wand and it slipped out of his fingers.

He let me take it. Why? "We were escorting them to dinner."

"With shackles and pointed wands?" I dropped the wand and resisted the urge to stomp on it.

"For their protection." His announcement was ridiculous.

"What?" I noticed the glares and frowns from the gathered witches and warlocks. At me and my rush to judgment? Or at my non-witch friends? "Surely, they're safe at dinner. They're guests. My friends."

The acolyte scowled. "They need to stay together so we can watch them."

Because they didn't trust them.

"Are they shackled when they're in their rooms?" I remembered they hadn't been restrained at the spa. Why now?

"Destiny," Cassia grabbed my arm and winked at the warlock. "He's a guard following orders. They're here and everyone is fine."

"They shouldn't be wearing shackles." I whispered-shouted in her ear. I didn't care if everyone heard me. "I need to talk to Stone."

I pushed forward again with Cassia at my side. She winked at the acolyte again. "We're their friends. Can we talk to them?"

The acolyte acted suspicious. Once he nodded, I went straight to Stone and wrapped my arms around him.

"Are you okay?"

"Fine. How about you?" He shook off my hug, embarrassed by me. "What did they do to you?"

Smoothing my dress, I quelled the fretting in my belly. "You don't like?"

"I do like." His eyes flashed with heat and his deep timbre sent flutters through my midsection. "You're gorgeous, dressed up or not."

"As gorgeous as Princess Ellery?" I pushed out my hip, hating the bit of jealousy that clung around my heart. The princess was engaged to someone else. I shouldn't worry about her.

"To me, you're the most beautiful." Not a direct answer to my question, but I'd take it as a win.

His shackles rattled, reminding me of more important things than what he thought about my clothes. "I'm going to demand they release you. All of you."

"Don't get yourself in trouble." Stone warned as I stomped off toward the acolyte guard whose wand I'd taken. He must be in charge.

The acolyte picked up his wand and pointed it at me again.

I wished I had one to point at him. "I demand you release my friends."

"Destiny." Cassia grabbed my arm again. "He can't release them without orders."

I reeled toward her. "Who ordered that they be shackled? Who can release them?"

"I can." Provost Morgane wended our way in a long, black dress.

Just great. The woman who disliked my friends and probably hated me.

"Why are my friends shackled?" I didn't come right out and accuse her of ordering their restraints. "I want them released."

Her gaze narrowed and I could see hate in her expression. "They are not witches."

As if that explained everything. It didn't.

Cassia shrugged and kept her mouth shut. She wasn't going to step out of line. She'd grown and become stronger during our adventures, yet wouldn't stand up to one of her own. This was important to me. They were important to me. I didn't understand how Cassia could stay silent.

I'd do this on my own. "They are *guests* at a welcome dinner."

Provost Morgane arched a brow as she studied me. Respect flickered in her eyes giving me an ounce of hope. "I'll take the heat for releasing them if you promise me something."

I hesitated. She'd been against my friends from the second we'd arrived. She'd known they'd end up in the moat if they stepped on the bridge. But Stone and the others appeared miserable. Locked up, embarrassed, stared at. I had to do something to help.

"What?" I used the single word to cut the charged atmosphere. I held my breath waiting for her response.

Cassia tensed and didn't blink.

Provost Morgane took in both of us. "That you will discuss succession with an open mind."

My brows arched. I had no idea what she was talking about. King Zacharye was the ruler and at some point he'd have children to succeed him. I was fully behind him and his new government and didn't mind discussing it with her. "Sure."

"Very well." She flicked her wand so fast I couldn't have stopped her if I wanted. "*Alliges no.*"

The atmosphere electrified. The hairs on my arms rose. The area around my friends glowed in a greenish light. I tensed. What if she changed my friends into frogs? The glow and the shackles dropped to the ground with a clank.

The noise freed my tension and anxiety. My friends were free, kind of. They were still surrounded by the acolytes.

Stone rubbed his wrists and the others did the same. None of them smiled in relief or celebrated.

Without hesitation, I ran to Stone and jumped in his arms which automatically wrapped around and stayed there, warming me.

"You're welcome," Provost Morgane trilled and whisked away, but not before reminding me, "Don't forget my request."

Request or blackmail?

Cassia strutted to Lukas. She gave him a kiss on the cheek.

He blushed. His brown hair was curled in tight swirls. He acted uncomfortable with Cassia's closeness.

Still standing by Lukas, she directed her attention to me. "As soon as you're done talking to your friends, I want to introduce you to a few important people."

I huffed, understanding diplomacy. If I wanted the coven to teach me, they needed to know and trust me. "Come with us, Stone. And Lukas too."

"As much as I'd love to stay on this hunky guy's arm, I think the first time you meet some of the council witches it would be best done alone." She patted him on the shoulder.

Their relationship must be progressing quickly. While I'd always sensed something between them, they were both shy. Being home had made Cassia bold, but not outspoken about her friends. I wished being at the coven gave me a similar confidence with my magic.

"Do you mind?" I squeezed Stone's hand. We were finally together again, and yet always apart.

"This is important to you. You need to convince them to teach you about your powers." He squeezed my hand back and let go. "I'll stay with the others."

He wanted to protect our other friends. He didn't fully trust the witches even though the shackles were gone. I could tell by his wary gaze as it roamed over everyone and everything. He kept watch.

I understood his wariness. The witches had been welcoming to me and Cassia, but not really anyone else from our group.

Cassia grabbed my arm and tugged me forward. She seemed to be dragging me everywhere. "You're going to love the members of the council. They can teach you everything you need to know."

"Excuse me, Counselor Drabek." Cassia crossed her wrists making the sign of respect. "I'd like to introduce you to Destiny."

I made the sign with an awkward jerk. I'd never been taught.

"Nice to finally meet you." Counselor Drabek wore a bright red dress with feathers trailing at the bottom of the skirt. Her blond hair had been pinned up in an elaborate style. "Can't wait to see what Mistress Lita does with you."

The comment thudded in my head.

"And this is Counselor Barkridge."

Counselor Barkridge wore a tailored white suit and had a monocle in one of her eyes.

After a quick greeting, I was introduced to Counselor Ebonywood, Counselor Trevils, and Counselor Shade. I'd never keep them straight.

We worked our way up to the head of the table.

"Where are your parents and your sister Jinx?"

"Oh, they're sick." Cassia pouted her brightly colored lips.

"I'm sorry. Wouldn't you rather be with them than at this stuffy dinner?" I remembered her reunion with her sister. They'd both been so happy to see each other.

"No." She waved a dismissive hand. "I think their excitement of my return made them ill."

My brows furrowed. The two of us had experienced plenty of excitement and we'd never gotten sick. Injured. Attacked by a dragon. Tattooed. But not sick.

Bong. Bong. Bong.

"What is that?" I wanted to cover my ears.

"It means Mistress Lita will be arriving soon and it's time to take our seats." Cassia tugged me toward the head of the table.

I ground my foot. "I don't want to sit up there."

"You're the guest of honor." She continued to pull me forward. "You have to sit next to the mistress."

Uncomfortableness settled in my gut. "Why aren't you a guest of honor, too?"

She'd returned home after a long absence. They'd known her. While I was an unknown witch who may or may not have family, who might belong.

"I am, sort of. I'll be beside you." She pulled out a chair decorated in black netting with sparkling stones. "And Provost Morgane will be next to me."

Oh, goody. I really didn't want to have to discuss the bargain I'd made with her during dinner.

"I want to sit with *our* friends."

"They'll sit together and be fine." Cassia winked. "You miss your hunky Stone."

Slipping into the chair she'd pulled out for me, confusion wrangled inside of me. She'd really come out of her shell. Winking and gushing and openly flirting with Lukas. I considered the area where Stone and my other friends sat. Not mingling, barely talking except for hushed whispers to each other. They didn't want to be here.

Neither did I. Everyone watched every move I made. It forced me to go slower, to be careful about each step I took so I wouldn't fall on my face in the strange high heels.

Mistress Lita apparated to the head of the table, wearing an elegant black gown of tulle and lace. One shoulder dripped down with embroidered black flowers and wrapped around her waist in a hug. The long gown displayed her right leg through a straight slit. Her arms were covered in long, embroidered gloves.

Everyone quieted and regarded her with respect.

"Destiny." She assessed every inch of my body, stopping at my forehead and frowning. "You look almost like a real witch."

"Thanks." I bit my lip. She hated the banshee mark but I didn't care.

Simon, the first acolyte I'd met, pulled out the ornate chair at the head of the table. Mistress Lita stayed standing, although she bent slightly as if it took effort to stand straight. When we'd first met, my perception was that she was strong and powerful. Had it been an act?

Cassia took the regular black wood chair next to mine. Everyone else followed suit and took their seats.

A tinkle filled the air. Silver goblets appeared filled with a bubbling brew. I peered down the table at my friends. Their glasses were filled too. Finally, my friends were being treated as equals.

Trolgar picked up his glass. The acolyte next to him knocked his hand. He dropped the glass and the liquid spilled onto the black tablecloth.

"Oaf," a witch sitting close to my friends said.

"Who let heathens in?" a warlock asked and peered at me.

I choked and pressed my hands into the table about to stand up.

Cassia grabbed my wrist. "Everyone is supposed to wait for Mistress Lita to drink. The guard didn't mean to knock his glass, only to stop him."

Understanding that she didn't want me making a scene didn't make me less angry. I hated that my other friends were down there while I was up here, hated that they were distrusted and disliked, hated that they stuck out.

"Attention." Mistress Lita picked up her glass. "I want to welcome a lost daughter of the Inferis Coven."

Gazes swung toward me, and I felt each like a bullet. I hated the attention. I wanted to meet a few witches who could teach me how to use and control my magic. I didn't want this dinner and I didn't want my friends ostracized.

Mistress Lita paused with the goblet halfway to her lips.

The crowd clapped and shouted a welcome.

My cheeks warmed and the imaginary bullet holes didn't pierce as deep. This wasn't the false welcome I'd received from the banshees. The coven didn't need my half witch powers. They could help me figure out my skills and maybe find a distant relation. I smiled and gave a little wave.

Mistress Lita sipped from her goblet and raised it high again. Her toast wasn't finished. "We're also happy Cassia has returned home to us and her loving family."

More polite applause.

Cassia gave a princess wave, soaking up the love.

Swiveling toward the mistress, I waited for her to say more welcoming words. When she didn't, I stood next to her and raised my glass. "I'd also like to introduce you to my friends who are guests here as well." I wanted the witches and warlocks to know my friends shouldn't be disparaged or bullied. "Stone, Lukas, Helartha, Trolgar, Gnit, and Pith are heroes in the battle against the Regent Theobald."

The crowd hissed at the regent's name, confirming they weren't on the evil man's side. Good thing because I'd been fooled before.

Mistress Lita cleared her throat, looking slightly annoyed that I'd interrupted. "Thank you, Destiny. Many of you are aware of Destiny's special combined magic."

Why had she wanted to erase part of my heritage but not the power that comes with it? I slouched in my seat.

"Destiny will be training with us on how to control her unusual powers," Mistress Lita continued.

My chest constricted. I didn't want everyone to know I couldn't control myself. I wondered how many of them had heard about the explosion in the spa or my attack on Damien and the witches teasing Trolgar. I peered down the table and didn't see any of them. Maybe they'd been punished. Lifting my chin, I held in a smirk.

"Destiny mentioned she's also interested in finding familial relationships." Emotion threaded through Mistress Lita's voice. She dabbed at her eyes. "It's been difficult to keep this secret all day. I wanted everyone important in the coven to hear the announcement at once."

I straightened and something fluttered in my stomach. She knew someone related to me, otherwise she wouldn't have mentioned it. Peering down the table, I assessed everyone's nose, chin, and eyes. I could be staring at an aunt or a cousin.

"I named Destiny when she was a baby." Mistress Lita dabbed her eyes again.

My blood froze. I knew the story. A witch had named me and connected me to the Wicked End Prophecy. Resentment flared and anger sparked. It had been her who'd saddled me with a terrible divination.

"Destiny is almost seventeen and great things are expected of her," Mistress Lita continued with emotion. She tilted her head up and stared down everyone seated at the table. Presence radiated off her and I understood why she was such a formidable leader. "Because Destiny is part of *my* family. She's my great granddaughter."

Chapter Seven

The crowd's gasp was nothing compared to my sharply indrawn breath scraping with painful longing.

Excuse me, I was what? A million words spun in my head, each of them more upsetting. Mistress Lita had greeted me. She'd known all day and had said nothing. "What?"

"I'm your great grandmother." She bent down and wrapped her arms around my torso.

Stiffening, I stayed seated. Everything about the contact seemed awkward. Besides hugging Stone and my friends, the last person I'd hugged was my grandfather. My eyes stung. I didn't even remember the feel of my parents' arms around me.

Angling out of Mistress Lita's arms as she stood erect, I pivoted toward Cassia. "Is it true?"

"Yes!" She clapped her hands together. At least one of us was happy.

Mistress Lita beamed at the gathered group. She'd wanted to make a splash with the big announcement.

"Why didn't you tell me, Cassia?" We'd spent weeks together as captives of the banshees. More time in the dungeon beneath the human palace. "Why didn't you say anything?"

"I didn't know until I spent time with my sister. Jinx told me everything. She swore me to silence until Mistress Lita made the announcement tonight." Cassia's sisterly bond was tighter than our friendship.

I shrunk in my seat. Mistress Lita was the old witch who named me, the one who'd given me the Wicked End Prophecy. It hadn't been any old witch as I'd believed. It had been my great grandmother. I didn't know what to say.

Though she wasn't old anymore. How was that possible? How could this fierce woman, who appeared to be around my mother's age when she had died, be a great grandmother? It didn't make sense.

She raised her goblet again. "So not only is this a welcome to the Inferis Coven. It is a welcome to the family." Mistress Lita, no, Great Grandmother, took a sip.

Did she not notice my distress?

She finally sat down and food magically appeared on our plates. An acolyte stepped up and whispered in her ear, preventing me from catching her attention. I had so many questions.

I gaped at Cassia. "You knew I was attached to the Wicked End Prophecy. How could you not know I was Mistress Lita's great granddaughter?"

My friend clanked her empty glass on the table. "I didn't know the two were connected. If you remember, I didn't know much about the prophecy either."

True. But she'd known enough to make me worry. I still worried.

"Because if you knew, you would've told me?" She was my best friend.

"Of course, I would've told you. In the dungeon under the palace or when we were captives of the banshees." She shivered. "I didn't know about your relationship to Mistress Lita or anyone else."

"Anyone else?" My mind whirled.

"I meant generally. If I'd known anything else important, I would've told you." Cassia picked up her fork with a load of orange potatoes and shoved it in her mouth. She smiled with a closed mouth and waved her hand indicating my plate.

I couldn't eat. I could barely think. "So there's no other relation I should know about?"

"Not in the coven." She shoveled more food into her mouth and turned to Provost Morgane on the other side.

Twisting toward Great Grandmother, the title didn't sound right on my tongue. I waited for a chance to speak to her, to ask her questions. Many, many questions. But witch after witch and acolyte after acolyte came up to speak with her in almost a choreographed action. I got to my feet unsteadily. If Great Grandmother didn't have a second to discuss the announcement with me—an announcement that changed my life—I didn't need to stay by her. I really didn't want to ask personal questions in front of an audience anyhow.

"Where are you going? You haven't eaten." Cassia swallowed a big gulp from her magically refilled glass.

I snatched my goblet off the table and stalked to the other end. A couple of witches tried to stop my progress. I ignored them. The tingling laughter, clinking glasses, and buzzing gossip clattered in my head. The festive mood made everything worse.

When I reached my friends, the acolytes—or guards—blocked my way. Again.

"I'm saying hi to my friends." I refused to be put off. I'd already talked to them once so there shouldn't be a problem talking to them a second time.

The acolyte jerked his head in a nod and stepped to the side. The earlier acolyte arresting Trolgar hadn't listened to my pleas. Maybe now that everyone knew I was related to the mistress, I'd have a few perks.

"Hi everyone." I took hold of Stone's hand. "How's dinner?"

"Not as good as yours." Trolgar pointed at his plate filled with a gray mush.

"The chefs didn't know what they would eat," the guard explained the poor quality of food for my friends.

"Ridiculous." I grabbed the acolyte's plate. "You don't mind sharing, do you?" I handed the plate to Trolgar. "Can you ask the chef to twitch their fingers and get my friends real food?"

The acolyte picked up a plate from another acolyte and handed it to Gnit.

"Are you ready to leave?" Stone certainly was. He probably wanted to leave the second he arrived.

"We all are." Gnit scowled.

"You have to finish the potion helping you breathe in the coven." The acolyte picked up a mug near Stone's place and handed it to him.

Helartha made a face. "The drink is disgusting."

"It makes me sick." Pith clutched his stomach.

I remembered when they'd first arrived and couldn't take in oxygen. "You should drink it. I'd hate for you to choke again."

"*Hvitspyd.*" Stone downed the drink and dropped the empty mug on the table. "Happy?" He sneered at the guard. "Let's go so we can talk somewhere private."

The acolyte didn't respond.

Stone put his arm around me and I welcomed his protective warmth. I peered at my great grandmother. She watched every move I made, or at least every move my friends made, and whispered something to Cassia.

Cassia, who'd been talking with a tall warlock, nodded and rushed to our side.

"Where's everyone going?" She grinned at Lukas. "Did I mention how hot you look in those clothes?"

He glanced down and tugged at the jacket. "Not really my style and it's been a long day."

"I get sick after drinking the stuff." Helartha's skin appeared a little green.

"There's going to be dancing and fireworks." Cassia wiggled her butt at Lukas and giggled.

"I'm not sure your warlock friend would want us present." Jealousy oozed through Lukas' tight lips. His gaze narrowed on the guy she'd been talking to.

"He's a friend." She grabbed Lukas' arm and tucked her body in close. "I want to dance with you."

"No dancing for me tonight." He shook his head. "Have fun."

"I couldn't have fun without my friends." She whined and pouted.

I didn't understand how she didn't realize none of us wanted to be at the dinner party. She'd been so perceptive in the dungeon. She must be distracted by her happiness at finally being home.

"I want to see Violet." Gnit crossed his arms and stuck out his small chin.

So did I. "I asked Mistress Lita ab—"

"Your great grandmother," Cassia squealed. She was more thrilled than I about the relationship.

"I asked about seeing Violet and my great grandmother," I smirked at Cassia, "said we'd see her soon. I'll push tomorrow."

I was exhausted. I hadn't slept last night after the happenings at the banshee camp and only had a short nap. We'd been busy at the spa all afternoon. I rubbed my forehead. I'd barely had a moment to myself.

"Okay." Stone ran his fingers through what used to be long hair and fisted his hand. "I want to walk you back to the academy and get some sleep."

An acolyte stepped up. "You cannot go to the academy."

Stone glared. "I know I can't go in the stupid building. I'm escorting Destiny back. In private."

The man went on alert. His body stiffened and his gaze darted around between Stone and I and Mistress Lita. I tilted my chin, daring him to say no.

"Lukas can walk me back too." Cassia yawned. "The guards can escort everyone else to their quarters."

"Guards?" I know I'd been referring to them as guards in my head, but no one had called them guards out loud. I'd had enough guards in the past couple of months.

"Not guard guards." Cassia clapped her hand over her mouth. "Escorts to their lodging."

"Prison," Pith muttered.

"Is it bad?" Pivoting around, I bent down to talk to him. He'd been in the human dungeon, captured by the banshees, and now he still felt imprisoned. "I know they had a hard time accommodating us."

"It's actually pretty nice." Helartha clutched her stomach looking as if she might hurl. "I need to go now."

"Destiny," Trolgar bent down. "I haven't been home in months. Now that I know you're safe, after we see Violet I'm going to head out. If that's okay with you."

My heart squeezed with sadness. "Yes, of course. You should go see your family."

I remembered how much I had wanted to find Grandfather and now meet new family. I scrutinized Mistress Lita. She'd been proud announcing our connection and yet ignored me now. At least she'd been much nicer and more accommodating than the provost. But I refused to automatically trust her even though she was family. My friends were my family, even if my great grandmother said otherwise. I'd be sad for anyone to leave. I understood though and wanted my friends to be happy.

After saying goodnight, the acolytes escorted my friends to where they were staying. Stone kept his arm around my shoulders, while Cassia and Lukas strolled behind us.

Stone tugged me closer. "By your expression earlier, you had no clue that woman was related to you." His warm breath tickled at my ear. "How are you feeling about the announcement?"

I slowly sucked air in my lungs while trying to decide. "I'm not sure. She didn't act grandmotherly when we first arrived." I glanced at the guards trailing behind us. "She doesn't look grandmotherly either."

"How can she be your great grandmother?" Stone rubbed my arm. "Maybe witches don't age. Enough about her, how do you feel?"

"I'm shocked. Numb, really. Why wasn't she involved in my life?"

Why hadn't she visited when I'd lived with Grandfather? Or before when my parents were alive? With my memories returned I would've remembered her if she'd been around. And why hadn't she helped me escape the banshees? Her message, or should I say threat, had shown up after I was safe. Frowning, she must've known where I was, otherwise how else had the message found me?

Stone shrugged, lifting his arm. "Hard to say."

"I wish she would've told me first instead of stunning me with the news in front of the entire coven. I didn't know how to react." I shifted in his arms when we reached the drawbridge. "I wish I could stay with you."

"Me too." He perused around before lowering his head toward me. "I'm not doing my job protecting you."

Dissatisfaction itched across my skin. I didn't want him thinking of me as a job. "Is this part of your job?"

I wrapped my arms around his neck and pulled his face down. Standing on tiptoes, I touched his lips with mine. His immediate response had me smiling against his mouth.

He wrapped his arms around my waist and lifted me slightly off the ground. It was like floating or levitating, except it wasn't magic, it was love. The urge to speak my feelings had me starting to break off the kiss. Until his tongue slipped inside my mouth and I wasn't thinking at all.

"What're you doing?"

Lukas' sharp voice had me pulling away from Stone. We both turned.

Cassia had her arms around Lukas' neck similar to how I was with Stone. Except Lukas stood stiff and unbending, glaring at her.

"Getting a goodnight kiss." She sounded peeved. "Don't werewolves kiss goodnight?"

"They do when they're a couple." He stepped out of the circle of her arms. "We never talked about or agreed to anything."

I thought they'd make a cute couple. Obviously, Cassia did too. I also knew that werewolves mated for life.

She stuck out her hip. "Don't you want to kiss me?"

"Yes. Maybe. At some point." His cheeks brightened. "I don't want our first kiss to be on display." He jerked his chin at the waiting acolytes.

Heat flooded my face. I hadn't thought about kissing Stone in front of anyone. Of course, this wasn't our first kiss.

"Fine." Cassia stuck her nose up and stormed to me. She yanked my hand and whispered, flinging a finger at the drawbridge. It began to lower.

"You two," one of the acolytes indicated Stone and Lukas. "We'll take you back to your rooms."

My heart ached. I hated how Stone and I were separated and didn't get to finish our kiss. There were so many things we needed to clear up between us. But Lukas was right. I didn't want to have a private discussion with the acolytes listening.

"Goodnight, Stone. Goodnight, Lukas." I waved.

"Let's go." Cassia kept hold of me. I couldn't tell if she was hurt or angry.

"You can let go of my hand."

She did as I asked when we got to the other side of the bridge. "No one wants to hold my hand or kiss me. Not even you." She pouted.

"You were gripping my fingers too hard." I shook my hand trying to get the sensation back.

"I can't believe a werewolf rejected me." She stomped up the stairs. "Lots of warlocks want to kiss me. They know I can help their careers."

I reeled back. "They kiss you to advance their careers?"

She halted on a step. "You know, because my family is important. So is yours." She grinned. "You could have any warlock in the coven. All of them would want you."

My stomach flipped. I wasn't about to go around kissing warlocks. "I only want to kiss Stone."

"Don't get me wrong. Stone is a hunk." She fanned her face at the top of the long staircase. "But you're a powerful witch and..."

"And banshee."

"Yes, and banshee." She used a spell to open my room. "You're powerful. And Stone has no power whatsoever. No magic. You don't think...at some point...he'll get frustrated with your status and your magic?"

Her words drilled into me. "We won't be here long."

"You don't think he'll get tired of protecting you? Basically, being your personal guard." She threw open the curtains and peeked out the window. "You don't think he'll come to resent you? Especially if you take him away from what he wants to do in life."

Cassia must know about the offer from King Zacharye. The offer Stone had accepted without telling me, and delayed to come here. Guilt churned causing my throat to burn.

She faced me. "Did Stone want to come to the coven?"

"Not exactly. But we're just here for a short time."

"It takes a while to train." She stepped to the door. "Years at the academy."

I sunk onto the bed. I'd pictured a few weeks. I didn't want to wait years to be with Stone. "I'm a fast learner."

She snorted. "You'll need to be. Distance doesn't make the heart grow fonder." Bitterness laced her words as if she spoke from experience. "Distance makes your differences become more noticeable and the chasm between widens."

Stone and I already had a chasm. We hadn't said we loved each other. He'd made plans for our future without consulting me. He acted more like a guard than a boyfriend. I didn't want him to stay at the coven if he'd rather be somewhere else.

At the palace with the princess. And the new king.

I had nothing to be jealous or worried about. Stone loved me. He just hadn't said it yet. And I needed to stay at the coven. I needed to learn. But how long would he stay if we couldn't spend time together, knowing that he wasn't welcomed by the witches and warlocks?

Chapter Eight

The following morning, I pounded on Cassia's bedroom door. "Cassia!"

Last night, she'd shown me her huge room right next to mine. I'd asked why she wasn't staying with her family and she said she planned to visit them every day. Mistress Lita wanted her near me to help me adjust. Cassia would never spy on me like another pretend friend. She was a real friend. She only wanted to help me feel more comfortable in the new surroundings.

When she didn't answer after several more knocks, I gave up. Maybe she'd ended up at her parents' home to help take care of them during their illness. I didn't begrudge her time with family. I just wanted her to come with me to see mine.

Mistress Lita was waiting to see me. I swallowed. Great Grandmother.

To get to her office I had to climb down out of my tower, through the main part of the academy, and up the stairs to her suite of rooms. This place needed an elevator. Or I needed to learn to apparate.

I paused at the bottom of the stairs. The grand hallway was as gloomy as before. The doors were closed on the balconies above. The floating candelabra glittered with dim light. The witches I passed were serious and in a hurry. They barely glanced at me.

Taking a corner, I heard giggling. Three girls wearing matching school uniforms came around the corner. I recognized them. They were the ones who'd made fun of Trolgar with Damien. I flattened my lips.

They slid to a stop in front of me.

"Destiny." The girl with straight black hair waved, pretending we were friends. "You didn't come to the after party."

"I," I'd hated how my friends hadn't been welcomed, but I decided to be more diplomatic. "I was tired."

"Cassia partied the night away." Another girl from the same trio swayed her hips. Her larger lips were painted a bright pink.

"She did?" That wasn't the Cassia I knew. Then again, she had old friends at the coven. Maybe she loved parties and dancing and there'd been none of those things in the dungeon or with the banshees. At least not for her. She deserved a little fun after what she'd been through.

"Her and Damien." The third girl chuckled and wiggled her eyebrows in a suggestive way.

I frowned. Cassia had been mad when Lukas hadn't wanted to kiss her. I hoped they would work things out.

"What about you and the god-like giant?" My pretend friend glanced down. "Is he that big everywhere?"

My cheeks flamed and I tilted my chin up. "I wouldn't know."

"Really?" The one with the pink lips giggled. "When you get tired of him—"

"Or he gets tired of you..." The third girl elbowed her friend.

My heart thumped. Stone and I might not have committed to anything specific in our relationship, but we'd never get tired of each other. Right?

"Send him my way." Pink lips bumped her hip against her friend's.

I didn't want to stand around gossiping about my relationship with Stone. I had a mission before Trolgar left. "Can you direct me to Mistress Lita's office?"

Pretend Friend gave me quick directions and I was on my way. Yesterday, they'd been mean to me and today they'd been nice. Rounding my shoulders, I had to get used to the fact that witches and warlocks would treat me differently because I was related to the mistress. That was the reason for their change of mind.

I didn't need to make new friends who might favor me because of my ties to Mistress Lita. I had old friends, good friends. Violet had been part of our team and I wanted to ensure she was okay.

My knees quivered as I approached Mistress Lita's door. She was powerful with her magic and in the coven. Was she disappointed by the fact that I was part banshee and insisted on keeping my mark? Disappointed I couldn't control my magic? And after her welcoming announcement, disappointed I didn't want to stay? Although maybe I hadn't made that clear yet. Everything was happening so fast.

Taking a deep breath, I lifted my hand to knock.

The door flung open on its own. Or probably with magic. I'd have to get used to everyone having powers.

The scent of burning sage hit me first. I held in a cough as I entered. A dark fireplace with intricate carvings flared and faded. Trepidation tripped through me until I spied the rest of the room.

Bright colors with pretty blue and yellow walls, flowers in vases, and a striped couch and chairs. A coffee table sat in the middle of the furniture holding a flower teapot and tray. Everything in the room appeared new. Mistress Lita must have recently redecorated.

"Destiny, come in." Mistress Lita sat at a wooden desk and lifted a fine-boned China teacup with a trembling hand. Square reading glasses perched on the tip of her nose and dark circles hung under her eyes. Last night she'd had a few gray hairs. Today, her long dark tresses were half white. "I see you found the clothes I left for you. How did you sleep?"

The dream jolted my mind and I wiped my hands down the deep purple pants I wore. Snippets of other scenes had played in my sleep last night too. "Not well. I had a dream or a nightmare." Maybe a memory.

She must not have slept well either. Her gaunt face and raspy voice made her seem older.

She reached into a drawer in the desk where a pile of papers flipped magically. "I can give you a charm to hang in your room to stop nightmares and banshee wails." She pulled out a circular talisman in a quarter moon shape. "I should've put it in your room before you arrived."

I tucked in my chin. "What if I don't want to stop my banshee wails?" Like I'd refused to get rid of the mark.

"At the Inferis Coven we don't have much death."

That would explain why she didn't age. I compared her again to the woman in my dream. How could they be the same? Maybe the dream witch had been a great, great, great relation. Lita was too young to be the woman from the memory, although she'd specifically said she'd named me. A family name then?

"Are you ready to learn the witch way?" Realizing Mistress Lita wanted me to learn magic as much as I did gave me leverage.

I straightened, standing tall. "After my friends and I see Violet."

"She's not conscious." The mistress' lilt went flat. "I'll take you to talk with Provost Morgane who will give you your schedule for tomorrow."

"No." I pressed my foot into the ground. I needed to be firm. "I want to see Violet first."

"You sound like a child."

"I am a child. Sort of." I'd be seventeen in four days. I felt as if I'd lived several lifetimes. I wouldn't back down. "I want to see Violet this morning. With my friends."

"I thought you wanted to learn magic." My great grandmother was disappointed. "With your witch and banshee background, you'll need to possess exceptional control with your combined powers."

Part of learning control was taking control. "Trolgar wants to go home. He wants to see Violet before he leaves."

"You can't just show up to the medical facility." Mistress Lita set the teacup down. "We'll need to arrange a visit with the witch doctor and such a large group will be disruptive."

I crossed my arms. This was too important to give in because Violet was important. I went along with the spa and the clothes and sitting at the head of the table while my friends sat at the other end. It was time for my great grandmother to give a little. "This isn't a negotiation."

Holding my breath, I didn't twitch a muscle on my face. I couldn't exhibit a second of doubt. This was too important.

"Of course, we can arrange a visit." She nodded regally and added a soft smile. "Follow me."

She didn't waste time.

"And my friends?" My bones tensed. I refused to go without them.

"Simon."

The acolyte apparated next to me.

I jumped. I had to learn how to set a warning spell for when someone apparated near me. If there was such a thing.

"Get Destiny's friends and bring them to Dr. Everbleed's office." Mistress Lita ordered and he apparated out of the room without a word. "Let's go."

She led me out of her office, down the stairs, and across the drawbridge which was down. Crossing the moat, I peered into the water. I swear I saw something stalking my friends yesterday. She led me to the same building the spa had been in except we went around to the back.

A sign on the metal door said *Medical Laboratorium* and I shivered. It sounded like a place to do experiments, not healing.

"Wait here while I make sure your fairy friend is ready to be seen." She entered the building before I could respond.

Perspiration already soaked the silk blouse I wore. The dreary clouds must be heavy with moisture because mugginess clogged my senses.

Violet was unconscious and in hibernation, although knowing Violet she'd want to be more than presentable. It's the reason why I'd put her in my discarded dress right after she'd been frozen.

"Destiny." Helartha rushed ahead of my ragtag group of friends. She'd put on her old clothes and her red hair was back in a braid.

Simon led the group. Bringing up the rear was another acolyte.

Stone, who sported a new red bruise on his cheek, carried Gnit who grimaced and held his leg. My friends had changed back into their own less formal clothes.

Worry threaded through my veins. I hated that we were separated. "What happened?"

"Misunderstanding, miss." Simon's flat tone explained nothing.

Stone gave the acolyte a dark glower. "The guard wasn't specific when he said he was taking us to the *laboratory* and Gnit panicked."

Similar to what I'd thought. A chill ran down my spine with memories of the dungeon, the treatment there, and the experimental auraguillotine which sucked majiks' powers and souls.

"Naturally, he put up a fight." Lukas stood beside Stone, a protector in his own right. "I think Gnit broke his leg."

"And Stone protected Gnit." Helartha tugged on her braid.

Of course, he did.

"And lost." Pith jumped up, raising his hand.

"They used magic against us." Trolgar stressed this point because he understood using magic against other majiks wasn't allowed in the coven. He'd learned that the hard way.

And now it had happened twice. My mouth dropped open. "What?" I glared at Simon. "That's illegal and they're my friends. Guests of the coven."

"They attacked us." He sneered and glowered at my friends. "We had to defend ourselves."

"Or explain better." Stone's sarcastic remark told me he believed Simon had tried to scare my friends on purpose.

"Are you okay?" I stroked Gnit's arm.

"Good thing we're at the laboratory." Stone scowled at Simon. "Most people and majiks call them hospitals or medical offices."

"The witch doctor can fix the goblin in seconds." Simon snapped his fingers.

"His name is Gnit." I hated the way Simon treated them. "If the witch doctor can fix injuries in seconds, why isn't Violet okay?"

Simon didn't say anything.

"Welcome." Dr. Everbleed made a dramatic exit from the building, flinging her arms wide, truly welcoming me and my friends. No warts or green skin. She wore a white lab coat and a splashy dress in varying colors. "I'm Dr. Everbleed, the witch doctor."

Her gaze stopped at me and her nose twitched.

"How's Violet?"

"What's wrong with her?"

"Will she live?"

My friends asked at the same time.

"Why are you working here and not at the spa?" I wanted a real doctor to be caring for Violet.

"The medi-spa is used for cosmetic procedures which I handle." Dr. Everbleed glared at me while running her finger over her nose. "Warts, for example."

I hunched my shoulders. I'd only wanted to stop her from removing my banshee mark.

"Gnit is injured. Can you treat him?" Stone stepped to the front of the small crowd.

"Of course. Come in. Come in." She waved us inside. "Destiny, I'm sorry about our misunderstanding yesterday."

"It's okay." It wasn't, but the attempted removal of my banshee mark was in the past.

"Let me see your little friend." She brought us into an office and pointed to a chair inside. "One of my assistants will take you to see your fairy friend while I examine him."

Stiffening, I didn't want to leave Gnit alone.

Reading my mind, Helartha stood next to him. "I'll stay."

Leaving two of our friends behind, a young witch wearing high heels clicked down the long corridor. The rest of us followed. The long corridor had fluorescent lights and machines beeping in the hall. The sting of alcohol tickled my nose.

Lukas stepped next to me as we strode down the sterile hallway. "Where's Cassia?"

"I don't know. I pounded on her door this morning and she didn't answer." I didn't tell him about her late night partying. I didn't want to add more ammunition to his possible jealousy.

Beep. Beep. Beep.

A steady beeping caught my attention when the assistant opened the door at the end of the corridor. "Here is your friend."

We stepped into the room which had a large window peering into an adjacent room. The interior area had various machines with tubes and wires. Lit candles circled the room in a pentagon shape. A hospital bed sat in the middle of the space and in it lay Violet. Her long blond hair splayed across the pillow. Her face appeared shrunken, paler, and slightly purple. Her thin body shivered beneath a pile of blankets.

"How is she?" Stone's protective instincts sharpened his tone.

"The same," the medical assistant demonstrated no compassion.

Maybe after working in the medical field for awhile someone couldn't get upset about every sick or injured person.

"What're you doing to heal her?" I shook, observing Violet made me cold.

"What about the wounds?" Trolgar shadowed his eyes and peered through the glass.

The assistant squinted down her nose at him and turned to talk to me. "We bandaged up the external wounds. Internally..." She shrugged.

"Is Dr. Everbleed a real medical doctor or some crackpot?" Lukas snarled.

"We're doing our best." The assistant raised her hands, wiggling them as if preparing to do a spell against him. So much for not being allowed to do magic against other majiks.

I stepped in front of my friend. Guess, I was a protector too.

Doubt sewed through me. That's what I'd thought about the banshee healer helping my grandfather. She'd helped him to his death. My heart frayed around the edges. "Have you consulted with the fairies?"

Violet was a fairy. Helartha and Gnit had brought her to the witch coven at Cassia's suggestion because we'd been in the middle of the battle against the regent. The coven was closer than the fairy castle and Cassia believed they'd have the medical knowledge and the magic to cure Violet.

Staring into the room, the witches definitely had medical equipment. A monitor hung above the bed displaying a zigzagging up and down graph.

An IV pole stood tall dispensing a clear liquid. Another machine with a keyboard attached sat beside the bed. The screen was blank.

The coven had magic. But because she was a fairy did the witches not know how to heal her?

"Great idea, Destiny." Stone championed. "I've got contacts with the fairies."

The fairy princess.

"So does Dr. Everbleed." The assistant competed with Stone. "We've been discussing her case back and forth."

"Who are you talking to?" Stone postured into a leaning forward, more threatening stance.

I tensed, wondering if I needed to hold him back.

"None of your business." She started to pivot away.

He grabbed the assistant's arm. "Violet is my business."

"Then why don't you go visit your contacts?" The ends of the assistant's lips lifted. She dared him to leave.

My heart squeezed. I didn't want him to leave, especially to go to the fairies. "I'm sure there's a way to send a message. You're a witch."

"You're a witch." The accusation sliced my psyche.

I was a witch, just not a very good one and this woman knew it. I thought medical people were supposed to do no harm. Shaking my head, I remembered the bird delivering a message to me. "I don't know how to send messages magically yet."

The woman smirked in a superior way. "Who do you think we should contact?"

"Commander Gardenia." Stone didn't hesitate.

The medical assistant waved her hand and an acolyte apparated. "Take this...Stone and help him send a message."

The acolyte nodded and led Stone away. I wanted to follow, but I needed to see Violet up close.

"Sorry I'm late." Cassia barged into the room. She wore a stunning deep peach dress with a low cut bodice and flared skirt. Her hair had been tugged back into a messy ponytail and her makeup didn't cover the shadows under her eyes. "Where's Dr. Everbleed?"

"Cute outfit." Helartha wiggled her eyebrows.

The dress displayed Cassia's curves. Even with the tired eyes, she looked gorgeous.

"Thanks." Cassia flashed a minimal smile until her gaze landed on Lukas. Then her lips opened in a broad grin. "Hellooooo."

The werewolf shuffled his feet. "Hi."

"So you've seen Violet." The medical assistant swiveled in the other direction.

I wasn't ready to leave. "I want to go inside and talk to her."

"She's unconscious." The assistant kept walking.

"I'd like to hold her hand and say a few words." My pulse slowed to a sad rhythm. Violet had saved us and I wanted to thank her.

The witch scanned our group. "Well, you can't all go in there. It would be disruptive."

Cassia raised her hand. "Why don't the others take a tour of the medical laboratory? Destiny, Trolgar, and I will visit with Violet. When the others get back from the tour, they can see her."

The assistant peered down the hall, probably wishing the witch doctor would show up to disallow us. "The patient might get too tired."

"She's been sleeping for weeks." Frustration balled in my gut. "We're not going to make it worse."

"You can take the rest of them to see the lab where the doctor does research." Cassia's suggestion came off as an order. How much clout did her family have?

After a few grumbles, Lukas and Pith filed out. Cassia opened the door to Violet's room.

"Only a few minutes." The assistant stood by the window to watch. "You don't want to do anything to alarm her."

Slipping Violet's cold hand from beneath the blankets, I squeezed. "Hello, Violet. It's Destiny." I felt a little silly talking to an unconscious fairy. "Thank you for sacrificing yourself so the rest of us could get out of the dungeon."

Her finger twitched.

My pulse quickened and excitement shot through me. Maybe talking to her was getting a reaction. Maybe she could hear me. "We escaped, and Prince Zacharye is now king. Majiks are equal."

Or they will be once the king got everyone else in line. At least the evil regent was finally behind bars and awaiting trial.

"We brought you to the Inferis Coven because it was close, and Cassia believed the witches could help you." I exchanged glances with Cassia and Trolgar. "Cassia and Trolgar are here too."

Cassia came closer to me. "We wish you'd wake up."

Violet snatched her hand from mine. She sprung into a sitting position, her body creaking with the movement. Her hand curled and her untrimmed, long nails stretched out wildly. Her fingernails clawed down from my cheek to my chin.

Acute pain burned the skin on my face. Shock shuddered through my bones. I took a step back. "Ow."

Cassia whipped out her wand and forced Violet down. The fairy continued to struggle against the magical force. Her shoulders wobbled back and forth. Her legs kicked out.

I sucked in a sharp breath.

Dr. Everbleed ran into the room and flicked her wand. The straps, which had been laying loosely off the sides of the bed, wrapped around Violet's chest and arms holding her down. Violet twisted trying to get loose.

I knew how she felt.

"Step back." The witch doctor flicked her wand again.

Violet quit struggling and her eyes closed.

Gasping, I held my palm against my scratched and bleeding cheek. Stunned, my body went numb.

Violet had attacked me.

Chapter Nine

S haken, I sat on a chair in Dr. Everbleed's office. When Violet attacked me, I didn't know how to react. I couldn't strike back.

"It's good she woke up, right?" My voice quivered with shock and pain from my injury. My moving lips tugged on the skin and the sharp ache reminded me again that a friend had attacked me. Maybe when we'd first met she might've physically hurt me, but not now.

"Yes and no." Dr. Everbleed dabbed at the scratches with a cotton ball soaked in antiseptic.

I jerked, remembering how the banshees had forced my grandfather into unconsciousness. "Did you give Violet a sedative?"

"Too dangerous." The witch doctor spread an ointment on my cheek. "We want her to wake up."

"She will." Cassia sat on the arm of my chair, keeping her arm around me. This was the compassionate witch I knew.

"What did you do to Violet?" Gnit lay on a cot with his ankle in a cast.

"I used a mild calming spell. If our patient gets rattled by anyone else, I might need to do something more dramatic." The witch doctor dabbed my cheek harder.

"What happened?" Mistress Lita apparated into the room. Her skin appeared mottled and looser under the eyes. Her lips were cracked and dry. "Simon sent a message that I needed to come immediately."

I didn't know what to make of her sudden aging and it was probably impolite to ask.

"Destiny has a few scratches." Dr. Everbleed stepped away taking a bloody cotton ball with her.

I felt woozy. The scratches were worse than I'd thought.

"I leave you for five minutes and you get into trouble." Mistress Lita threw up her hands and paced toward me. She must be overprotective, the same as Stone. "She will not have another abomination marking her face."

My insides hardened. My banshee mark was not an abomination. "It's a scratch. And I'm proud to bear the banshee mark." I'd keep saying it until it sunk in.

"The scratches might scar." She bent down and held my chin in her hands. "Don't worry, sweetie. My magic never leaves a mark. Unless I want it to." The last bit she said under her breath.

The coldness in her tone chilled. It sounded like a threat.

She wiggled her fingers and mumbled something.

Heat scalded my cheek for a second and then the torment was gone.

I ran a hand across my now-smooth cheek. No pain. No indentations. "Why couldn't Dr. Everbleed perform that magic?"

Mistress Lita smiled in a secretive, superior way. "It's special magic."

"Dark magic," the doctor muttered.

The combined words shadowed my soul.

"What?" I wanted to be sure I heard correctly.

"Here's a mirror." Cassia snapped her fingers and a mirror materialized in her hand, interrupting my thoughts.

Anxious about what was done to my cheek, I took the mirror and held it up. "Thanks."

My cheek was as white as snow. No marks or lines or deep scratches. My skin was perfect, better than before. My gaze flipped to my forehead. The banshee mark was still there. My shoulders relaxed.

"What happened?" Stone rushed through the door and kneeled by my chair. "I swear I can't leave you alone for a second."

I could take care of myself. "Violet was upset and attacked me. Any word from the fairies?"

"You look okay," he admitted begrudgingly.

I smoothed an agitated hand over my no-longer injured cheek. Stone hadn't seen the injury, but I wanted to look more than okay to him.

"Dr. Everbleed has been in contact with a fairy healer." He nodded at the woman, showing he'd been skeptical of her claim. "They've suggested several things. The fairies want her sent to Queen's Academy."

"Yes, yes." The witch doctor stood and stepped toward a metal counter holding potions and salves. "But after this latest attack, your friend appears more unstable."

The banshees had forced my grandfather to travel and he'd taken a turn for the worse. "The doctor has a point."

"Fairies want to take care of their own." Stone stood ready to press the fairy healer's request. He'd spent a lot of time living at their castle.

"Since King Zacharye is now in charge, aren't we all one?" Dr. Everbleed snapped the cap on the antibiotic.

"There is no fighting between the different majiks. We're here to help each other." Mistress Lita shooed Cassia away and sat in her place. She put her arm around my shoulders.

Stiffening for a second, I forced myself to relax. It felt good to be with a family member who cared for me. My spirits rose. I agreed with her philosophy too.

"The others are back from their tour." Dr. Everbleed stepped toward the door. "You understand they won't be able to visit the fairy today."

Touching my cheek, I understood. I didn't want anyone else to suffer.

The group gathered by the door as I told them the news. Concern for me, disappointment about not getting to see Violet, and surprise at what had happened crossed their expressions.

Pith angled his head. "It's odd Violet would attack a friend."

I agreed. She must not have realized who stood by her bedside.

"I can't wait longer for Violet to reawaken." Trolgar gave me a hug. "I should say goodbye."

My heart ached and I hugged him back. After the way he'd been treated the first day by Damien and the other witches I understood why he wanted to leave. "I'll miss you."

Everyone else hugged Trolgar and he stepped in the room to hug Gnit laying on the cot. "I'm ready to leave too."

Understandable since one of the acolytes had injured him.

Another round of goodbyes took place. My eyes burned and I sniffed. My group of friends was getting smaller.

"I can fully heal your friend's ankle." Mistress Lita had stood by and watched our sorrowful goodbye. She must care a little about my friends. "His traveling will be easier."

"And quicker," Lukas muttered.

Only I'd heard his comment. I'd need to ask him what he meant. At the moment, I wanted to watch my great grandmother's special magic.

Dr. Everbleed removed the cast and my great grandmother waved her arms in a circular pattern. Sparks shot from Mistress Lita's fingers, arced, and wrapped around Gnit's small ankle. "Flex it."

Gnit's wary gaze landed on me before he crooked his foot. "It doesn't hurt." He hopped off the bed and danced a jig. "It feels great."

"I'll help Trolgar and Gnit exit the coven." Cassia flashed a grin. "Do you want to come with me, Lukas?"

He ran a finger under his collar. "Um, sure."

Watching the four of them leave the building, I hoped Cassia and Lukas figured things out between them.

"I'll signal an acolyte to take the rest of you back to your rooms." Dr. Everbleed twirled her wand and Simon and another acolyte apparated.

"But Stone..." I wanted to stay with him.

"Stone," Mistress Lita took hold of his thick arm. "Would you be interested in a tour of the perimeter protections for the coven? I think you'll find it interesting and quite reassuring."

My great grandmother wanted to assure Stone I was safe. I appreciated that she cared enough about me to satisfy him.

"Sure." Stone's serious expression told me this was something he was interested in observing.

"Simon, you will show our giant friend around." She dropped Stone's arm and ogled me.

Simon crossed his wrists in a sign of respect. "Yes, mistress."

"I'll go with you." At least I'd be with Stone even if we weren't alone.

"Now that you've seen your friend, we need to discuss your education." Her voice firmed and she added a soft smile making her new wrinkles deeper.

My desires pulled in different directions. She was my great grandmother. I wouldn't be at the coven long. Stone and I would have the rest of our lives together. "Okay."

The sooner I began, the sooner I'd finish and we could leave the coven. "I'll see you later." I frowned as Stone marched away with barely a wave.

Mistress Lita held out her hand covered in dark spots. "Will you trust me to apparate together? It will be much quicker."

The fact that she asked calmed my nerves. There was no pressure and I wanted to begin learning right away. I took hold of her hand. "I want to learn how to apparate soon."

"For you, it should be easy." She snapped her fingers.

My body was flung into a black void. Clinging to her hand, I was yanked through complete darkness. A light switched on and we landed in her office. I stuck my hand out for balance, still feeling woozy from this form of travel.

"Whoa."

"Are you riding a horse?" Her sharp tone made me regard her. She flashed a quick smirk. "Kidding." She walked to her desk with no stumbling, used to apparating. "You will begin classes tomorrow."

Her announcement struck through my center, jarring me.

"Classes? As in school?" I'd never been to school. I'd had a tutor when I was a small child at the palace, and then grandfather had taught me.

"The best. Inferis Coven Witch Academy." Mistress Lita's boast brought me back to the present. She leaned against the desk. "The best witch teachers will bring your magic up to par."

Her insult slashed at my confidence. Remembering the spa incident with the witch doctor and others in my past, I might not be worthy of being related to her. I needed teaching. Lots of teaching.

"You'll find your academy uniform, spell books, parchment, and anything else you'll need in your room."

"Uniform?" I scrunched my face remembering the three girls in the hall. Peeking at my current outfit of designer pants and silk shirt, I'd hate a uniform. I wasn't one to fit in.

"A requirement at the witch academy."

"I don't really want to go to school. I thought I'd just study with a few really good witches and..." I snapped my fingers, wanting to be good.

"You can't use magic to learn magic." She crossed her arms and I could see brown spots on them too. "I thought you wanted to learn to apparate and many other things. There is so much the academy can teach you."

"I do want to learn." I gulped, realizing this was going to take more than a few days or weeks.

Leaning over, she took hold of my hand. "Do you know your family history?"

The change in topic had my mind swiveling. "Just what Grandfather told me and what I learned from the banshees." I sank into a chair.

"Not your banshee side." She swiped her hand in the air, dismissing half my heritage. "Your witch side."

She might dismiss my banshee side. I didn't. My grandfather's heritage meant a lot to me especially now that a good leader was in charge of the clan.

"Not really." I knew my mother was a witch although she'd worn the mark of a banshee. "I didn't know about you."

Her expression relaxed. "Of course not. When your mother married that...that..."

I tensed. "My loving father."

"Yes, your loving father." Her lips tightened into a slight smile. "She left our family and our heritage."

"Is that why you placed the Wicked End Prophecy on my head?" I fisted my hands. "Because you were mad at my mother?"

She pressed her other hand to her chest in shock. "I foretold the prophecy. And it was awful to forecast such dread on my own great granddaughter, especially after what happened to my own daughter."

My grandmother. I'd never heard anything about her. "What happened?"

Mistress Lita dabbed at her eyes. "My beautiful Angelita died when she fell into the Dark Angel's Veil waterfall."

My sympathy bled thinking about a young witch falling into a waterfall to her death. My entire family had died in awful circumstances. "I'm sorry. Drowning must've been a terrible death."

Mistress Lita sniffed. "Right before your mother turned seventeen, she left the coven."

"Why did she leave?" I wanted to learn more about her.

"Silly really." She fluttered her hand. "She fell in love."

Beaming, I was glad my father made my mother happy during their short lives. My mother had left the coven and married someone she loved despite their differences. She'd had me and brought me to the coven one time to be named. We'd never visited the coven or my great grandmother again.

My brow furrowed. "Why didn't we ever visit? Why didn't you visit me?"

"I tried to visit." She squeezed my hand. "After your parents died, I tried to find you. I searched everywhere, even questioning Anvers Snow's banshee clan. The man hid you away so well, even my best acolyte hunters couldn't find you."

She'd tried to find me, even used coven resources to search. She'd wanted to meet me again, possibly spend time with me, even teach me about being a witch. Warmth enveloped me. If she'd found me, I'd be a stronger witch and we'd have a closer connection. I loved Stone and my friends but I yearned for a familial connection now that I'd lost my grandfather.

"What exactly does the prophecy mean?" I'd thought when the banshee clan planned to use my powers to help Regent Theobald that was what the Wicked End Prophecy referred to. I'd fought against them and freed myself but still had the prophecy attached to my name.

Mistress Lita stared at me so intensely I thought she'd see deep into my soul. "I don't know."

I sat straighter, ready to jump out of the chair. "You prophesied it. How can you not know what it means?"

She pushed away from the desk and hobbled. "I thought it might be about you growing up in the human palace, especially once the evil regent took charge. When I learned you were with the banshee clan, I thought it might happen because of them."

Her thoughts about the banshees were similar to mine. Maybe we weren't so different.

"One can only surmise about a prophecy. Until it comes true no one really knows."

Clenching my fists again, I couldn't believe she didn't know. "Why foretell the prophecy? Why not stay silent?"

"In a coven, it's the grandmother's right to name the child, and since your grandmother was gone it fell to me." Mistress Lita placed her arms on the fireplace mantle and squinted into the flames. "I believed the prophecy was a way to bring your mother back to the coven."

The confession seemed forced. "Why didn't she want to visit?"

"I wanted her and you to stay at the coven." Mistress Lita choked up. "To keep both of you safe."

My great grandmother must've been lonely after her daughter died and my mom left. "And my father?"

"He was a banshee. He couldn't stay at the coven." Anything sentimental fled her voice.

She'd wanted my mother to take me and leave my father. I stood up. "We were a family."

"Until they both got themselves killed." Her hard tone blamed them. "I didn't know where to find you." She wailed in an all-alone tone. "That man, Anvers Snow..."

My chest contracted with anguish. "That man was my grandfather. He took care of me and now he's dead."

"And I'm sorry." She didn't sound sorry. "He kept you away from me. He hid you so I couldn't find you."

"For my safety." I'd resented our hermit existence, but now I understood. The banshee clan expected me to return and be married off. The regent searched for banshees to use in his sinister scheme.

"From me." She moved so fast I couldn't react before she took hold of my chin in a gentle hand. Her eyes gleamed with unshed tears and her lips trembled. "You don't fear me, do you, my child? Your great grandmother?" She asked the question as if speaking her biggest fear. She didn't want me to be afraid of her.

To be my great grandmother, she had to be at least fifty. She looked about thirty yesterday, young, strong, and confident. A day later, she appeared older. Had bringing me to the coven aged her? Maybe the gray hair was a new style or maybe I was just that much of a handful.

My heart tugged. She was intimidating at times and soft at others. She was family, the only family I had left. "No, of course not."

Still holding my chin, she turned my head one way and the other, examining every inch of my recently-fixed skin. Her gaze dug into mine, deeper than before. I felt she could see my soul and every truth.

Smashing my lips, I wanted to yank my chin away. She had no right to know my deepest thoughts and feelings.

A flame flared in her pupils and extinguished. It must've been the reflection of the fire.

"Call me Gigi. It's what your mother called me." Softening, she brushed my chin with her thumb before letting go. "Come and sit next to me."

Her words suggested something lonely and grandmotherly, like she was about to impart wisdom. She wanted to connect with me. Maybe she didn't understand the best way to approach that. She sat on the couch and I took a seat at the other end. I wiped my sweaty hands on my pants. She might be my great grandmother, but I didn't know her and didn't think I was ready to call her Gigi.

She scooted closer and took my hand once more. "You've arrived at a very important time."

It *was* an important time. King Zacharye had defeated his uncle and he'd reunite the kingdom. I'd discovered I wasn't the last banshee. And I'd learned I was half witch. "I'm so glad I've met you. Is there anyone else I should meet?"

She held up her hand. "Before I say anything, you need to agree to the Secretum Bond."

My gaze widened. "What? Why? What is it?"

"It will make it so you can't speak to anyone about the information I reveal." Her persuasive voice hinted this was a good thing. "What I'm about to tell you is top secret coven business."

"What if I don't want to know coven business?" I'd learned too many secrets recently. "I'm not staying long."

Her smile fell and her pupils became duller. She glimpsed away as if gathering her thoughts. Taking a deep breath, she rotated back toward me. Her calm expression should've warned me. "Do you normally make snap decisions before learning everything there is to know? Like when you insisted your friends cross the drawbridge."

The cutting slight and her disappointment rang in my ears. I should hear her out. The thought reminded me of what Provost Morgane had asked of me. "No."

"I understand this might be confusing for you and you have your plans set for the future." Mistress Lita's reasonableness conflicted with my actuality.

I had no set plans. Stone and I hadn't committed to anything. He'd taken a position without consulting me. His words and his actions confused me. She had a point. I might learn more about her, my grandmother, and my mother. "I want to learn about the coven, magic, and family."

"Make the bond and I'll tell you everything." Her gaze seared into me.

Finally, someone willing to tell me everything. I tilted forward, temptation straining my muscles no matter the risk. I'd been kept in the dark my entire life. So what if I couldn't tell anyone else? Stone had kept secrets. "What will this Secretum Bond do to me?"

She chuckled, probably at my paranoia. "It's a secrecy pact which will not allow you to divulge what we've discussed to anyone."

My nerves tingled. She thought I was being ridiculous. Agreeing to learn only obligated me to silence and since I knew nothing now, what was the harm. "Okay. I will agree to the Secretum Bond."

Her dark orbs flared with light and gleamed. Muttering, she stuck her hand out. A black thread sprung from her finger and shot toward me. I froze and my eyes widened. The thread wrapped around my neck and tightened.

My hands jerked up to yank the thread away.

"Stop." She flickered another finger at me. "Sorry sweetie, this is part of the process. It won't hurt...for long."

My hands were forced down. I couldn't reach up. I couldn't move. My breaths came in faster pants.

The thread wrapped around and around my neck. With each circle it became tighter and tighter. Panic bolted from my throat to my torso to my center. I couldn't breathe. I opened my mouth and no words came out.

"It's the bond reacting." The gleam flared again. "It will end soon."

My lungs constricted and my pulse slowed. I refused to be killed by a string. And my great grandmother. Is this why my grandfather kept me hidden from her?

She jerked her wrist and her hands went into a fist. At the same time, the black thread burned around my throat. The scalding pain fired. She yanked her fist inward, toward her. The thread sizzled around my neck leaving a trail of ashes behind.

The scalding and pain evaporated.

I exhaled slowly afraid the agony might return.

Between us, the thread burned like a wick going toward her. She opened her fist, welcoming the flame, and then she squeezed her fingers capturing the fire.

The second I could move, my hands went to my neck. I grazed only smooth skin. No welt or scar.

She shook her hand and pressed the palm to her chest. "Don't worry. The bond doesn't leave a mark on the outside."

What about the inside? After seeing that I'd be scarred for life.

Mistress Lita stood, paced to the fireplace and watched the hot fire dance. "One of the coven's biggest secrets is that we guard the secret Gates to the Underworld."

I inhaled sharply. "As in H...E...Double L?"

"Correct." She whirled around with more energy than she'd displayed earlier. "A few witches and warlocks are aware of our important role."

I drew in a shaky breath. The coven must be important for it to have such a critical task. Those stuck in the Underworld were bad. If anyone escaped, there'd be chaos in our kingdom. And no one would want to go there purposely before they died.

"Our line has held the leadership position forever." Determination gave a hard edge to her voice. "We protect the kingdom and the coven."

What did that mean for me? I'd realized earlier I was a protector by nature. "How long have you held the position?"

Her uncomfortable laugh gave me the shivers. "A woman never shares her age."

How witches aged was a complete mystery to me. Maybe they had a secret potion to stop aging and she needed to take a sip. A large sip.

She took my hand and held it in hers. "But a seventeenth birthday is special. It's when a young witch decides her path."

Confusion swirled in my mind. I turned seventeen in four days and had no clue what direction to go. I was taking it one day at a time. Learn to control my magic, discover my heritage, figure out things with Stone.

"There's a ceremony at midnight the night before you turn seventeen where you announce your decision."

"There is?" Did I have to announce I wouldn't be staying in the coven?

Mistress Lita straightened her spine and held my gaze. I felt she was facing one of her worst fears and it wasn't me. "If the line doesn't continue, the Inferis Coven will die as I know it."

The fire in the fireplace burst with higher flames, sending black smoke up the chimney.

My body tensed waiting for an explosion or an attack. Her dire statement speared through my center. Familial obligations weighed on my mind like a crown. I barely knew her and knew nothing about the coven, and yet I felt a sense of connection and obligation. Even if I wasn't staying, I didn't want the coven to die.

"Our family line has done great things." She thundered with pride. "And I refuse to let things change."

The leadership position had been in my family for ages, almost a royal line or dynasty. It was good to be part of a strong heritage. It hadn't been that way with the banshees. I'd only been important because I was the only one with powers. "Sometimes change can be good."

I'd changed. I'd gone from overprotected and ignorant about myself and the kingdom to becoming someone people could count on, someone who understood the workings of our world, someone with internal strength and magic.

"My leadership," she tugged on my hand bringing my full attention to her, "our family's leadership must continue." Her serious expression had dread filtering through my veins. What did she expect from me? Her eyes darkened as they stared into mine, willing me to concede. "You and I are the last of the family."

My mind ticked faster and faster. "If you expect our family's leadership to continue, that means..."

"You are next in line to lead the coven."

The pronouncement came from nowhere and landed in the center of my soul with a thud. She expected me to become the leader? I guess that was better than being forced to marry the future leader of the banshees. But I'd just arrived. I knew nothing about running a coven or even how to be a witch. My magic was atrocious.

My mouth opened and nothing came out.

Her gaze narrowed in a calculating expression. "I was fearful it would end. But now, I have you."

Chapter Ten

"This is the Witch Academy provost's office." The next morning, Cassia tapped on the black door. "She'll meet with you and give you your schedule."

"I wasn't expecting to go to school. And I'm not staying to become—" My words stopped. I opened my mouth again and again, similar to a fish. I couldn't speak what I'd been about to say. Bitterness flooded my mouth as a warning. I couldn't talk about not wanting to become the leader.

I'd just discovered I was a witch. I knew nothing about being a witch or the Inferis Coven. I didn't know what my future plans were. I needed to talk to Stone, except I couldn't tell him. I couldn't tell anyone.

Cassia scrutinized me. She knew I wanted to say more.

I couldn't share with her because of the Secretum Bond. Anxiety took up residence in my gut. Remembering Mistress Lita's calculating expression I knew she was going to try to convince me. But I knew nothing about how the coven worked. Her math didn't add up.

"I thought I'd work with a few well-trained witches and be done. Not actually attend the academy." I repeated the same thing I'd said to my great grandmother.

"School is the best way to meet the popular witches." Cassia shimmied her hips in the uniform. "There are parties and wand competitions and soirees with warlocks."

"I'm not a big party person." I didn't think she was either.

"You could be." She bumped her hip against mine and when the door opened, she waved. "See you later."

"Come in, Destiny." Provost Morgane's formidable greeting put a tremble in my step.

I moved across the threshold and entered a different world.

A black square rug had a pentagon drawn in red and in the middle was a cauldron bubbling with an orange liquid. Not a welcoming sight. No floating candelabra, only lanterns with a strange blue glow barely lighting the room. The windows were covered by heavy black drapes and on each wall stood a different hutch, some with rounded tops, others open to reveal potion bottles and ancient books.

"This is almost as impressive as Mistress Lita's office." And so different.

"Not quite," the provost snapped. She studied me as her thin red eyebrows arched. I thought she'd been much older than Mistress Lita yesterday. Now, I wasn't so sure.

With all the inspections I'd received, I was treated as a strange specimen from another world. She'd met me before. No need to study so intensely.

I shifted my feet. "I'm not sure the witch academy is the right place for me."

"Finally, something we agree on." Was she referring to my shocking line in leadership, to being half banshee, or to my friends being welcomed here? Either way, her voice came across as an insult.

I stood a little straighter refusing to be intimidated. I'd promised to keep an open mind while I learned. It was clear Provost Morgane didn't like me. I wanted to prove to her I could be a talented witch. Plus if I said yes to ruling, I'd be her leader and she'd hate it. I held in a smirk.

"How your great grandmother thinks you can keep up with a third year's work is beyond me." She was the first one who dared disagree with Mistress Lita around me. Everyone else fawned over her.

"You have zero skill and zero knowledge about being a witch." Provost Morgane drummed my own doubts into me.

True. "I, um, didn't know I was a witch until recently."

"Part." The single word sliced.

She'd never let me forget my banshee half. Neither would most others if I became the leader. Of course, I wouldn't. I wasn't staying. I firmed my lips.

Circling around me, she peered down and examined me from every angle, searching for faults. It wouldn't matter that I'd dressed in the black and white uniform, that Cassia had done something to my hair to make it shine and stay in place covering my mark. The provost's inspection told me I'd never fit in at the academy in her view. She'd never accept me as a future leader.

Internally, I huffed. I didn't want to become the leader or fit in. I wanted to learn and get out. I wouldn't stay and I wanted to shout it from the pointy rooftop. I didn't need to make more enemies. "I'm not sure why I'm here."

"Neither am I." She raised a thin brow, tempting me to say more. Did she know about how coven leadership was transferred? She must if she was the leader of the academy.

I licked my lips about to ask. A bitter taste flooded my mouth. I couldn't even speak of the transfer of power to those who might know. "What I mean is..." I bit my lip. "I need to learn how to control my powers."

"Most certainly." She snapped her fingers and a sheet of paper materialized in her hand. "Your classes are Runes, Spellcrafting, Arts of Alchemy, Familiars, and Wand Works."

My head spun. "I'm not sure I can keep up."

"I agree." She reeled around. "But your great grandmother wants you in classes with witches your own age."

"And warlocks." There'd be parties with them Cassia had said.

"Warlocks have separate classes."

My brow furrowed. "Is that fair?"

"Separate but equal." Provost Morgane's words popped.

"That didn't work so well in the past." I remembered when majiks were kicked out of the human schools.

A feathered pen appeared in her hand and she scratched something onto my schedule.

"After school you will have flying training." She grimaced as if picturing me in the air, "And to cap it off, you will have tutoring. With me."

She didn't sound happy. I wasn't happy either. We were oil and vinegar. So much for my vow to stay away from her. And when would I ever see Stone and my friends? "That's a busy day. When will I have free time?"

"In my academy, you are not special. You will not be given special treatment because you're learning or because you're the mistress' great granddaughter." The provost rolled her eyes. "You will earn your free time like everyone else when you learn to become a proper witch."

⟫⟫⟫ ⟪⟪⟪

Taking a deep inhale, I stepped through the doorway of my first witch class. Flutters the size of fairies flew in my stomach. I couldn't tell if I was excited or terrified.

Class had already begun. My legs trembled. Old wooden chairs with trays were arranged in groups. The teen witches leered at me except for a group of girls giggling in the corner.

"Ah, Destiny." The witch teacher had long, straight black hair on half of her head. The other half was bald. "You've arrived."

"Um, yes." I held my schedule with a surprisingly steady hand. "Sorry, I'm late Miss Serafin. I was meeting with the provost."

"Very good." She scanned around the room. "Do you know anything about the magic of gems, symbols, and stones?"

Stones. My heart bumped. I hadn't seen or talked to Stone since yesterday. Obviously that's not what she meant. "I know about walking through crystalline limestone."

"We all do, dear." She patted my arm. "Why don't you join—"

"Miss Serafin," the girl who'd teased Trolgar raised her hand. Her dark hair had been pulled back into a wavy ponytail with long bangs cascading around her narrow face. Her pressed uniform must've come right from a dry cleaner. "We'd love to have Destiny in our group."

Wariness had the hairs on my arms rising. She'd bullied my friend.

"Excellent. Raven, Aster, and Arabella are my most advanced students." The teacher pointed to them. "They'll be excellent tutors to help you catch up."

"Move, Arabella." The first girl, Raven, pushed Arabella off a stool and smiled, waving at me. "Come sit."

Lumbering, I felt awkward taking the other girl's place. The three of them seemed to be attached at the hip.

I perched on the edge of the chair. "Hi."

Arabella conjured another stool and squeezed in next to the third girl at the table, who must be Aster. All had dark hair, but their complexions varied in color.

"I'm sorry we got off on the wrong foot." Raven flipped her hair back and grinned in a trying-too-hard way. "I didn't realize the troll was your friend."

Aster clutched her feathered pen. "How did you meet a troll?"

"How did you become friends with a troll?" Arabella shivered.

Each question lobbed at me one after the other. "You don't have to worry. Trolgar is sweet and left yesterday. So did Gnit, my goblin friend."

Arabella scrunched her nose. "Goblins are so cute, in an ugly way." She compared him to a baby animal, not a majik. "Like the ugly dolls we loved as kids."

And a doll. I didn't know what to say. He was cute but more importantly loyal.

"So are the giant and the werewolf." Aster smacked her lips. "Hunky and hunkier."

"The werewolf belongs to Cassia." Raven defended my other friend as if Lukas was Cassia's property.

Why were they so interested in my friends now? It didn't matter. I wanted to learn, not gossip. "So what are we supposed to be doing with the rocks?"

The shiny stones had been carved into oval shapes with symbols etched into them. They laid in the desk tray in varying shades of purple, red, and green.

Raven giggled and the other two followed. "They're runes."

"In the past, witches and other majiks used them to make predictions and send messages." Aster picked up a green rock with etched symbols.

Peering closer, I wondered if I could get a message to Stone even though he wasn't far away. I missed him and with the schedule the provost had given me, I'd be busy all day. Every day. Mistress Lita told me I could communicate with him whenever I wanted, there just hadn't been time to learn how. "How would I send a message?"

"Oh, we have more modern ways to send messages throughout the coven." Aster pulled out a notebook with a feathered quill attached from her school bag. "Runes are old and a school requirement."

"Mistress Lita had a bird carry a small scroll to me." I remembered the threatening invitation. "The scroll was blank when one of my friends opened it. As soon as I touched the scroll, the writing revealed itself."

"It's a spirit animal totem." Arabella leaned in to whisper. "My cousin is in the Witch Secret Service and they use the animals to send secret messages when they're spying on other majiks.

I didn't understand the need. We were no longer at war and the majik factions should be working together. It must've been before King Zacharye was in charge. "What other ways can witches send messages? To other majiks or even humans?"

Raven shrieked with laughter.

The teacher tapped her wand on the desk. "What's going on girls?"

Had she wanted to get caught?

"Nothing. We're teaching Destiny about runes." She appeared innocent of the gossiping.

"And what have you learned, Destiny?" The teacher questioned me in a disbelieving way. Either she didn't believe Raven or she thought I was stupid.

"Um, um…" I was stupid. If I was going to do well in my classes and learn quickly, I needed to focus.

Another girl in class raised her hand. Her frizzy hair stuck out from her head.

"Yes, Lavender?" The teacher nodded at the girl.

"Teacher's pet," Raven muttered.

Lavender's shoulders slumped when she heard the tease. "Nowadays runes are used to foretell the future."

I sat on the edge of my seat. Maybe I'd finally get my answer. "To make a prediction or a prophecy?"

The teacher focused on me in a glaring, accusing way. "Yes, a prophecy, which you'll study in more advanced classes. Some, like your prophecy, are a curse."

CHAPTER ELEVEN

Spellcrafting was the second class of the day.

Stepping into the room, I spotted Cassia in the back corner and dashed to sit by her in the back row. This class wasn't going to be so bad.

"How was your first class?" Her vest and shirt were unbuttoned to a low point on her chest. Her last classroom must've been hot inside.

"The teacher spooked me about curses." I quickly explained what happened. "She tried to place blame on me about the prophecy and then she clamped up and wouldn't talk about it anymore."

Cassia leaned in and I could see the mounds of her breasts. "Your prophecy?"

"The teacher inferred it was a curse." A dark chill settled in my bones. The name of the prophecy was bad enough, now I had to think about it being a curse. And no one knew what it meant.

"Oh my stars." Her concerned expression comforted. "What did the teacher say?"

I shrugged. "Not much. It was the way she said it as she looked at me."

"She must've been trying to throw you off or make you uncomfortable. You know what the prophecy says, you just don't know its exact meaning. Right?" She tilted closer to watch me.

If I knew anything more, I would've told her. I shook my head.

The room was similar in design to the last one but instead of desks there were long tables. The table I sat at had graffiti etched in the wood. Neither Raven, Aster, or Arabella were in the class.

"Don't you think it's strange that warlocks aren't allowed in our classes?" If this was the best witch academy, why wouldn't warlocks want to be trained here? The magic was the same.

Cassia gave a dismissing wave. "They don't understand the deepest aspects of our witchcraft." She wiggled her eyebrows. "They're in flying class with us and their uniforms include snug shorts."

The only muscles I wanted to see were Stone's. With the banshees it was the males who ogled the females. Here it was the opposite. I didn't prefer either option. With King Zacharye leading the kingdom, all different majiks would be equal so males and females should be equals too.

I leaned in to whisper. If I spoke quickly maybe I could get the information out. "I learned I was—" A bitter taste coated my tongue and it stuck to the roof of my mouth.

She angled her head waiting for me to continue.

Except I couldn't.

I needed to say something. Anything. "I'm worried about our friends. With us in school all day, what're they doing?" I worried they might be sitting around doing nothing, bored out of their minds. "Is there some way to get a message to them?"

"I'll take care of it." She made it sound easy.

I fisted and unfisted my hands. Raven, Aster, and Arabella couldn't focus long enough to explain how to send a message.

A woman wearing a decorative blue caftan waddled in. Her dark hair was wild and frizzy and her eyes were lined with heavy makeup. "Okay, ladies. Quiet down. Everyone flip to chapter seven and take out your wands."

I didn't bring any of the books from my room and I didn't have a wand.

Cassia slouched in her chair, opened her book, and took her wand out from the satchel hanging off her chair. She stared straight ahead as if afraid of talking in front of the teacher.

I raised my hand. "Excuse me."

The teacher startled and adjusted her square glasses further down her nose. "Who are you?"

My midsection flitted. "Um, I'm—"

"Stand up and talk. I can't see you." A glowing beam came out of the end of her wand to shine a light on me.

The last thing I wanted. I put my hand up to shield my eyes. "I'm sorry. I'm Destiny and I'm a new student."

"A new student? We don't get those very often." The light continued to shine as the teacher squinted at me.

Other students twisted in their chairs to stare and murmur.

I was on display, highlighted and talked about. My skin heated. I'd thought by now the rumor mill would've spilled my story to everyone at the academy. The rumor mill fed by Raven, Aster, and Arabella. And don't forget Damien. He seemed to be friendly with every teenage witch.

"The provost didn't inform me. I'll check with her after class." The teacher turned off the spotlight. "In the meantime, you can use a loaner until you get your own wand."

A wand flung at me like an arrow.

I ducked out of the way and the wand struck the wall right behind my head.

Boing.

Spinning around, I gaped. The wand went in a direct path level with my head. If I hadn't moved it would've struck me right on my banshee mark.

The class giggled.

"Take it," Cassia whispered.

I wrapped my fingers around the wand and pulled it out of the wall. Sitting back down, I noted its heavy weight. It was gray and had a piece of black tape wrapped around the middle.

"Now that we've wasted part of our class, let's get to work." The teacher lectured about things I didn't understand.

Enscorcell. Hex. Captare. Spellbind.

"Do a Decimare Spell with no power. Practicing." The teacher flicked her wand in a large circle. "We wouldn't want to injure our fellow classmates."

She zeroed in on me and I realized she'd probably heard about one of my earlier mishaps.

"Like this and this. Swish." Her wand waved in concentric circles, each time getting smaller. "You can practice with power at home and hurt one of your male siblings."

The girls laughed.

I didn't. It must be a joke I didn't understand because I didn't have siblings.

I went from Spellcrafting to the Arts of Alchemy class. Not recognizing the few people in the room, I took a seat in front hoping to soak up as much knowledge as possible. A crow cawed and the rest of the girls filed in, gossiping and giggling. They watched me as they passed. No one said hello.

One of the last girls to enter was Lavender from my first class. She took the open seat next to me. Her dark skin contrasted with her wild red hair. She didn't wear any makeup and her uniform was too big. She didn't glance in my direction.

A cloud of smoke burst at the front and the teacher apparated. More than apparating, her entrance was pure showmanship. Her blond hair was in a tight bun high on her head. Her white dress floated around her. The long, bell sleeves fluttered around her wrists, and the high collar was tied high on her neck.

I rubbed my neck.

"Hello ladies, let's wait until lunch to finish your gossip." She smiled at the group, then frowned when she spotted me. "You must be the famous, Destiny."

My cheeks warmed. I wasn't famous. The last teacher hadn't known I existed. I shook my head.

"You're not Destiny?" She floated next to me.

"No, I am Destiny." I blew trying to cool my cheeks. "I'm not famous."

"Oh, we all know about you." Her words came out harsher than I'd expected. "I'm Miss Shadowmend. Let's begin." A thick book dropped on my desk and I jumped. "At this point, we're studying theory. Soon we will get into Alchemy practice. Who read the assigned reading and can answer a few questions for a prize?"

The class grew excited.

She held up a round, glowing globe. "Is the transformation of one material to another using alchemy actually possible?"

Everyone but me raised their hands high. They wanted to be called on.

The teacher picked a dark haired girl and she answered.

"Correct!"

The glowing globe floated into the student's hands.

"And since you didn't get to read the assignment," the teacher snapped her fingers and a rolled up parchment floated to me. "It's an alchemy properties poster. I assume you'll read the text tonight and will know the answer by tomorrow."

My head dropped. A full day of classes, tutoring, and homework too. "Is there going to be a quiz?" I'd never had one of those and I didn't know whether to be excited or terrified.

"Never." The teacher made the idea seem ridiculous. "We don't do quizzes in this class. Learning should be fun."

A bunch of prizes floated down. More parchment posters, jewelry, and notebooks. Each of the girls grabbed one.

⇥⇤

Entering the cafeteria, I experienced the same feelings and insecurities as when I entered the dungeon prison for the first time. Fear, abandonment, loneliness. The clatter of trays and pots and spoons. The din of low level talking followed by high-pitched giggles. The strange smells.

My pulse zipped around my body and my stomach did somersaults. At least I didn't give a banshee wail. No one would die here today. In fact, I hadn't wailed since arriving at the coven. I didn't know if that was because no one had died—I hoped so—or the charm Mistress Lita had given me was working.

Splashes of light filled the cavernous room from the arched stained glass windows lining one wall. The images showed witches dominating other majiks. The visual reminded me of the Reximus Palace ballroom except there humans dominated.

Row upon row of long tables with benches were filled with witches and warlocks wearing some form of the academy's black and white plaid. They ate, gossiped, and giggled. The witches hung out in packs and the males flirted from group to group.

I missed Stone's teasing grin. Knowing he was close made the feeling worse.

Not able to spot Cassia or even Raven and her two besties, I took the first open table. The crowded cafeteria was noisy and I wasn't used to being around so many witches at one time.

Food magically appeared on my tray and it wasn't appealing. I pushed my tray away.

Lunch was my only free time during the day. I wouldn't waste it here, sitting alone. Standing, I swiveled out the cafeteria door knowing exactly where I wanted to go.

But I didn't know how to get there.

All the hallways looked the same. I headed to the left and found a dead end. Pivoting around, I headed back the way I came, moving quickly past the cafeteria entrance before anyone could spot me. Taking a right around the corner, I bumped into something solid.

Losing my balance, I grabbed wildly, weightlessness emptying my lungs. "Ah."

Strong fingers gripped both my arms stopping my fall. "I got you."

"Th-thanks." The last thing I needed was to make a spectacle of myself by falling.

I peered up at my rescuer. Damien. My spirits sank. He wore a black shirt and pants, and a vest in the same plaid as my uniform.

"Are you okay?" He set me on my feet and flashed a dazzling smile. Not teasing like the last time, more flirtatious. "You seem a little dazed."

"No." I yanked on the skirt of my uniform. "I mean, I'm fine."

"Are you sure?" His lips twitched as if he knew girls fell for his sexy teasing. "Because the cafeteria is the other way."

His inviting tone had me studying him more closely. His short curly hair had been shaved by his ears, making the curls on top stand out more. His thick dark eyebrows were expressive in an arched angle. Wide, strong nose, square cut jaw, and dimples would have most believing he was gorgeous.

I wasn't most. I was already in love with Stone. "I needed air."

Damien laughed and I didn't understand what he thought was funny. Didn't witches and warlocks need time alone?

"So we meet again." He reached out his hand and clasped mine. "Damien."

It was just a handshake and yet it felt like so much more. "I know."

"You remembered my name." He kept my hand in his. "And you are?"

I also remembered how he'd teased Trolgar with Raven and her friends. I tried to slip my hand from his grip. "In a hurry."

"That's an interesting name." Damien didn't sound offended. "What happens if you're not in a hurry, In A Hurry? Do they call you Slow?"

Furrowing my brow, I tried to decide if he was being flirty, confusing, or mean. "I'm not slow."

"You're also not in a hurry." He squeezed my hand a little tighter.

"I'm in a hurry to get someplace." I gritted my teeth and yanked at my hand. "Would you let me go?"

"If you'd told me your name, you'd already be on your way. You must want to spend more time with me." He flashed his white smile again, trying too hard.

"As if." Didn't most at the academy know my name? I was introduced at the dinner. Of course he hadn't been there. "Destiny, sorry."

"Nice to meet you Destiny Sorry."

"No, I meant—"

He laughed again. His uniform had a crest on the upper left of the vest. "I know what you meant."

With his concentrated stare, I shifted my feet and yanked my arm. "Will you let go of my hand? I need to get going."

"Where would you be going? The warlocks' bathroom?" He released my hand and waved at the door I'd been about to enter before I bumped into him.

My cheeks heated. "Sorry, I'm—"

"Destiny Sorry." He grinned.

I wanted to say I was Destiny peeved now. This conversation was taking too long. I had a short time during lunch and I needed to find Stone. "I'm trying to find my way to the front door. I'm new at the Academy."

"Oh, I can tell." He wiggled his eyebrows in a fun, flirty way again. He wasn't making fun of me exactly, just having fun. "You're going the wrong way."

"Which way is the exit? Please." I tacked on hoping he'd give me directions and let me be on my way.

Pointing, he gave me directions and then grabbed my arm when I pivoted away. "I don't think it's a good idea for you to leave the building."

It didn't matter what he thought. Even if I couldn't find Stone and my other friends, fresh air would be good for my mental health.

"But don't worry. I'll keep your secret." He winked hinting that we were conspiring together.

"Thanks, Damien." Racing away, I felt his stare on my back.

The dark hallways got wider as I followed his directions. Finally, I was in the grand hallway near the wavy stairs. The large front door loomed in front of me. Finding the exit shouldn't have been difficult.

The large, heavy door was closed. Glancing around, I hoped someone nearby would open it. I didn't know if I needed a spell or what. I did know I needed to get outside. Maybe it was the girls' hammering gossip, or the new things I'd learned, or the strange environment, but I needed to see my friends. True friends. I didn't know what they were doing or how they were being treated.

I tiptoed across the foyer and reached for the black handle. The iron beneath my fingers was hot. I pushed down the handle. Sighing with relief that it wasn't locked or spelled, I went to push the door open.

Alarms rang.

The high pitched whirring strained my ears.

I shoved the door closed and the alarm stopped. I sagged against the wood door.

A net dropped out of nowhere and scooped me up. My feet tangled in the ropes and I plopped into the center of the net as it raised higher and higher.

My pulse pounded and fear charged through my bloodstream. I was caught like a fly in a spider's web.

Chapter Twelve

"I don't care who your great grandmother is, you will obey the rules." Provost Morgane apparated into the foyer and tapped her foot on the floor way below me. Her bright red hair popped bigger, more electrified as if anger had given her a new appearance.

I wondered if embarrassment had given me a new look. Red face, staticky hair, pretzel shaped body. I pushed and kicked at the net trying to get free. I couldn't move and I was failing.

Failing at the academy's rules, written and unwritten. Failing at making a good impression. Failing at classes and learning. When I needed to succeed and fast.

A group of students gathered to watch the spectacle. Their wands pointed at me in accusation and ridicule. Or were they prepared for an attack? Either way, right now I was their enemy. Raven smirked, standing with her posse. Damien's lips twitched, holding in a chortle. It seemed like the entire school watched me struggle in the net.

My burning cheeks scalded. "I didn't know I couldn't leave during lunch. I didn't know it was a rule." I yanked my skirt down. Hopefully, my underwear wasn't showing. "I wanted to see my friends."

Provost Morgane's glare lasered through me. "Are your friends more important than rules?"

They were. But I understood I couldn't speak my mind here and now. Embarrassment morphed to anger pulsating in my veins. I wanted to shout, how could I follow the rules if I didn't know them, instead I gave a squishy smile. "Can you get me down first and then we can talk?"

"*We* will not be talking. You will be listening." She roared and I swear a rush of wind came out of her mouth.

The net swayed and yet the imagined wind didn't cool my cheeks. Everyone would hear me being rebuked. I punched with my legs again. "My legs are cramping."

My complaint had her gaze narrowing. "Rules are rules."

"Provost Morgane," Mistress Lita apparated beside the academy's head. Cassia skidded to a stop behind her. At least I had two friendly faces in the crowd. "Destiny is—"

"I know, your great granddaughter." The provost finished my great grandmother's sentence.

Mistress Lita's mouth went rigid, and then she loosened her muscles and smiled. "Our new student has not been informed of our rules. Has she?" My great grandmother was sticking up for me using logic.

"I didn't know I wasn't allowed to leave the building."

Both women scowled.

I pressed my lips together, knowing when to shut up. I'd let them discuss the next step.

"First, let's get Destiny down." Mistress Lita flicked her hand and the knots on the net began to untie.

Uh oh.

I was going to fall and hit the ground. Hard. Wouldn't that be punishment enough? To fall in front of the entire academy, witches and warlocks.

The knots slipped and my body jerked.

I held my breath. I hoped she could heal my body like she had my cheek. The ropes from the net sliced my skin. My pulse thrashed and air blitzed out of my lungs. Struggling, I started to free fall from forty feet. My body tumbled a little as the ropes untied and I remembered why I was no longer afraid of heights.

Because I couldn't fall.

Exhilaration lit me from the insides. I could fly.

"Warlocks." Mistress Lita commanded with a single word.

Twisting and turning, I ended up face down. The floor rushed at my face through a kaleidoscope of colors. The guys' dark uniforms blurred together in a single group. They positioned themselves below me. Their arms reached up to catch me.

They were only in my way.

I jerked my arms up before sweeping their fingertips. My falling body stopped and I surged upward. Now in firm control, I flew higher and a grin slipped onto my face. This was one power I could control.

"Look at her," Arabella pointed.

"She's flying!" Raven squealed.

Aster waved her hands. "Pretty cool."

"And different." Damien had dropped his arms and studied me from below.

Provost Morgane took out her wand and zeroed in on me.

Mistress Lita beamed. She scanned around noting everyone's surprised expressions.

Which was weird. I thought witches could fly. Although in the banshee tent Cassia had called it something else.

I lowered my arms and let my body slowly come to the floor. My heeled boots touched down with a click.

Cassia scrambled to me and halted. "You can fly without a broom."

"I showed you at the banshee camp." She'd levitated to the bed and I'd dive bombed on top.

"You did. Of course, you did." She galloped in and hugged me while peering over my shoulder. "With the excitement I forgot."

"Quite the demonstration." Provost Morgane's tone told me she didn't approve.

My shoulders dipped.

Cassia let me go and took a step back. "It was." She defended me.

"It was impressive." Mistress Lita held her chin high. "Fitting for our line."

My chest swelled with her acknowledgement.

The other students watched the exchange.

I yanked my skirt and straightened my shirt making sure my clothes were in the proper position.

"Attempting to leave the academy is an infraction of the rules." The provost's lecture was a blow to my ego, especially in front of the entire academy. "Destiny must be punished. No special treatment because of who she is or because she can fly."

I stared at the floor. The only special treatment I wanted was to be taught to use my magic as quickly as possible. I also wanted to ask why no one else could fly.

"Destiny is my great granddaughter as you pointed out," Mistress Lita used a reasonable voice. "I will provide the punishment."

Peeking up from my downcast position, hope fluttered. The head of the school should be in charge of students breaking rules. This was an exception to the rule and I was happy about it. My own great grandmother would not make the punishment too terrible.

"Students, get to your next classes." Provost Morgane's sharpness told me she was not happy with my great grandmother's pronouncement.

The shuffle of footsteps told me the students were leaving the foyer as she commanded. They listened to her.

Lifting my head, I watched them leave. Cassia scurried after Damien and grabbed his arm. I'd have to ask her about him.

"Destiny," Mistress Lita got my attention. "We will discuss your punishment at dinner in my suite tonight."

I nodded slowly. I wasn't eager to have the discussion.

Provost Morgane's lips contorted in disgust. "Get to class or you'll be punished for being tardy." She flung her arm and apparated out of the area.

"Mistress Lita," I wanted to discuss seeing my friends.

"You've caused enough trouble today." She must've sensed my next question. Her smile appeared strained. She'd stuck her neck out for me and I was grateful. "I'll see you at dinner."

She apparated away and my body sagged releasing the tension. That was part of the problem. My entire day had been scheduled and I didn't know how my friends were doing. It was the reason I'd tried to leave. Kicking the marble floor, I headed to my next class.

Familiars class.

Arriving at the room, I noted an entire menagerie of animals. A dozen cats, a parrot, a lizard, and a couple of dogs. Cassia sat in the back row holding a green, slimy snake.

Shuddering, I took the empty seat next to her. "I thought you didn't have a familiar."

She stroked the snake. "As soon as I returned to the coven, this little guy presented himself."

"You hate snakes." I remembered her saying something about it in the dungeon.

"The familiar picks the witch."

"And the warlock?" I couldn't get the image of her rushing after Damien out of my mind. I thought she liked Lukas.

"Warlocks don't have familiars. That would give them extra power." She made kissy faces at the snake.

I grimaced, though not only about the snake. The coven was unequal in the opposite direction from the banshee clan. There, males had the power and the females were slaves. Here, the warlocks were acolytes and guardians, subservient to the witches. Neither seemed fair.

The teacher apparated to the front of the room. She wore loose black pants and a large floral blouse. Long blond hair went to her waist. A small monkey clung around her neck. "Good afternoon, witches."

"Good afternoon, Miss Grim," the students responded.

The greeting hadn't happened in any of my earlier classes. This room had comfy chairs spread throughout the room. No desks or tables.

I was the only one without a familiar. But being different shouldn't rub me the wrong way. I was used to being unique.

"Today we will continue training your familiars." Miss Grim stroked the monkey's back. "You must instruct your familiar of your needs and desires. Learn to communicate so they can follow your orders without a word being spoken."

The witches stroked and spoke to their animals. I didn't think I'd ever witness such a strange sight.

"What should I do?" I whispered to Cassia. I really didn't want to draw additional attention to myself and I didn't want an animal, especially a snake.

"Miss Grim." Cassia raised her hand. "Destiny doesn't have a familiar."

All heads turned toward me. Great.

"At your age? You poor thing." The teacher tutted believing I should be embarrassed by my state. "I'm sure there's hope."

She made it sound as if I was desperate. I didn't want a familiar. Just another thing to worry about and I worried enough about Stone and my friends already.

"Maybe she doesn't have a familiar because she's part banshee." Arabella pointed out what she believed were my shortcomings.

I straightened my shoulders. "It's okay. I'll watch."

"For today, that's fine." The teacher's tone grew hard. "But if you want to pass the class, you'll have to take the final test with your familiar."

I didn't need to learn this stuff because I didn't want a familiar, and I didn't plan to be around long enough for the final test.

In Wand Works class, I pulled out the loaner wand. The teacher had us flicking our wrists and fingers, twirling the wand like a baton, and thrusting like a sword. Of course, with no magic.

I paired up with Lavender. She was in my Arts of Alchemy class and no one wanted to partner with her. Cassia had a long time partner.

"Okay, partners." The teacher clapped her hands. "Dueling with wands is an ancient tradition between warlocks. Of course, once witches started dueling, we were better. Now, we have our own tournaments."

Lavender leaned in to whisper, "Raven is the best witch dueler. She competes throughout the entire kingdom."

Nodding, I was impressed. She acted so confident. In classes, in competition, with warlocks. If I had that kind of confidence I'd learn this witch stuff faster, leave with Stone sooner, and have our future together sealed.

"Thanks for pairing up with me." I was grateful Lavender had been willing to pair up with a complete beginner. She'd already given me several tips.

"I'm grateful. I usually have to pair up with the teacher." She fake shuddered. "She can be forgetful and accidently use magic when we're practicing."

My eyes widened, imagining. "What happens?"

She giggled. "One time she changed my wand into an apple. I think she was hungry."

I laughed with her.

The teacher signaled for us to begin. "En garde!"

Using my self-defense lessons, I took a wide stance and held the wand out. Lavender did the same.

"Witches on the right advance."

The teacher directed and Lavender advanced.

"Witches on the left perform a feint."

I stepped forward, ducked, and struck her on the chest.

"You're good at this." Lavender's compliment raised my spirits.

Finally, something I was good at. Apparently better than the teacher who accidently used power against her. Thinking about this, my veins sizzled. Power exploded from my fingertips and into the wand.

No, not now. My uncontrolled powers couldn't go bonkers against my new friend.

The unfamiliar wand jerked in my hand pointing at Lavender's torso. Sucking in air, I wrapped both hands around it, struggling to point the wand down. The wand fought back as if it had a mind of its own. The wand jolted forward to point at her again.

My nerves ignited and a charge went through my bloodstream. The wand heated in my fingers. I could feel the power increasing. That couldn't be good. I had to calm myself. Blowing out a breath, I loosened my tense muscles and tried to communicate with the feckless wand. If I could control myself, I could control the wand.

With white knuckles, I forced the wand to the left. Sparks exploded from the tip like a missile. My body jerked and I watched the sparks of magic shoot out. "Lavender, duck!"

She did and the sparks hit the wall creating a smoking black hole.

My body drooped and I dropped the wand. That could've been Lavender. I didn't deserve a wand.

My friends, new and old, weren't safe around me.

Chapter Thirteen

"Everyone, grab a broom." Miss Hunt held a broom with colorful feathers tied near the end. She wore leather pants and a jacket. Her hair was pulled back into a ponytail.

I couldn't believe that with the technology available and the fact that witches could apparate to wherever they wanted, they were still flying on broomsticks. It reinforced the stereotypical image of witches in children's tales.

The group of about twenty students hurried to the brooms on a rack. We'd changed out of uniforms and into shorts and T-shirts. The training was held on the field surrounded by bleachers carved from stone where some type of sport was played. Possibly wand dueling in which Raven was the champion.

"The witch who got trapped in the net is here." A warlock pointed his chin at me.

"She can fly without a broom!" A witch snickered. "What's she doing in this class?"

"I heard she almost killed Lavender," another witch added.

I tried to ignore their taunts. With shaking legs, I slinked to get my broom. I refused to do anything else to embarrass myself on the first day. The witches, warlocks, and teachers probably thought I was the worst student ever.

Reaching out, I grabbed the top of the last broomstick. Acute pain lanced through my hand. I winced, trying not to make a bigger reaction. The broomstick had mangled my palm. Blood dripped from my hand and the skin throbbed.

"Destiny cut herself on the stibnite crystal," Raven tattled on my mistake.

Ashamed, I'd planned to hide the injury. Everyone would believe it was another thing I'd done wrong. None of them had sliced their skin. I scowled at the broom. A black crystalized rock had been fastened to the end of the broomstick. The rest of the handle was wooden.

The teacher examined my dripping hand. "Never touch the stibnite crystal end. It's sharp."

No kidding. "I didn't know." I was tired of saying the same thing over and over. I dropped the broomstick.

"Did you know the sweeping part of the broom is made of feathers from the Brimstone bird?"

I didn't know if she was kidding. I'd never heard of a Brimstone bird. The feathers at the end of the broom came in an array of blue, green, and gold.

Staring at the ground, watching my blood fall onto the grass, I shook my head.

She plucked a feather from the broom. "Hold out your hand."

Was I going to get my wounded hand slapped? Was this another way to embarrass me?

I held out my hand. A long red line with a deep slash and rough edges went through the center of my palm. She gripped my wrist and brushed the feather across my skin. It tickled and something more.

Murmuring what must be a spell, she crossed the feather across my palm again and again. The tickling became hot tingling. My body tensed. I wanted to yank my hand away. But Miss Hunt wouldn't harm me in front of the other students. My fingers curled on their own. I wanted to squirm and shift my feet. Closing my eyes, I thought about trying to make her stop with my mind.

The tickling sensation halted. Opening my eyes, I scrutinized my hand. The blood had stopped flowing. The wound stitched itself together. A white puckered scar formed. My jaw dropped.

"You'll probably have a scar." She flicked her fingers and the feather disappeared.

Why didn't she have healing powers like my great grandmother? The scratches on my face had been worse and I didn't have a mark.

"Damien will kiss it and make it better," a male I didn't recognize teased.

My face flamed and I caught Damien's gaze. He knocked his elbow into the blond guy next to him. Remembering what Cassia had said about the warlocks, I had to wonder if he liked me or if he liked the fact that I was related to Mistress Lita. Same with the witches.

"We've lost precious time training." The teacher's voice hardened. "Everyone mount your broomsticks and don't touch the stibnite."

The students chuckled.

I held in a huff. How was I supposed to know a simple broom could be dangerous? I tilted my chin up and watching exactly what the others did, I mounted my broom. I'd follow everyone else closely.

"Lift off," the teacher commanded.

What? No instruction? No spell? *No helmet?*

Watching everyone rise into the sky, I didn't even know how to begin. A few of the students wobbled. One shot straight up and back down, but ended up getting control of her broomstick before hitting the ground.

Raven flew smoothly around the arena. Aster and Arabella followed. Damien and the blond guy flew with a bunch of other warlocks. They zoomed around the edges going fast.

The teacher flew past me. "Kick the ground and hop."

Sounded easy. I could fly on my own so surely I could fly using a broom. I didn't want to stick out even more than I already did. I kicked the ground and jumped. And landed right back on my feet. I tried again and again. Each time I kicked the ground harder, more out of frustration than an actual attempt at flying.

Could any of them fly without the broom? A question I'd have to ask my great grandmother tonight. Everyone had exhibited shock this afternoon at my ability.

At this point, the students circled around the amphitheater at a swift pace. The buzzing above created a slow wind. The teacher waved her arms around and the students got into groups of three. They flew at each other, interweaving with precision.

Anxiety pinched at my grounded feet. I kicked and hopped again. Nothing.

Miss Hunt blew a whistle. "Everyone land. Training is done for today."

My shoulders sagged and I let my head hang. I'd never begun.

"You need to trust your instincts." Damien landed beside me. He got off the broom and took hold of mine. "You have to feel the wind beneath you. Let it lift you. And trust yourself."

I laughed. "Have you seen or heard about the mistakes I made today?"

He smashed his lips together and studied the ground. He knew because he'd witnessed most of them.

The other kids put the brooms away in the rack. Most of them avoided glancing in my direction.

"I can fly on my own. I don't need to learn this." I could use the extra time to study or see my friends.

"It's more than flying. It's about working as a cohesive unit in a battle."

I scrunched my brow. "A battle?"

"A sport, if you will."

"Oh, it's a team sport." Learning what witches do as a group would be a good idea.

"Listen." He placed my hands around the broomstick and held them there. "Most of us have been flying since we were little kids. This class isn't about the basics of flying. It's about learning formations and such."

"Synchronized flying." I smirked.

He stared at me. "I like your smile."

It wasn't much of a smile. I sighed. Even if he might be flirting, at least he was trying to help. "Okay. So I kick the ground."

"It's more of a push off the ground. The brooms are magical and they'll sense your confidence."

Why didn't anyone tell me this at the beginning?

He tapped my hands. "Not too tight. You don't want to choke the stick. Hold it loosely, hinting at a caress." He trailed his finger over the back of my hand.

I swallowed. "Got it." I lifted my hands off and his touch fell away. I re-gripped the stick a little more loosely.

"What if I take you for a spin?" He swung his leg around my broom and positioned himself behind me. "You'll experience how flying on a broom feels and it will give you confidence."

Doubt filled me at his suggestion and his closeness. "Okaaaaay."

We took off.

My stomach vaulted. I clutched the broom handle tighter. "I wasn't ready."

"You said okay." Damien's arms wrapped around my waist. "I'll keep you safe."

His response annoyed me. Why did everyone want to keep me safe? I could protect myself and fly without a broomstick.

At least he was trying to help, more than the teacher. I relaxed and cleared my mind. I needed to focus on the experience. The broom between my legs thrummed. My fingers relaxed around the handle. Air rushed against my cheeks and my hair streamed behind me.

Thrills cascaded down my spine. A different kind of thrill even though I could already fly. This was a new skill where I learned the witch way. A step in learning to control my magic.

We circled around the stadium and I saw the patterns cut into the stone seating, going higher in concentric circles. Moss grew between the rows. As he took the broom higher, we passed the edges of the stadium and the entire coven area spread out before me.

Heavy clouds hung in the sky. Rain would soon follow. The academy stood out among the other low-lying buildings with its tall spires and monstrous arches. The brownish water of the moat wrapped around the building and behind it came the caves and cliffs.

Veering to the left, the large flat building encompassing the spa and medical lab came into view. Behind was another low-lying building.

"The warlock dormitories." Damien pointed to the building I examined.

The dormitory sat beside a dark, fast-running river. "What's that river?"

"Helvete River." His voice in my ear tickled. "It comes from the Dark Angel's Veil."

My heart contracted. That's where my grandmother had died.

My great grandmother had told me the Inferis Coven protects the Gate to the Underworld. I wonder if the waterfall was a connection. "Can we go see the falls?"

"Soon." He swung the broom lower and went in between the medical lab and the warlock dormitory.

A small, squat building with peeling paint sat off to the side. Two people caught my attention. A witch with long blond hair, which stood out on its own because most of the witches had dark hair or had dyed their hair a fun color. And another blond. Tall. Male.

Stone.

My heart thudded. I thought he'd been stuck in his room all day.

The female blond had her hand on his arm and flirted with him. He leaned toward her. Even from this distance it appeared they were having an intense discussion.

Stone placed his hand on the girl's. Jealousy streamed through my veins.

"To Dark Angel's Veil." Damien maneuvered the broom in the other direction.

I swiveled my head. "Wait."

"If we don't return to the arena soon, it will start raining." He gunned the broom forward.

Stone and the girl became a tiny dot on the ground.

"There it is." Damien waved at the roaring, rumbling brown water. It wasn't a traditional waterfall pouring straight down. The dirty water hit a rock here, a boulder there. Narrower at the top, it widened buffeting the rocks below. No calm and clear lake at the bottom. Just a muddy river with a fast current. "Don't you think it's beautiful?"

I wouldn't have chosen that word. I would've said dark, bleak, other-worldly.

"Is that where the Gates—" My words stopped.

"We should go back now." He pointed the broom down.

We descended fast and my back pressed against the front of him. He kept one arm on the broom handle and the other around my waist. It was like riding a rocket going down.

Air caught in my throat. We'd crash any second.

At the last moment, he pulled up on the broom and his feet skidded on the ground. The broom stopped and we hovered.

"What did you think?"

I twisted around to face him. I'm sure my face flushed and excitement shined in my eyes. "It was amazing. Especially seeing more of the coven from up high."

He brushed at a hair clinging to my cheek. His hand paused.

A new group entered the arena. Not students. Not witches and warlocks. An elf, a brownie, a werewolf, and a blond half giant.

Stone's expression darkened as he glowered. His eyebrows thundered and his lips dipped into a deep frown. He wore the open V shirt, black leather tunic and leather breeches he'd arrived in.

"Hey!" I lifted my arm to wave and realized Damien's arms around me blocked my movement. He still leaned close after brushing my hair away.

My stomach fluttered. I pushed his arms off and swung my leg over the broom. "Hi! I'm so glad you guys are here."

"Are you?" Stone peered at me. He crossed his thick arms.

"Of course. I've wanted to see you all day." I scrambled toward him and my friends.

Damien dismounted and held the broomstick. "I'm Damien, Warlock Advisor." With his other hand he reached for a handshake.

"Stone." He kept his arms crossed.

My nerves teetered. "And these are my friends Pith, Helartha, and Lukas."

My friends seemed reluctant to take his hand, but each of them did.

"I see you're making new friends." Stone's accusation sliced.

My chest ached, especially when I remembered the blond witch he'd been talking to. "I bet you are too."

One of his brows arched and then his expression cleared. "Cassia said we could find you here."

"She was right." I wrung my hands wishing we could be alone to talk. "Where is Cassia?"

"She said she had to check on something and would be right in." He waved a hand. "I thought you were too busy learning to control your magic to spend time with me. With us."

He tacked the last part on because he didn't want to sound jealous.

If he was jealous, he had no reason to be. I shouldn't be jealous of some strange blond witch either. "I have been busy all day."

"Flying around with flyboy." Stone didn't keep his dislike for Damien quiet.

I hoped Damien didn't hear as he strutted toward the exit. He stopped when Cassia entered and spoke to her.

"I can explain." Even though I shouldn't have to. Stone should trust me. My mind pictured him and the blond. I shouldn't need to ask either.

"No need." His icy tone sent a chill in my direction.

I wanted to warm him up. "I tried to visit you at lunch."

He arched a skeptical blond brow. "Thanks?"

"Let me explain." I wanted to tell him about my day, about everything I'd seen and learned. And the mistakes I'd made.

"No need." He shook his head. "We came to tell you Pith and Helartha are leaving. Maybe I should leave too."

My heart crumpled. "No."

My gaze landed on my friends. They'd changed into their old clothes. "Why are you leaving?"

"I haven't felt well since arriving." Pith clutched his stomach.

"We feel nauseous." Helartha appeared a little green.

"And I want to spend more time with Iban." Pith gave a bashful grin.

"I hate sitting around doing nothing." Helartha kicked the dirt. "The elves need help rebuilding now that the regent is no longer in charge. My experience will be better utilized assisting them."

Stone's expression didn't change. He probably believed the same thing about the entire kingdom. Maybe what he'd said earlier wasn't about hurt or jealousy, just that he was bored and searched for an excuse to leave.

"We escorted you here safely," Helartha waved her hand around the arena.

"And we checked on Violet." Pith's anxiety shrilled. "It's time for us to go."

I took hold of Pith's hand. "I understand." And I did, even though I'd miss them. "What about you, Lukas?"

He angled his head to watch Cassia talking to Damien. "I'm going to hang around for a bit."

Because of Cassia.

She strutted over after Damien left. We all hugged and promised to try and stay in touch, if I could learn to send messages outside the coven.

Cassia and Lukas walked Pith and Helartha out of the arena and the coven.

My eyes stung. "I'm going to miss them."

"Are you?" Stone recrossed his arms and glared.

"Is this about Damien again?" My temper spiked. "He was teaching me to fly on a broomstick."

"I don't think that's all he was doing." Stone grabbed my hand. "You can't trust everyone. Especially flirtatious guys."

Like him. I remembered his flirtatious attitude when we'd first met in the dungeon. I saw him with the blond witch. Is he saying I shouldn't trust him?

"I'm not naïve. I didn't accuse you of anything when you were with some blond witch earlier." By saying it, I kind of was accusing him and displaying my insecurities.

His green gaze widened. "What blond?"

I jerked my chin at the sky. "I saw you when I was flying." I didn't add that it was with Damien.

"The only witch I talked to was Cassia and she's not blond." He wouldn't even admit he'd met someone.

The strange witch shouldn't—didn't—matter. I gave him a short smile and squeezed his hand trying to make us both feel better. "I did try to see you today. There are enchantments to keep witches in."

His body tensed. "Are you a prisoner?"

"If I was, I'd refuse to stay." His concern became suffocating. I wanted to shout that I could take care of myself. "There are rules and I didn't know them. No leaving the academy during the school day."

His jaw dropped. "You enrolled in school?"

"I didn't really have a choice." I needed to calm him down, not rile him up. "I mean, that's how they're going to teach me. I go to classes and once I've mastered my magic, we'll leave."

"How long will that take?" His disbelieving question suggested forever. Did he not believe in me or was he in a hurry to leave? He'd accepted a position without telling me and obviously he wanted to get to work.

My great grandmother wanted me to stay forever. She wanted me to become the leader. But I couldn't tell him that because of the Secretum Bond. I hated keeping secrets from him, but I had no choice.

I forced a big grin. "Have you heard from Princess Ellery or King Zacharye?"

"Simon helped me to send a message telling them where I was temporarily." Stone emphasized the last word.

The emphasis rubbed against my nerves. I was already under so much pressure. I tipped my head down. "I'm going to learn as fast as I can."

He gripped my chin and tilted my face to his. "I know you are."

Our gazes connected and so did our hearts. The link drew us closer. He believed in me. My body leaned toward his. He bent his head and his lips lowered to mine. The immediate zing took me away from everything. All my worries and concerns.

I responded to the kiss. Our argument was silly when we had this between us. Protection, caring, compassion, love.

"Destiny." Provost Morgane's harshness brought me out of the romantic haze. "You're embarrassing yourself."

Flustered, I wanted to shrink. Stone's arms loosened around me.

"You're late for tutoring." The provost tapped her foot.

Stone stuck out his chest, posturing. "No one *was* around to *see* until you magically apparated." He blamed the magic.

"You stay silent." She flicked her fingers. "Destiny would be better off, if you couldn't open your mouth."

"Mmmrhmmm." Stone struggled to speak.

Panic shredded my lungs.

He couldn't open his mouth. Angry creases formed around his lips. His eyes widened and his nostrils flared. He used his fingers to try to pry his lips apart. He swung accusingly at me.

Guilt slammed into me. At least he could breathe through his nose so I wasn't worried about him dying. The guilt balled into rigid knots of remorse in my stomach. He was silenced because of me, embarrassed because of me. "Provost Morgane, take the spell off him."

She kept tapping her foot as she assessed both of us.

Stone's cheeks went red. Rage flashed in his pupils.

My panic boomed higher. He'd be furious with her, me, and the witches. He was helpless in the coven and was only staying to be with me. "I thought witches couldn't use magic against other majiks."

"He's half human." Her lips lifted on one side. "And has absolutely no power."

She emphasized his current predicament. Guilt, panic, and shame that she'd treat him this way caused the balls in my stomach to toss and turn. I didn't know a spell to counteract. I didn't know many spells. Another shortcoming.

I fisted my hands. "I'll tell Mistress Lita, my great grandmother."

Provost Morgane scowled and then she showed a hint of a smile. "Go ahead."

Balling my fists, anger roiled inside of me. I couldn't lose control and do horrible magic against the head of the academy even if she did deserve it. Blood pounded in my veins. My fingers heated and sparks lit up my palms.

I gripped my hands together trying to stop the onslaught. I glanced at Stone. His glued-shut mouth. His flaring nostrils. His wide eyes not exhibiting fear but fury.

She humiliated him on purpose. She wanted to dehumanize him and make him think less of himself. Make me think less of him.

Impossible.

The protective instincts inside rang loud, jarring me into action. It was my turn to stand up for him. I released my hands and let the power explode.

The broomsticks trembled in their storage rack. As one, they lifted and flew toward us. Their sharp stibnite points aimed right at Provost Morgane.

I didn't want to kill her. I wanted her to listen to me. "Wait!"

The broomsticks didn't stop. They missiled straight at her.

Horror ripped through me. Through my mind and my chest and my soul.

She wasn't concerned. Laughing, she flung her arm up.

The broomsticks fell to the ground with a thump.

She grabbed hold of my arm and we apparated away. "Don't mess with magic against me. Not yet anyhow."

Chapter Fourteen

Provost Morgane's statement about magic and messing garbled while we apparated. I understood it just fine. A direct attack against the powerful witch wouldn't work.

With her gripping my arm, I was flung into the black void once again. I needed to learn how to do it myself. The provost probably thought she was scaring me by apparating. She was, but not because of our form of travel. I'd apparated with my great grandmother before. My ribcage constricted. This time I didn't know where we were going.

My feet landed on a carpeted floor. My knees bent at impact and I stuck out my arm.

Provost Morgane let go of my other arm and I sank to the ground, breathing heavily. The room was dark. The light hadn't changed much from the black void.

An orange glow came from a cauldron near the ornate fireplace. The mantle had dozens of candles in different sizes and colors. The walls were lined with bookshelves filled with books and some framed photos featuring a young girl. A wood desk with spindly legs sat in front of an arched window.

The provost clapped her hand. "Lux."

An old lantern sitting on the desk flickered on. No other lights. I didn't understand how she could work in the dark.

Gathering myself, I stood on shaky knees. "Where's Stone?"

"Where you left him." She sounded uncaring and unconcerned.

I had enough worry for both of us. "Did you do anything to him?" With her parting threat I thought she might.

"No." She shuffled around to her desk and sat.

"What about the talking spell?" I pushed, Stone being my primary concern.

"I removed it when we left."

"Suddenly. With no warning." I raised my voice. "He'll worry about me." He always did.

She regarded me, deciding how to punish me for yelling. "He's your protector."

"He's more than that." I couldn't tell her how much he meant to me. "Stone helped save me from Regent Theobald's dungeon and from the banshees. He's going to work for King Zacharye."

I was proud of his accomplishments at such a young age. He'd done more than most of these witches and warlocks to help save the kingdom.

"Will he?" She sat back in her chair, considering. "Then why is he here?"

There were so many things I wanted to say. He cared about me. He wanted to be with me. He loved me. "He wanted to see I was safe at the coven."

"The real question is: Is he safe?" She trilled higher.

The bumping of my heart morphed into a fast beat. A panicked beat. An angry beat. I pulled out the loaner wand and pointed. "What did you do to him?"

She flicked a finger and my wand broke in two, falling onto the floor. "Nothing."

I licked my lips. First stopping the broomstick attack and now easily breaking my wand. She'd told me not to mess with magic against her. "You threatened Stone."

"It was a threat." Her calm expression and easy-going tone belied her words. "But not from me."

"What do you mean?" My gaze darted around the room. "From who?"

"Any number of places." She sounded bored with the conversation. "He's living in a coven filled with witches and warlocks. Your giant has no magic. No status. Except his friendship with you."

Everything she said riled me up. I'd worried about Stone sitting around doing nothing, but hadn't thought he might be in danger.

The provost waved her hand. "Take away the magic stuff, how will he feel knowing he relies on you?"

He'd hate it. I smashed my lips together to stop from speaking out loud.

"The giant is very independent. He plans to work for the new king." Provost Morgane's reasonable assessment cut through my heart. "You'd think he'd want to be there to help the young king settle the kingdom and repair damage done by the regent."

She was right.

"You shouldn't have apparated me away." I returned to one of my original concerns, ignoring my own worries about Stone staying at the coven. What if he started to resent me because he believed he was stuck?

"You were late for tutoring." She opened a large black book sitting on her desk. "I'm a busy witch."

I was busy too. I hadn't had a moment to myself. I barely saw Stone and Lukas, my only two non-witch friends hanging around. And now Stone would be worried about me. I could picture him trying to force his way across the drawbridge demanding to see me. "Is there a way to get a message to Stone? I want to tell him where I am and make sure he's not worried about me."

"I'll teach you. It's my job." She took out a small piece of parchment from her desk. "What's the message? Nothing too gushy."

I shifted my feet and focused on the tall ceiling with dark wood beams. "Say I'm fine. I'm in my tutoring session and learning to send messages."

She wrote with the tip of her wand. "That's it? You don't want to add *hugs and kisses, Destiny*? Or *love, Destiny*." Her emphasizing certain words heated my cheeks.

I swallowed the heart-shaped lump in my throat. "Just sign my name."

She signed the paper with a flourish. "Place your wand at the corner of the note and say the following incantation. *Mitte Nuntius Stone*." She demonstrated.

Sparks shot from her wand and burnt the edge of the parchment. The edges curled into themselves and changed to smoke. The brown smoke dissipated into the air.

"Looks easy." It seemed easy enough. I repeated the incantation to myself. "How is the message delivered?"

"The smoke reforms into paper and it will appear in his hand."

My spirits lifted. I could communicate with Stone whenever I wanted. My lifting spirits stumbled to a stop. "How does he reply?"

She grinned. "He can't. *He* doesn't have magic."

The insult to Stone chiseled through my head. I ignored it. At least I could send him messages. I could tell him what time and where to meet. Glancing at my grandfather's old fashioned watch around my wrist, I yawned. It had been a long day and there was more to come.

"Before we begin, let's get you your wand. It will help you control your powers." Provost Morgane took the pieces of the loaner wand. "Tell me a few of the things you can do."

"I don't need a broom to fly." Smirking, I remembered everyone's shock at seeing me fly instead of falling out of the net.

"I witnessed." Did she disapprove of my flying or the fact that she didn't know in advance? "I'll speak to Miss Hunt about teaching you attack and defense formations without a broom. Both your hands are free to hold weapons."

My brows furrowed. Damien had mentioned something similar. "Attack and defense?"

"Oh, you know, flying positions." She opened a drawer in a large cabinet. The drawer was filled with neatly aligned wands. "What else can you do?"

Around a hundred wands of different colors sat in the drawer. Short and long wands. Sparkly wands. Curved wands. Two toned wands. Wands with stars or other elements at the top.

Mind control was the first thing I thought of. I didn't want to share the information. "I've crushed and tossed boulders." I remembered injuring Drago, the dragon. "Although, I don't know if it's witch magic or banshee magic." One of my issues was figuring out which was which.

Her hand went straight to a black crystal wand. "Very impressive. Maybe you have some other kind of power." She snorted and held out the wand. "This one."

The thin wand twisted around itself coming together at the top in an iridescent diamond.

I shrugged and took the wand from her hand. My palm warmed. A flame flared through the center of the black crystal reminding me of something. "Was that fire inside the top?"

"Fire from the Underworld." She nodded, expecting as much.

"Is a wand supposed to be warm in my hand and spout fire?" I hadn't seen anyone else's wand do something so strange.

"Not a normal wand. It's called Obsidian's Fire." She spoke slowly, apprehensively. "Wave it around."

I did as asked. The wand grew hotter. "Is it supposed to burn?"

Her smile turned sly. "For you, possibly."

It was weird. The wand felt right in my hand. The wand connected to me, which was odd with the name Obsidian's Fire. "Can I try a simple spell?"

She studied me and the wand in my hand. "Say *Aperta Secreto* and point at the filing cabinet."

"What will it do?"

"It will open the unlocked bottom drawer and bring me the file on wand assignments so I can register yours."

"Why?" Silly to use magic for such a simple task.

"It will demonstrate your control."

Giving a quick nod, I pointed my new wand at the filing cabinet. I said the spell and the wand heated and power throbbed through my hand. Excitement hummed in my bloodstream. If the wand could help control my power, it could be the answer to my magical mistakes.

The bottom drawer slid open and a single black file popped out. The file flew out of the drawer and flopped open on the floor.

"That's a top secret file." Provost Morgane's mouth dropped open and she clutched at her chest. She acted horrified and yet something wasn't authentic about her reaction.

I'd obviously retrieved the wrong file, but nothing to get upset about, even if the word *secret* was in the spell. "I'm sorry. I didn't mean..." At her expression, I trailed off.

Her face expressed alarm. Wide eyes filled with fear and her lips pinched together. "Give me the wand back." Provost Morgane held out a shaky hand. "I made a mistake."

My fingers wrapped tighter around the wand on their own, refusing to let go. My body told me this wand was mine. "I want this wand."

"Mistress Lita will never approve."

"I'll talk to her. Tell her the wand fits me even if it does burn a little." A lot.

The wand was weightless and I sensed a connection to my soul. Was that even possible?

"We'll discuss this again. Just leave." Provost Morgane bent down and picked up the top secret file.

But not before I read the heading on the top page: *Dark Angel Succession.*

⋙ ⋘

Pounding on Cassia's door, I hoped she was inside. She spent a lot of time with her old friends and family, which I totally understood. But I missed seeing her and I needed to tell her about what I'd read in the file.

The door flung open and Cassia stood there half dressed. The room behind her was smaller than mine and messy. "Destiny, I thought you'd be in tutoring for ages."

"I got out a little early." I stepped inside and slammed the door.

Piles of clothes sat on the bed and lay across a chair. The drawers in the dresser were mostly open and the closet was overstuffed with items in many bright colors.

Quickly explaining what happened, I finished with, "I accidentally read the top of the file and it was entitled *Dark Angel Succession.*"

Cassia's eyebrows arched and her skin paled. Then, her lips lifted in a slow smile and she laughed. "I didn't know Provost Morgane was still pulling that joke."

Confusion rang in my head. "It wasn't a joke to me."

"The spell she told you to say was to take out a fake secret file." Cassia studied the ceiling while continuing to chuckle. "The provost has been using the trick for years every time a witch gets their first wand."

I shook my head slightly. While I'd been angry at myself for my magic not working correctly, I'd been more upset about what I'd read. "The top secret file said something about a Dark Angel." Something tickled the back of my brain. I'd heard the term before.

"An old legend." She dismissed me with a wave of the hand. "Most witches know about the fake legend. For them it's scarier because they think they removed a top secret file and are going to get punished."

I flopped onto her messy bed. "Provost Morgane was angry, fearful."

Cassia's gaze narrowed, calculating what I'd said. She smiled again. "All part of the act. Don't worry about it."

I let out a breath I didn't know I'd been holding. If I didn't need to worry about a Dark Angel I'd switch to my next concern. "I need you to take me to where Stone is staying. Can we apparate?"

"Apparating by students is tracked."

Between trying to leave at lunch, the mistakes I'd made in class, and the accident in the provost's office, the last thing I needed was to be found breaking the rules. "I'm already in enough trouble."

Cassia giggled. "You don't know the half of it."

"What?"

She tucked in her red shirt and threw a dark cloak at me. "I said you don't know the half of it. The witches are gossiping about you and Damien." She sang his name.

"Ridiculous and you should tell them so." My pulse throbbed. I didn't want these rumors getting back to Stone. "Stone and I are…"

"You're what?" She paused at the door and wiggled her brows.

"Nothing official, but…you know."

"I do know." She flashed a wicked grin before leading me down a back set of stairs and through a narrow hallway.

My muscles tensed. "Where are we going?"

"We can't go out the main door. Provost Morgane would know. Lux." Cassia's wand lit up. "Light yours."

I slipped the wand from my belt and held it up. "Lux."

"The Obsidian's Fire wand." Awe spiked in her voice. "Does Mistress Lita know?"

Her question made me tremble. "I'm going to tell her."

Cassia nodded. "This way."

I wasn't comfortable with sneaking around. I shouldn't have to hide where I was going. I needed to talk to Stone. Our last kiss had been interrupted and I wanted to confirm he'd received the note the provost had sent. I wasn't sure I trusted her. Maybe she'd burnt the note and it hadn't gone anywhere except up in smoke.

Creaking brought me out of my thoughts. A dark passage opened.

"A secret tunnel?" My jaw dropped and I stared at Cassia. "How do you know about a secret tunnel?"

She winked and laughed. "How else would I meet up with the warlocks late at night or sneak out to a party? The warlocks don't live in the academy."

The warlocks lived and studied separately. It was an interesting dynamic, an unfair dynamic because they didn't seem to have the same resources.

She put her finger to her lips in a *be quiet* sign.

My gut clenched. What was the punishment for breaking another rule? My great grandmother had already gotten me out of trouble once today. I didn't know if she'd do it again. I guess I'd find out at dinner, which I'd have to be at soon. I didn't care if I was late, seeing Stone was more important.

Cassia seemed okay breaking rules. I guess after escaping from the human dungeon she'd become a rebel. "This way."

The dark tunnel sloped down. The damp walls smelled musty and the *drip, drip, drip* of water told me we must be close to the moat. I shivered.

"Help me." She got on her knees and pulled on a rusty ring. A panel lifted from the ground.

I got down to help raise the square door and peered into a dark hole with an old ladder going down into the blackness. "You're kidding."

"After a time or two you don't even notice it's creepy."

"You hated the tunnels in the human dungeon."

"I...I did but I've been using this tunnel for years." She scooted to the edge and climbed down. "You want to see Stone, don't you?"

I did. Throwing my leg over the side, I started going down the ladder. I jumped down at the end into a stinky puddle of water. "Where are we?"

"Under the moat." Satisfaction oozed. "Almost there."

Despite all the wards, this passage was completely unprotected.

Ducking to walk through the narrow tunnel, I worried the entire thing would collapse and we'd drown. Cassia stopped and I bumped into her. The tunnel ended.

Air whistled from my lungs. "It's a dead end." Why would she lead me astray?

"It's crystalline limestone, silly." She chanted a few words and grabbed my hand, pulling me through. We exited on the other side with a plop.

Night had fallen. No stars were visible in the sky. The moat swirled behind us and I hunched my shoulders glad we hadn't been exposed to the dirty water.

"Come on." Cassia grabbed my hand and pulled me toward the stadium.

We edged around the outside and ran past the medical building. The roar of the waterfall was louder, closer.

She pointed. "That's where the warlocks live. Easy peasy for partying."

Damien had pointed out the dormitory.

Cassia stopped at a small, squat building between the medical lab and the warlock dormitory. An acolyte dressed in black stood at the door. He clutched his wand in his hand.

"I'll distract him." Cassia smoothed her hair. "You go in." She sauntered out, swiveling her hips in an obvious way. "Hello there."

The acolyte raised his wand. "Hello."

She directed his attention away from the door.

My stomach knotted. I dashed forward and opened the door, slipping inside. "Stone?"

The building had seen better days. Bricks had fallen out of the walls and the floor was scuffed and dirty. Silence greeted me.

"Stone? Lukas?" My spirits sank.

"Destiny?" Stone's blond head peeked around a corner. His green eyes gleamed when he spotted me and he grinned. "What're you doing here?"

"Visiting you." My pulse picked up its pace and I beamed tremulously. Finally, we were together and alone.

His smile faded. "You disappeared on me." He took it as a personal affront.

"Did you get my note?"

"Yes." He continued to frown. "At least I knew you hadn't been kidnapped. Again."

His sarcasm sliced through me. I crossed my arms. "I can take care of myself."

"That's my job." His intensity rubbed against my own insecurities. It was like a play we over-rehearsed.

I hated how he believed I was a job. "Is that all I am to you? A job. Someone to protect."

His broad shoulders dipped and his anger fell away. He took my hand and I sensed our core connection, yet it felt tenuous at the same time as if it might fray. "No."

Bumping his hip suggestively, I couldn't let this opportunity slip past. "Well anyway, I'm here now."

"That you are." His lips twitched and he pulled me against him. "For how long?"

Disappointment wormed through my chest. "I have to meet Mistress Lita for dinner."

"You mean, your great grandmother." He pulled back and arched a brow.

"Yes." I sniffed. Was he mad about me leaving or the relation?

"Come here." He yanked on my hand and brought me up close again.

Zings sizzled up my spine. Smiling, I raised on my tiptoes for his kiss.

"Oh, sorry." Cassia walked in. "Is Lukas here too?" She must still be interested in Lukas even though she flirted with others.

"Back there." Stone's slumber-ish voice showed his desire.

I hated that I had to leave him alone so often.

She skipped toward where Stone had indicated and stopped to stare at us. "Aren't you going to join us?"

I hadn't seen much of her or any of Lukas. But I also wanted to spend time alone with Stone. "Be right there."

Stone's heavy-lidded eyes opened wider. He angled his head in a questioning way.

She winked. "Take your time."

Thinking of her and Lukas' situation, I wrung my hands. "I'm sorry about what you saw with Damien. You're not jealous are you?"

"I don't know." Stone considered. "The warlock would be a better fit for you."

My heart jolted. "You fit me."

He laughed and stood taller. Using his hand, he measured the height difference between us. His expression went serious. "A warlock could help you navigate the ins and outs of the coven. He could help you learn quicker, teach you to fly on a broomstick."

The slight hint of jealousy bolstered my emotions.

"I can't help you learn your magic or control your powers." Stone agitated his hands in a helpless way. Not at all like him. "When you disappeared, I realized I can't even protect you at the coven."

I wished I could prove to him that I could protect myself while also showing I needed him. I wished I could share my other concerns about coven leadership. Bitterness flooded my mouth thinking about the Secretum Bond. I wished I could make him feel better about the situation. But I could take this from bitterness to bliss. "You can help me with this."

I stood on my tiptoes again and brushed his lips with mine.

He bent his head and wrapped his arms around me tighter. The kiss filled with punishment and passion. He was angry at himself for being unable to protect me. I had to communicate to him that I could protect myself. I put more power and pressure into the kiss. I wanted him to know we were equals.

"Excuse me," Simon's whimpering cut across my bliss.

Pulling apart, Stone kept his arm around my waist. Why did we keep getting interrupted?

The acolyte held out a small electronic device. "I've received an encrypted message for Stone from King Zacharye."

"You have?" Confused, I didn't realize witches had the hi-tech communication devices. My pulse raced. It reminded me of how the banshees had hi-tech equipment while living a nomadic life.

"When I sent a message to the fairies about Violet, I also sent a message to the king."

Stone took the device and clicked a couple of buttons.

Holding my breath, I waited for him to explain or share more. Just as he was a confidant to the king, I wanted to be his confidant. Guilt trampled my thoughts. Of course, I couldn't tell him everything. "What does it say?"

His expression went blank giving nothing away.

"Well?"

"King Zacharye...requests...my presence." Stone's unfocused answer and seriousness showed he was deep in thought.

"You knew the king wanted you by his side." Stone had sacrificed to stay with me, to protect me. Maybe he should've gone with the king.

"King Zacharye needs me now. Something's happened." Stone's clipped tone told me there was more in the note.

"What?" I realized establishing a new government was time consuming and had risks, but the biggest danger, the regent, had been arrested. The kingdom was under control. Stone had promised to arrive as soon as he could, as soon as I was done learning.

"I'm not at liberty to say." Stone's voice chilled. He surveyed the area.

Simon stood right next to us and Lukas and Cassia had come out of the back room.

It must be because of them he wouldn't share. Surely, he'd tell me later. "How urgent?"

"According to this message, very urgent." Stone rubbed his chin.

"Are you going?" My love plunged downward. He'd promised the king he'd arrive after his time at the coven.

Tension stretched between us. Between all of us. My heart ticked out each silent second.

He cleared his throat and pulled back his shoulders. "It wasn't a request. The king commanded me."

Chapter Fifteen

Loneliness wrapped around my heart.

Stone was leaving. I could see it in his expression and sense it by the way he held his body. He wouldn't deny the king's demand.

"Aren't you supposed to be at dinner with Mistress Lita?" Simon held a parchment burnt around the edges. The parchment hadn't been in his hand earlier.

My chest squeezed, sending sadness through my veins. "Tell Mistress Lita I have to cancel."

"No." Stone grabbed my arm. "She's family. Besides, I have to finish deciphering the message."

There was no doubt in his voice. He was leaving. He had to go.

"I'll walk back to the academy with you." Cassia slipped her arm through mine. "Bye Lukas."

The werewolf frowned and furrowed his brow. We'd ruined his plans for the night.

My sadness gnarled. This couldn't be my goodbye with Stone. "You can't leave tonight."

"Tomorrow." Stone's immediate response disheartened me. He already bent his head toward the device, not paying attention to me anymore.

Would I ever be as important to him as serving the king? Of course, working for the king gave Stone a purpose he didn't have here. Here, he had nothing.

Cassia ushered me out of the building and we trekked back to the academy. She said the spell for the drawbridge and I didn't even pay attention. I was too numb. Stone leaving was best for both of us. He could assist the king and feel purposeful, and I could focus on learning.

We crossed the bridge and she walked me up the stairs to Mistress Lita's suite of rooms, where my friend said goodbye.

The door opened without a knock.

"You're late." My great grandmother's voice quivered. "I was worried about you."

She didn't sound that worried and she obviously knew my whereabouts. Simon had found me with Stone.

A round table set for two had been added to her cheery room. A nice and intimate dinner for me and my great grandmother. It was just the two of us now. I'd lost my parents, my grandfather, and now possibly Stone.

"Sorry, Mistress Lita." I couldn't even muster true regret. "I was busy."

"Call me Gigi. Your mother did." Her sweet suggestion warmed my bones. "Look at this beautiful flower." She held up a plant with small black buds. "Once dried it can become a potent herb in a potion."

"What does it do?"

"This and that. And it's hard to find. Only grows near the waterfall's edge." She pouted her lips, seeming concerned. "Enough about this. How are you? You seem upset."

Her sympathy almost undid me. My eyes burned and I heaved. I slumped into the seat next to her. "Stone," I held back a sniffle.

"If he's hurt you, I'll take care of him." The threat sent a chill through me. Just like Stone, she'd protect me from anything.

I had yet another champion. I wasn't sure if I appreciated it. I'd saved Stone from the cave in, I'd discovered the tunnels in the human dungeon to plan our escape, I'd taken control of the banshee clan. Surely, I could take care of myself. Why didn't anyone believe me?

Not that I didn't appreciate her support. Through my unshed tears she appeared even older. "Stone received a message from King Zacharye."

Her mouth opened in surprise. "This Stone is important to the new king."

She'd come to realize how paramount he is to the kingdom and to me.

"He is." I pulled my shoulders back. I was proud of him.

She poured tea into the cups. "What was in the message?"

"I don't know." We hadn't had time alone to talk. "But the king commanded him to return to Reximus Palace right away."

"We can make arrangements for him to leave tomorrow." Mistress Lita's efficient movements mirrored her words.

A sob escaped. "I don't want him to leave."

"What would he do otherwise? Stay here and sit around?" Her assessment was the same as the provost's and my own thoughts. "This Stone is a man of action. He's a confidant of the king. Why would he stay?"

I couldn't claim our love out loud. I believed he loved me. What if he loved his duty more? "He's my protector." I pulled out the lame excuse.

"Hah." She snorted. "You don't need a protector. Soon, you'll be stronger than him, more powerful than him. Then what will he be?"

She spoke slowly, hinting that he was a lowly creature. He'd still be my guy. In the future, we'd have a more defined relationship. He'd said so himself, although it wasn't a promise. And we wouldn't be staying at the coven.

"How would it be if you two stayed together?" It was a rhetorical question. She snapped her fingers and fully filled plates with Cornish game hen, dark rice, and corn sat on the table. "With your powerful magic, he'd lose his sense of self. He'd have no purpose here. He'd be lower than a warlock."

Her display of power and confidence proved I'd be able to do that soon.

"What has he been doing since he arrived?" The challenge in her question said she already knew the answer.

"Not much." Slouching back in the chair, I let the sadness change into a private pity party. Sitting around is not something Stone had ever done in his life.

"And will he be happy with that? Will he stay happy with you?" Her questions stabbed with sharp points. Correct points.

If he stayed while I learned, he'd start to resent me, hate me even.

Mistress Lita straightened and her lips pursed together in triumph. Decades of leading the coven must've worn on her. Whatever her true age, she was beautiful. I wondered if this was how my mother would've appeared if she'd lived. Had she always known she wanted to be the leader? Of course, she'd have known her lineage since the moment she was born. I hadn't. It had been a shock discovering I was half witch. But I knew I didn't want to end up alone and controlling.

If I didn't want to become leader, I didn't need to stay at the coven. Professor Nilsen at Reximus Palace might be able to help control my magic and maybe Cassia would come with me. I knew I couldn't lose Stone by keeping him tethered to the coven, a place he didn't want to be and had no purpose. And I didn't want to stay in the coven without him.

Things solidified in my brain. "You're right."

Mistress Lita's smile grew brighter. She believed she'd gotten what she wanted.

My next statement was going to wipe the smile off her face. "I'm going to leave with Stone."

➤➤➤ ⫷⫷⫷

After sending Stone a one-way message that I was going with him, Mistress Lita convinced me I should attend classes in the morning to learn what I could before leaving the coven. She'd tried a tepid attempt at convincing me to stay, but she must've recognized I'd made up my mind. Stubbornness must run in the family.

Of course, Stone couldn't respond to my message so I didn't know what he thought about my decision. My gut twinged. I'm sure he was thrilled. Stone and I needed to stay together. Too much of our lives had been spent apart.

Miss Shadowmend, the Arts of Alchemy teacher, had sent us on a scavenger hunt to find a rare plant called Death Weed which can be dried and used in potions. The prize was a unique magic potion book that I really wanted to win.

Remembering the plant from Mistress Lita's office, I described it to Lavender and she agreed it was the same item. We worked as a team trying to gather the plant with black flowers. I'd miss her when I left. The thought weighed me down. According to Mistress Lita, the coven would die. Did that mean she would die too? What about Lavender and even Raven, Astrid, and Arabella? What about Damien and the warlocks? What about Cassia and her family?

I didn't want the witches and warlocks to die. Why couldn't they pick a new leader? Why did it have to be me? I didn't even know these people a few days ago. Why should it be my responsibility to stay?

We picked the plants close to where the Dark Angel's Veil waterfall cascaded into the river below. The green, scrub brush plant with black petals stood out and grew in abundance. None of the other witches from class had picked this location. Maybe they didn't have inside information.

"There's a bunch over there." The potion book prize would help me teach myself about alchemy. It was something I wanted to bring with me when I left.

"Not a good idea, Destiny." Lavender's voice quivered. She hadn't wanted to come anywhere near the waterfall and I'd had to convince her.

This morning it was finally sunny and I was happy to be outside.

She shook the basket to get my attention. "We're not supposed to get close to the Dark Angel's home."

"The Dark what?" I sucked in a breath so intense my ribs pierced my lungs. Cassia had told me it was an old legend.

"The Dark Angel guards the Gates of the Underworld." Lavender trembled, fearful of saying his name.

"I thought the coven guarded—" My words stopped and bitterness flooded my mouth. I couldn't speak of it because of the Secretum Bond. Maybe the bond was not about me sharing secrets. Maybe it was about me not asking questions and learning more than I was supposed to. "Tell me more."

Her gaze danced around confirming we were alone. "He's a guiding leader of the coven."

I paused my picking. "He's a leader?"

"Not a leader exactly. It's a coven secret." My friend ducked her head. "I'm not supposed to know much, but my mother... I can't talk about him."

I wonder if she'd agreed to a Secretum Bond.

"So the Dark Angel is real?" I had to know if Cassia had lied about the file being a joke.

"Of course, he's real." Lavender chuckled darkly. "Once upon a time he was a warlock from our coven."

"How long ago?" I picked another plant. Might as well learn truthful history while I worked.

"A long, long time ago." She picked another plant. "A new Dark Angel is chosen when the current one's Death Mate dies and joins him in the Underworld."

I stared at her. "You know about the...the..."

She angled her head. "The Underworld? Sure. The current Dark An-gel has held the position for at least a century. I don't know who his Death Mate is but she's lived an impossibly long time or something in the process went wrong. The warlocks have been competing for the position for decades. No one new has been chosen."

"Only a warlock can become the Dark Angel?" When she answered yes, I let out a breath. I needed to focus on winning, not legends. "I really want to win this prize. I could use the book when I leave."

"I can't believe Mistress Lita is allowing you to go."

"She doesn't have a choice." This was my decision.

I waved Lavender over to a spot where the plants grew in large bunches right next to the edge. The steep drop had me getting on my knees to keep my balance. I didn't want to fall in like my grandmother had. Spray from the waterfall hit my uniform.

"The water doesn't burn you?" Lavender levitated the large basket hold-ing the plants we'd collected so far. She didn't step any closer.

"We'll be careful." I pulled the plants. "Bring the basket over here."

She took a step and used her wand to bring the basket closer to me. I dropped the plants in. "Should be plenty to win." She grabbed hold of the basket. "We should head back."

The water rushing down the falls grew stronger and louder. Steam start-ed to rise. The water at the bottom bubbled in an ugly brown brew.

Fascinated, I stood and watched.

The bubbles grew bigger and bigger. Some of them took on a darker color, almost black. They began to form a shape. Or was a shape emerging from beneath the waterfall?

Instead of stepping away, I stepped closer. An urge drew me toward the edge.

The shape became a man. Or part man. He had long gray hair and small horns protruded from the sides of his head. His nose was flat with wide nostrils and his pupils glowed with flames. He didn't wear a shirt and his sagging center showed that at one time he'd been muscular. Now he just looked old. He wore a ragged cloth around his waist and his legs were covered in hair.

"Destiny, run!" Lavender grabbed my arm and tried to pull me away.

"Who steals from the Dark Angel?" The man roared and his body seared with heat.

My bare legs and face roasted.

Lavender's fingers slipped off my arm and her body stilled.

My mouth opened to speak and nothing came out. Peering at an unmoving Lavender, I tried again. "We weren't stealing. We were picking plants for class."

The Dark Angel's expression darkened. His horns glowed red. "Witches from the academy?"

I began to nod and a lump formed in my throat. Maybe I shouldn't tell him anything. "I didn't know the plants were yours." Although Lavender had warned me to stay away. "I didn't realize..."

Fear boiled inside me like the water below. A plan formed in my mind. Probably a stupid plan but I had to protect Lavender and myself. Slipping the Obsidian's Fire wand from my pocket, I didn't know a spell to use. But he didn't know that.

"Leave us alone." My hands trembled as I pointed the wand at the man.

The water bubbled more and steam rose around the Dark Angel. His angry frown deepened and he raised his hand to strike.

If he was dark, I needed to try light. "Lux."

The tip of my wand lit. Nothing scary or formidable. The stupid spell and my false bravado failed.

"Have you learned how to use *my wand* after only a day?" His voice thundered. Heat licked off his body and tried to wrap itself around me.

His wand? My mind swirled. How could this be his wand? And how did he know I'd only had it for a day? I'd told Stone and the mistress I could protect myself. Maybe I was wrong.

The Dark Angel controlled his laughter. "For that miserable attempt, I'll want payment for my Death Weed."

"Okay, Mr. Dark Angel." Rubbing my hands on my skirt, I didn't know what to call the man. "How much do you want?"

He laughed again at my confusion and panic. How could the man know me so well? Could he read my thoughts?

"She's holding my plants. She stole them." His finger snaked out and he pointed at Lavender holding the basket. "I'll take her."

Before I could react, a brown wave of water swept from the river and wrapped around Lavender. The strength of the wave, or the magic, carried her down beneath the flow of water. She never moved or screamed.

My eyes popped. My heart hammered. My pulse sped around and around my body.

"No!" I screamed for her. It was my fault we were near the falls. She'd warned me to stay away. "Don't take her! Take me instead."

The Dark Angel gave me a mysterious smirk as he began to sink beneath the river with his payment in tow. His black gaze pierced mine. "We'll meet again, Destiny. Soon. Very soon."

Chapter Sixteen

The Dark Angel's parting statement chilled even though everything was blazing hot. A promise from someone called the Dark Angel was definitely a threat.

I stood frozen to the spot for a few seconds before panic crept into my consciousness. My new friend was gone. My breath came out in shallow pants. She'd been taken and I'd been threatened. I'd tried to use magic. My shoulders dropped. I'd been defenseless.

If I was so powerful, why did I feel so helpless?

Provost Morgane apparated with a group of five witches. "What happened? An alarm went off."

Blinking a couple of times, I processed what she said. "You have alarms in case someone falls in the river?"

"There's more than water in the river." The provost peered over the edge. She swiveled around to face me and her eyes bugged out of her head. "Where's my daughter?"

"I don't know. Who's your daughter?" I didn't care about her daughter, unless...unless—no time for conjecture. "We were picking Death Weed for class," I heaved, "a bit too close to the edge," I heaved again admitting the last part, "and the Dark Angel took Lavender into the river."

She could have drowned or boiled to death. Panic bubbled like the river. My insides scalded and baked about to burst with fear and sorrow. Lavender might be dead and it would be my fault.

Provost Morgane's expression went pale. She wavered as if blown by the wind. Sinking to her knees, she grabbed her head in her hands. "Lavender!"

My mouth dropped. Lavender was Provost Morgane's daughter.

The other witches didn't move. They must not know what to do. Their expressions held disbelief and fear.

"Do something!" I dropped to my knees beside the provost. Desperation flayed me on the inside. "You're a powerful witch. Can't you zap this Dark Angel with a spell? Conjure or apparate Lavender back?"

The provost wept, rocking back and forth. "My daughter!"

I lifted my hand to pat her back, wanting to comfort. I wasn't sure how or if she wanted my touch. She was a leader in the coven. Surely, she knew how to deal with this situation. "There must be something we can do." When she didn't answer, I raised my head to the other witches. "Isn't there something we can do?"

One witch shook her head. The others stared at the ground.

I processed their reactions. Were they giving up without a fight? If witches were so powerful, they should be able to do something against this Dark Angel. I was told my grandmother had fallen into the falls. Was that a lie? Had she been taken too?

Mistress Lita apparated in front of us, her tulle cape blowing in the wind. She wore a black leather corset with straps. The tulle repeated in the wispy skirt and beneath were black lace stockings and short boots. A few strands of white hair loosened from a bun. I'd never seen her hair up before and couldn't get a good look at the full color.

My chest lessened its constriction. Thank the elves she'd arrived.

"Mistress Lita." At her stern glance, I used the nickname she'd wanted. "Gigi, we need your help. Lavender was taken by the Dark Angel. Provost

Morgane is inconsolable. None of them know what to do." I waved at the unhelpful witches standing there. "I don't know what to do. How can we get Lavender back?"

"*We* won't be doing anything." The provost lifted her head and scowled. "You've done enough, haven't you Destiny?"

The provost automatically blamed me. I hung my head. She was right. My pulse beat faster and sweat formed on my brow. Lavender had tried to tell me not to get too close and I didn't listen. I'd antagonized the Dark Angel by attempting a spell.

"We'll place blame later." Mistress Lita stepped to the edge of the falls and peered down. Her body wavered and she appeared leaner and shorter than last night.

"Do you see anything?" I scurried beside her, not caring if I fell in or got in more trouble. "Is Lavender alive?"

"She's alive for now." The mistress expressed no emotion. "I'll need a clear account of everything that happened."

As a leader, she must not be able to express her feelings.

She hobbled beside the provost. She didn't bend down or kneel beside her. "You must pull yourself together, Provost Morgane. I'll start discussions with the Dark Angel. This has happened before."

I gasped. My great grandmother could just pick up a phone or send a message and talk to the scary half man? I thought Regent Theobald had dark vibes, but this man's aura was obsidian black.

The provost raised her head slowly. She glared at the mistress. "We both know how this ends."

My pulse skyrocketed. More secrets.

My great grandmother's eyes hardened. "You can put together an extraction team."

"What can I do?"

"You're leaving this afternoon." Mistress Lita's voice chilled, sending a shiver through me. She'd never acted so cold. "Is this what you do, Destiny? Create problems and then leave?"

I faltered back. Did I create problems? After the rescue from the dungeon, I'd planned to fight against the regent. It wasn't my fault I'd been kidnapped and Stone and my friends had left to find me. I'd left the banshee clan with better leadership even though they wanted me to stay. And now, I planned to leave the coven while Lavender was in danger. If I was truly a protector, how could I leave now?

Provost Morgane stood and stepped into Mistress Lita's space. "While you're negotiating, don't give away all our secrets."

How many other secrets did the Inferis Coven have?

I was in a daze of guilt and disbelief. I couldn't get rid of the image of the Dark Angel grabbing Lavender with a wave and taking her. How could she survive the boiling temperature and being underwater for so long? Was this a rescue or recovery mission? Classes had been canceled while the provost put together a rescue team. I wanted to do something. I wasn't used to sitting idly by while someone else did the rescuing. Now, I understood how Stone felt staying at the coven.

My ribs constricted around my lungs so tight I couldn't exhale. I couldn't leave the coven now. I had to find Stone and tell him.

Using the secret passage Cassia had shown me, I made my way to where Stone and Lukas were staying. No acolytes were posted out front so I hurried inside. "Stone?"

"What's wrong?" The question was one he often greeted me with. He always believed I was in trouble. Is that why he stuck around?

I ran into his arms and they wrapped around me. How much longer would I receive his comfort? "I can't leave the coven."

His body tensed and he held me back slightly. His gaze narrowed in suspicion. "Why? Are the witches stopping you?"

"No." I stiffened, slightly insulted he'd suggest that. "I did something terrible."

He hugged me closer. "You'd never do anything terrible, on purpose."

His doubt poked me. "Of course not. But Lavender..." My chest tightened and my complex breath labored remembering how she'd been taken. "Lavender..." I took another harsh breath refusing to cry. "Lavender was taken by the Dark Angel."

"The what?" Stone tilted away to stare at me. "And who is Lavender?"

"She's a witch and we were working on a class assignment." I gave him a summary of what happened. "The Dark Angel is..." I licked my lips trying to stop the bitter taste in my mouth. "My great grandmother is going to negotiate with him and Provost Morgane is putting together an extraction team and I...I..."

"I'm sure your new friend will be okay." Stone kissed the top of my head and rubbed my back. "Powerful witches are working to find her."

"She was taken and it's my fault." The wail morphed into a determined thread. There had to be a way I could help. I was resourceful. I'd rescued others before.

His arms wrapped around me like a trap. "What're you thinking?"

"Nothing."

"I know you. You're plotting something." Keeping his arms around me, he pulled back to stare and analyze my expression.

I ducked my head, hating how he knew me so well. If there was something I could do, I'd find it. He'd do the same thing, he just didn't want me doing anything rash. "I can't leave the coven right now."

"Because you're going to do something stupid." He inferred I'd attempt a rescue.

"No!" Lifting my head, I looked straight at him. I didn't know what I was going to do. But I couldn't sit around and wait for others to do the work of finding Lavender. I couldn't abandon her. "I can't leave because I messed up again. I can't go out into the kingdom without learning to control my powers."

Without knowing what happened to Lavender.

I thought I could leave. Between the books I could take from the coven and the assistance of Professor Nilsen at the palace, I thought I could learn outside the coven. Seeing the Dark Angel made me realize I knew next to nothing.

"It wasn't your magic that got this girl kidnapped." Stone's logic didn't matter.

"It was my fault we were by the waterfall and I have to stay until I know she's okay. And clearly, I haven't learned enough to stop being taught by powerful witches." I was even more convinced. I couldn't go out into the world, lose control, and get my friends in more trouble. I had to know what I could do with my magic and how to control it. I had to learn the secrets of the coven.

His eyes flashed with a million emotions as if fighting with himself. "You understand, I have to leave."

My heart cracked in two. I'd hoped he might delay. "Could you ask King—"

"No." The single hard word cut through my hope. "I've delayed my appointment long enough. King Zacharye needs me. I can be useful there. Here, I'm doing nothing. I can't even protect you, especially if I rarely see you."

I understood in my head what Stone said, but my soul already felt alone. With Lavender missing, I wanted to be useful too. If I told him, he'd rethink staying because he'd want to protect me. I couldn't use my farfetched plans to keep him close. As a half human and half giant he'd only get in the way. Stone would complicate matters.

I forced myself to nod.

"You're safe in the coven, with the family you always dreamed of." His voice cracked. "They'll find your friend, you'll learn, and eventually you will join me. And Cassia is here with you."

"And Lukas."

Stone glanced away and back again. He frowned. "Lukas is going to take Violet to the fairies."

Upset shook me to the core. Three more friends were leaving. But I understood Violet would be in a better place. Stone was supposed to leave this afternoon. "How soon?"

"Simon said he could arrange transport for us any time today. I was waiting for you to finish your morning classes..." Stone sputtered. He didn't want to exhibit his anticipation. "You understand why I have to leave?"

His urgency to leave hurt. This would be goodbye for now.

"Yes." Pain slid across my throat.

The tension in his body released. He was relieved to be going, to be leaving me.

"You understand why I can't go with, don't you?" I stood on tenterhooks waiting for his answer. I'd been so sure about leaving last night. Now I wasn't sure about anything. I did know I needed witches like my great grandmother, teachers, and even the provost to guide me. And I had to ensure Lavender was found.

He nodded and took hold of my hands.

"I'll learn as quickly as possible. Then I'll join you at Reximus Palace."

But still looming was the whole I'm-supposed-to-be-the-future-leader-of-the-coven secret. The thought made me want to laugh after what I'd done this morning. No one would want me to become the leader.

My mouth flooded with bitterness. I couldn't even tell Stone what my great grandmother expected.

"Of course, you will." He squeezed my hands, not sounding so positive. "This isn't goodbye forever. It's goodbye for now."

"At least I get to tell you goodbye this time." I joked while my heart was breaking. Another kidnapping might be easier on my emotions.

He took possession of my lips in a devastating goodbye kiss. My mouth clung to his in desperation. Another separation and I didn't know when we'd be together again. I didn't want to let go.

He broke off our kiss. "We need to tell Cassia goodbye."

She'd be upset about Lukas leaving. We could commiserate with each other.

Holding hands, we strolled out to find Cassia already talking to Lukas.

"Oh moons!" Cassia held both of Lukas' hands. "I can't believe you're leaving before we..."

Even with my heart breaking, I arched an amused brow.

"Before we what?" Lukas asked the question I'd been thinking.

She must not have seen Stone and I standing there because she stalked up to Lukas and grabbed his face between her hands. "Before we did this."

Plunging her lips onto his, she smooched him. Her hands ran through his hair and down his back wanting to paw every part of him. He didn't move, shocked probably.

She stepped back from him. "Hmm?"

"Well, goodbye...Cassia." Lukas was taken aback. He hadn't expected a goodbye kiss.

Guess their relationship hadn't gotten that far.

I observed Stone to get his impression and held in a sigh. I couldn't believe we were going to be apart for who knows how long. And I wasn't about to tell him I loved him right before he left. I knew we had a special connection but we had to survive another separation. He had to do what he had to do. And so did I. We were both independent. We'd come back together, right?

Simon apparated between us and created a portal. "Violet is ready to be transported. Dr. Everbleed has assured me she's in a comatose state in a protective pod."

"Goodbye...Cassia." Lukas sidestepped her and wrapped his arms around me. "Goodbye, Destiny."

His hug was quick, eager to leave. He stepped into the portal, waved, and he was gone.

"Your turn." Simon created another portal.

Stone hugged Cassia goodbye and stepped over to me. "Goodbye, Destiny."

He squeezed my hand and released. My fingers slipped out of his large hand and coldness wrapped around my skin. "Bye."

I took a shaky breath trying to control the show of emotions as my world fell apart.

Stepping toward the portal, he glanced back one more time. Then, he rushed forward and bent his head to mine. Our lips brushed in the sweetest, saddest kiss. He whispered bye against my mouth, turned away, and walked into the portal.

I touched my hand to my mouth, never wanting to forget the feel of his lips on mine.

The portal closed and my heart closed with it.

CHAPTER SEVENTEEN

And then I was alone.

Simon apparated away and Cassia made excuses to see her family. Loneliness swept through my soul. Stone had left out of duty. Lukas had gone to take Violet home. My other non-witch friends had left because of illness or family responsibilities. Even though Cassia was at the coven she'd been different since returning to her home. And my new friend Lavender had been captured.

Thunder boomed and dark clouds scudded above the area. The weather matched my mood. Dark and gloomy. Sad and lonely. A little helpless.

Stone left and took the sun with him.

Rain poured from the sky. I stood there and let the heavy wet drops fall on me, weighing me down. Taking a deep breath, I took a moment to be somber and sad. And then, I shook the feeling off. I had things to do. Saving Lavender and learning to control my magic. Once I accomplished those things Stone and I would be together again.

With that belief deep in my heart, I marched through the pouring rain, back to the academy. Back to where I'd face recriminations about Lavender, scorn for my terrible magic, and my daunting great grandmother and the secret binding us.

Classes were canceled because of the Lavender emergency, which didn't help my goal of learning, although I wasn't in the mood to sit in a classroom. But I also wasn't in the mood to be stuck in my room. After changing out of my wet clothes and into simple pants and a sweater, I decided to visit Provost Morgane hoping she'd calmed down and would talk to me rationally. I wanted to know who the Dark Angel had taken before and why? Had it been my grandmother or someone else? What had happened to them? And most importantly, how could the information help save Lavender?

I couldn't shake the image of the monster taking Lavender or the words of his final threat. The threat had implied something personal. I was at a loss of what to do. Yet I knew I had to do something. I had powers no one knew about. I had experience rescuing others. I was strong and determined to help because Lavender was my friend.

Turning the corner where the teachers' offices were located, I stopped when I heard whispering.

"You don't think it's an unusual coincidence that she asked me to replenish the Death Weed supply this morning?" I peeked around the corner to see Miss Shadowmend, the Arts of Alchemy teacher, talking to Provost Morgane outside her office door. "The mistress even gave me the extraordinary prize for the winner."

Mistress Lita had been involved in the competition? That didn't seem like something she'd participate in. She was more involved in administration than education.

"The spell book would be tempting for someone who needs to learn magic quickly." The provost wrung a white handkerchief through her fingers. She was already grieving.

"And wants to leave."

They were talking about me. I'd been desperate to win the spell book because I thought it would help me learn after I left.

Provost Morgane dabbed the handkerchief to her cheek. "We can't worry about why it happened. We have to do something to save my precious daughter."

"What can we do? We have no access. No way in or out."

"The Dark Angel protects his victims from the boiling water. What if a witch jumped into the river encased in a spell to protect their skin from burning?" She threw out an insane idea.

"There is no spell. You're talking crazy," Miss Shadowmend chastised. At least one of them was thinking straight. "You'd be sacrificing yourself."

"It's not as if this coven hasn't seen a sacrifice before."

The provost's absurd response startled, but it wasn't said in a comical way. She sounded bitter which meant sacrifices in the coven were real. My pulse pounded faster, worried about more secrets I'd uncover.

"And will happen again *very soon*."

I swallowed the lump in my throat, feeling ill. Another sacrifice soon? Wasn't Lavender a big enough sacrifice?

"And there's nothing we can do to stop it." Provost Morgane's defeat hit me hard.

Miss Shadowmend placed a consoling hand on the provost's arm. "I'm surprised you'd want to stop it after what happened to your daughter."

Swirling around, I couldn't listen anymore. I'd talk to Mistress Lita about this sacrifice and saving Lavender. Surely, the mistress must know how to save my friend. She communicated with the Dark Angel.

On my way to dinner, I bumped into Damien. "Sorry, I wasn't watching where I was going. I was thinking—"

"About Lavender." Damien grabbed my arms to steady me. "I was searching for you. I was worried."

"Yes." The weight I'd taken off with my wet clothes returned.

"I'm sure the provost's team has a plan to perform a rescue from the River Styx." The concern for my friend was revealed in his voice.

"The river what?" A shudder rocked my body. First coven sacrifices and now this. "You told me the river is called Helvete."

"That's what the river is called above ground. Below ground it is called the River Styx and it leads to the Underworld. The Dark Angel is its guardian."

I shook my head slightly trying to get the relationship straight. I thought the coven guarded the Gates to the Underworld. "How do you know this?"

Damien puffed out his chest. "I'm a Warlock Advisor."

"Excuse me?" The more I learned, the more confused I became. Although I did remember Mistress Lita saying something about the warlocks' involvement. Maybe Damien could talk about it. "Tell me more."

"The coven guards the entrance. The Dark Angel decides who gets on Charon's Boat to sail the River Styx into the Underworld."

"Will Lavender go down the river?" Blinking a few times, I held back my emotions. Angst, fear, devastation at losing my friend. "He's the devil."

"Close." Damien chuckled with a husky timbre. "The elder warlocks have met the Dark Angel."

"How? When?" I thought it was impossible to get to the Dark Angel without going through the boiling river and falls. The teachers had made it seem very difficult.

Damien angled toward me. "I've actually seen the Dark Angel in his lair."

"You have?" Heck, I hadn't known the Dark Angel actually existed until today.

"Warlock elders report directly to the Dark Angel. One day another warlock from the Inferis Coven will take his place," Damien boasted.

"Only warlocks can take the Dark Angel's place?" I'd never want the position. "Why would anyone want to?"

"It's a huge honor." He straightened, standing taller. "Live for however long you want. Decide who goes to the Underworld. Infinite powers."

"Alone." I knew how that felt. "The Dark Angel is by himself, all alone, for eternity."

"He takes a Death Mate."

My feet rooted to the floor holding back a dark shiver. The Dark Angel was old and evil. "Did he choose Lavender as his Death Mate?"

Damien grinned. "No. The current Dark Angel picked his Death Mate a long time ago. He waits for her to die and they pass through the gate together, then another Dark Angel is chosen. My understanding is he took Lavender as payment."

"Because I picked his stupid plants when Lavender warned me not to." My stomach thrashed in turmoil.

Damien stroked a finger down my cheek. "Hey, it's not your fault."

"It is my fault and Provost Morgane and other witches are discussing ridiculous plans." My back ramrodded straight. "I have to do something."

"I'll tell you what, I'll talk to a few of my friends and see if we can help you." He bopped the tip of my nose with his finger. "Maybe we can figure something out together."

"How can you help?" I shouldn't question the offer but cynicism spread through my veins. "Why do you want to help me?"

His cheeks reddened. "Well, I...I like you."

Shifting my feet, I peered at the ground. I had to be straight with him even if it meant losing his assistance. I lifted my gaze. "I'm with Stone."

"For now." Damien spoke with confidence.

"Forever." I added forcefulness to the single word.

"The giant is gone." He clearly had information sources of his own about who was coming and going from the coven. Which could be helpful in my new quest.

"Doesn't matter." But it did. "Stone and I have been separated before."

Damien lightly chucked me on the arm. "I'm willing to take my chances. Are you?"

Did the challenge refer to him or his plan? "On a way to help rescue Lavender, I'm willing to take chances." I wanted to be perfectly clear.

"Okay. I'll talk with my friends and get back to you." His regular smoothness had a rough edge.

Maybe he wasn't as confident as I believed. But I needed his help and didn't want to lead him on. "And you're going to help me even though we will never be a couple?"

"Help you and Lavender. And myself." He flashed a broad smile. "She's pretty cute and her mother is the provost."

My brow furrowed. I wasn't sure what that had to do with anything until I remembered Cassia's words about how the warlocks would date anyone with familial power.

⟩⟩⟩⟩⟩ ⟨⟨⟨⟨⟨

That evening, I sat at the table with Mistress Lita in her suite of rooms antsy to begin our discussion. Acolytes, always dressed in black, served the first course of salad. I didn't understand why we needed anyone to serve us when she could snap her fingers and have food materialize.

I opened my mouth to talk. She silenced me with a raised hand. Her formidable demeanor and how she always seemed in control was the exact opposite of me. Chaos churned in my gut about Lavender and impatience tromped in my head.

When the acolytes apparated out of the room, Mistress Lita lifted her fork with a shaky hand. Her bun appeared a complete mixture of white and gray. The pronounced bags under her eyes were a sallow, yellow color and her cheeks were saggy. The skin on her neck sagged. "You decided not to leave with Stone."

It wasn't a gloat and sounded sympathetic.

Tears stung. Smashing my lips, I controlled my emotions. I had to keep myself together. "Yes. After Lavender... I realized I need to learn from the best, and you and the other teachers are the best."

"I'm the best." She stretched across the table and patted my hand. "I'm glad you decided to stay."

"I'm not staying forever." I used the cloth napkin to dab at my lips and discreetly swipe my cheeks. "I'm staying until Lavender is safe."

She yanked her hand back. "You are next in line. Do you want the coven to die?" The harsh black and white question slashed through me. "The night of Ascension is tomorrow at midnight."

It wasn't that simple. I didn't want anything to happen to her or Cassia. Or Cassia's family, Damien, Lavender, and even her mean mother, the provost. I didn't want anything bad to happen to anyone. I also didn't understand why it was my responsibility. "No, I don't want the coven or the witches and warlocks to die. But I didn't sign up for this. Leadership is not what I want."

I was a protector like Stone. Not a leader. Sure, I'd come up with successful plans and led in the past, but my ultimate goal wasn't to lead. Especially not at the Inferis Coven. I quivered. Not here with their inequality and sacrifices.

"You don't always get what you want." The edge in her tone bothered me because she expected the opposite for herself and schemed to get everything she wanted.

I never got what I wanted. I'd lost my parents at a young age. I'd had my powers and my memories taken away. I hadn't remembered Stone, been hidden by my grandfather, and imprisoned in a dungeon only to be freed, and then kidnapped by banshees. I felt alone at the coven even with my great grandmother by my side. I didn't know who to trust and who kept secrets.

"This entire situation has been a shock. Finding out you're my family, that I'm supposed to lead, the fact that I was even half witch surprised me." My bones weakened thinking about everything happening to me. Exhausted, I needed to be clear. "I'm going to learn to control my powers and return to Reximus Palace to be with Stone."

She scoffed. "Love is just another type of power. One you yield to get what you want. You will learn soon enough."

Offended, I threw down the napkin. "Learn what? How not to love?" I took a breath. "Who do you love?"

Because it certainly wasn't me. If she'd loved me, she would've found me sooner. She only reached out when she needed me and wasn't happy that I rejected her request to follow in her footsteps.

Her skin paled, possibly remembering someone she once loved. What had happened to make her so unhopeful about romance? "Love is weakness."

The words struck the center of my chest and shuddered to my core. Is that what she believed? She thought love was a weakness while I believed it was a strength. Did she use power to get love? "Does everyone in the coven believe love is a weakness?"

Cassia had said something similar about the warlocks. I'd never use power to gain love.

Mistress Lita nodded and took another bite. She was trapped in her own beliefs.

I never wanted to be trapped by my beliefs or my power, even if I was the one in charge. Damien said helping me could help him. I wasn't sure if he was referring to a powerful match with either me or Lavender, or something more nefarious. He definitely had ambitions.

At the thought of my new friend, I dropped my fork. "I can't believe we're sitting here having a relaxed dinner when Lavender's life is at risk."

"One must eat to nourish the body and mind." She took several bites of salad.

My skin itched for action or information. The way the provost had discussed the issue made it seem like there wasn't much they could do to save Lavender. Mistress Lita was supposed to talk to the Dark Angel. "What's the status of Lavender's rescue? Have you spoken to the Dark Angel?"

"I have." She set her fork down with a clatter. "Sometimes as the leader you have to make difficult choices."

Perching on the edge of my seat, I didn't appreciate where this was going. "What *choice* have you made?"

"The Dark Angel is unwilling to negotiate until after his Death Mate dies and joins him."

My pulse sped at full force. Damien had explained a little about the process. "When will that be?"

She arched a brow realizing I knew more than she'd taught. "He's been waiting patiently."

"For centuries."

She arched another brow. "Correct."

"Who would ever agree to become his Death Mate?"

"The role brings his mate a long life and tremendous power in the real world, and special powers for their offspring in perpetuation." Mistress Lita suggested the offspring should be grateful.

"Powers are not worth knowing you'll be sacrificed in the future." This must be the sacrifice the provost had spoken of. I'd never understand the reasoning.

Mistress Lita's eyebrows thundered together and her lips narrowed. She opened her mouth to talk and snapped it shut. The skin on her forehead crinkled and her lips twisted together. "There are ways around the ultimate sacrifice for the mate. If an appropriate replacement is found."

Something niggled in my brain but my immediate concern was for my missing friend. "Is that why the Dark Angel took Lavender? As a replacement?" I'd asked Damien something similar and he'd said no. "Since she's down there, will the Dark Angel force her to take the place of his first Death Mate?"

"Lavender is not an appropriate replacement." Mistress Lita scoffed at the fact my friend wasn't good enough.

"If it's not Lavender, what will happen to her?"

"She will stay in the Underworld and become a servant to the Dark Angel and his Death Mate when she arrives. For eternity." Mistress Lita delivered the news of my friend's demise with no emotion. "There will be no rescue."

CHAPTER EIGHTEEN

My leap of faith could be a huge mistake.

I wiggled my shoulders trying to get comfortable. I wasn't used to asking strangers for help, but I was living in an unknown place with rules I didn't understand. Provost Morgane didn't have answers. And Mistress Lita was willing to sacrifice Lavender. I couldn't live with that decision. I'd been so upset about my great grandmother's announcement, I'd ask for help from anyone willing to listen.

"We're here because Destiny has asked for our help rescuing Lavender." Damien caught the small group's attention.

We met in the warlock dormitory where Damien had smuggled me into his room. It was so different from mine and Cassia's luxurious quarters. The barracks room had two simple bunk beds for him and his roommates. Metal lockers were on one side of the bed and desks were on the other. No nice furniture or cozy spaces or even a view out a window.

The only one I knew was Damien and I didn't know him very well.

"Destiny is more important in the coven than us." Xenos had blond hair coming to a point on his forehead. He stood by the wall with his foot pressed against it. "Why don't you ask your great grandmother?"

His snideness told me he hated Mistress Lita. I understood. At times she came off as cold and cruel, though not to me. My ribcage constricted. The only time she'd been cruel was when she denied help for my new friend. "Mistress Lita declared there would be no rescue of Lavender."

"I wonder what Provost Morgane thinks." Ulrich was shorter and wider, with muscles flexing beneath his black shirt as he gripped the railing of the bunk bed.

If I was upset about losing Lavender, the provost must be devastated. "The provost is working with a team of witches."

"Unbeknownst to Mistress Lita, we think." Damien stood at the front of the other two warlocks and I presenting the facts, not making accusations or opinionated comments. He'd make a good leader.

Wringing my hands together, I had to speak my mind. I'd taken a risk coming to them. Mistress Lita would be furious since she'd basically declared Lavender dead because she refused to help rescue her. "I overheard the provost and some other witches planning a rescue and their ideas were terrible and risky."

Xenos lifted his chin in a challenge. "You think you can do better than experienced witches?"

I kept my head held high. "I rescued majiks from the dungeon at Reximus Palace. I freed the brownies and the female banshees. I helped capture the regent."

The guys nodded, considering me with more respect. I wasn't just an untrained witch. I had experience.

"With our help, she can do this too." Damien clamped his hand around Xenos' arm. "The witches don't know about our access."

The other two warlocks went rigid. Their silence spoke more than words.

"Now they do." Ulrich's sarcasm confirmed my realization.

Damien had already told me that warlocks had access to the Dark Angel. The shocker was that the other witches didn't know. I bet Mistress Lita knew. She knew everything.

"Smart move, Damien." Xenos shook off the other warlock's hand and scowled. "You blew our one secret from the witches."

The witches believed that only my great grandmother, as leader of the witch council, could speak to the Dark Angel. I clenched my hands, needing their help more than wanting to expose their secrets. "I won't tell."

"See. She won't say anything." Damien paced to my side and put his arm around my shoulders. "She wasn't brought up in the coven, didn't even know she was a witch until recently. She doesn't have the same prejudices of the other witches. Which is why I asked her to meet us alone."

Moving, I let his arm slip off me. I did believe the warlocks were treated unfairly. Our school classes were separate. The leaders were women. Leadership should be based on ability and knowledge, not your sex or who you were related to. Separate wasn't equal.

"I appreciate your help, Damien." I met each of the warlocks' gazes. "I do find some of the coven practices outdated."

"What do you think guys? Should we assist her?" Damien spoke to his friends. His tone suggested persuasion.

Their blank expressions didn't hint at their answers. I held my breath. I'd decided to trust them when I'd contacted Damien after my dinner with Mistress Lita. Would they trust me?

"If you think it will help *our* cause, I agree." Xenos leaned back against the wall in a relaxed pose.

Ulrich jerked his head in agreement.

"Thank you." I let my breath out in a whoosh. Now the important question. "So how can you guys help?"

Damien scanned the other guys, confirming what he should say next. "The warlock elders meet in secret with the Dark Angel on a regular basis."

"There's a way in that doesn't involve a boiling river?" My hope rose and I felt lighter than I had all day.

"More importantly, there's a way out." Ulrich smashed his fist into his other hand. He was ready for a battle.

Xenos' lips flattened, getting serious. "We can get you down. But you'll need to talk to the Dark Angel by yourself."

My heart stilled as fear pulsed through my bloodstream. The Dark Angel was a terrifying half man whose his image and parting words haunted me. The warlocks would be more versed in negotiating with him. "Why me?"

Ulrich and Xenos glanced at Damien, and the three stared at me. They weren't telling me something. Nerves pinged across my skin.

"We believe you're the best person to influence the Dark Angel to release Lavender." Damien's tentativeness didn't give me confidence. "Because of who you are."

Because of my relationship to Mistress Lita.

My gaze narrowed. I'd decided to take a leap of faith and trust them but I refused to go in blind. There was more to this than Damien liking me or the warlocks being nice. They wouldn't take a big risk out of pure goodness. What was their cause? "Why are you helping? What do you want from me?"

The three of them looked at each other again and then back at me.

Damien took a step toward me and took hold of my hand. His serious expression told me this was important. It seemed almost like a proposal which was ridiculous because we'd just met. He knew about my relationship with Stone.

"The Dark Angel picks his own successor." Damien winked. "At seventeen, I'm the right age as well as first in my class. I'm the Warlock Advisor and I have leadership skills. I'd be the perfect warlock to take his place when his Death Mate finally passes and the two of them sail down the River Styx."

"Why would you want the position?" My question exploded with disgust. I'd asked him before why anyone would want the role and he'd spouted stuff about honor and power. "I'd never give up my freedom for a position."

"Warlocks don't have much freedom anyhow." Damien squeezed my hand as if he held onto a lifeline. "And my plan is to make things more even between witches and warlocks."

The coven was even more unbalanced than I'd noticed.

Xenos jumped beside him. "We'll be his right—"

"And left..." Ulrich stood on the other side.

"...hand men."

Damien smiled at his buddies. "If the Ascension goes through, you'll be leader of the coven and I'll take the current Dark Angel's place."

I tilted back slightly. He must know Mistress Lita's plan to have me become leader of the coven. Everyone knew things I didn't. Becoming the leader wasn't solely based on lineage although it seemed witches and warlocks assumed that. "How do you know about..." bitterness flooded my mouth, "...that?"

Damien stood straighter. "The warlock elders keep us informed of upcoming changes and opportunities."

More than my great grandmother told me.

"Which makes the position and who will become the new Dark Angel important." Xenos poked his elbow into Damien's side.

"It's not that we don't want things to work out for you as leader, but being part banshee won't make it easy." Damien didn't stiffen or drop my hand when he mentioned my other half.

Ulrich popped up on his toes with excitement. "And if the witch Ascension goes awry, the Dark Angel will be in charge."

"You?" My jaw dropped and I pointed at Damien.

"Yes." His grin grew brighter already believing he'd won.

Mistress Lita told me if I didn't Ascend, which I wasn't planning to do, the coven would cease to exist, not that the warlocks would take control. She'd lied. And I couldn't tell them.

"Let's face it with you having recently arrived at the coven and not knowing what you're doing with magic, plus being part banshee..." Xenos trailed off.

I understood what he meant. He didn't believe I could do the job.

Heck, I didn't believe I could lead either.

My great grandmother had told me Ascension to leadership was a big secret. It's why she'd forced me to make the Secretum Bond. Yet the warlocks understood how the Ascension worked and planned a workaround.

All the oxygen cleared out of my lungs and I felt lightheaded. Standing on shaky legs, I was ready to dash out of the room. "I think I've made a big mistake. How can I trust you if you want me to fail?"

⤜⤜⤜ ⤛⤛⤛

I couldn't sleep. After my secret meeting with the warlocks, I had more questions than answers. The end of our meeting replayed in my head.

"You can trust us because we've told you everything." Damien had sounded passionate. "We've shared our secrets and our plans. More than your great grandmother has done."

He was right.

Mistress Lita had lied or, at the very least, not explained. She'd made me take the Secretum Bond so I couldn't even ask questions of the teachers or any of the witches and warlocks.

"We're risking everything to help you rescue your friend. And if things go awry, you can walk away from the coven just like you wanted."

They'd told me they could get me in to see the Dark Angel and they believed I could influence him to get Lavender released and get Damien promoted. Shivering, I rolled over and pulled the blankets closer around me. It must be past midnight. The day before my birthday.

If the warlocks got me in, I'd make their case if I had the opportunity. Though I hoped I could sneak in and get Lavender without being seen. But I had no idea what to expect.

Cassia hadn't been in her room when I'd returned. I wasn't allowed to tell her anything anyway. She'd lied about the Dark Angel so I couldn't confess my secrets. At least Damien hadn't forced the Secretum Bond on me. And they clearly hadn't been subjected to one either. They knew coven secrets.

Rolling over again, I threw the covers off. Sleep was not going to come so I might as well do something useful. Go to the library and study. If the rescue failed, I might be punished, kicked out by my great grandmother, or die. I swallowed hard.

Opening the dresser, I picked from a wide variety of clothes that had materialized after I arrived. Too bad I had to wear the academy uniform most days. Tonight, I put on a black top and pants to suit my dark mood.

Creaking the door open, I stuck to the walls and snuck to the library. The fact that Mistress Lita wanted me to become leader when I wasn't even allowed to freely roam the academy stuck in my throat. Another form of a cage and I refused to stay locked inside.

I entered the library and found a hidden corner behind the main desk. The library had tall walls lined with books and magical ladders on rollers sliding around to retrieve them. Most of the floating candelabra were snuffed out with a few in the center giving off a little light. The room opened to a large skylight where stars winked in the night sky.

Giggling caught my attention. "All those awful zaubers are gone so we won't need to make any more of the *Voluntatem* potion." Cassia's voice startled.

Frowning, Cassia wouldn't call our friends zaubers. She wouldn't laugh at them. I peeked around the corner of a bookshelf.

It was Jinx, not Cassia.

Wearing a sheer lace dress, Jinx strolled alongside another witch with bright pink hair.

"How did the experiment work? Did the potion divert the zaubers' will to stay?" The witch with pink hair slowed her pace as she trailed her fingers across the books sitting on top of a shelf.

I fisted my hands. They had to be talking about my friends. All majiks were equal now and yet they referred to them by the terrible nickname. But clearly the witches didn't believe everyone was equal considering how they treated the warlocks.

Thinking about what Pinkie said, I froze. The potion they discussed was supposed to help my friends breathe in this atmosphere, not be an experiment or force them to change their minds about staying. Sadness and aversion darted through my veins. My friends had left as a result of influence from external sources, not their own choosing. But maybe it was a good thing if the witches didn't care for other majiks, if they had been in danger.

"It definitely made them feel sick." Jinx's rough chortle rubbed me the wrong way. "An added benefit."

She was mean. Nothing like her sister.

"Well, the zaubers have left the coven so the experiment was a success." Pinkie took hold of Jinx's arm.

"Some had to be pushed out in other ways." Her high heels clicked on the wooden floor. "Mistress Lita was so angry."

My brows furrowed. I thought my great grandmother had come to respect my friends. She knew how much they meant to me, especially Stone. I quirked my head.

Pinkie stopped and peered back. "Remember when Mistress Lita cursed and took away the banshee clan's magic while trying to find her?"

They were talking about me. My great grandmother had told me she'd searched for me and I knew the Skjult Banshee Clan had no magic because a witch had cursed them. The witch was Mistress Lita.

Shock trickled into numbness. Why wasn't I more surprised? She'd been nice when I arrived, especially compared to the provost but there'd been times she'd acted hard and uncompromising.

"Well, she finally found the tribreed." Jinx's tone lowered and I heard the hate.

For me or the mistress? I thought she liked me because I was her sister's friend. Obviously, I'd been wrong.

Pinkie sauntered forward again. "It will be good when the Ascension Ceremony is over and things go back to normal."

Normal? It wouldn't go back to anything resembling normal if I supervised the coven.

"Tomorrow night." Impatience nipped in Jinx's voice. "I'm getting tired of the pretense."

She'd pretended to like me and my friends. I had to tell Cassia. She was my best friend. I had to take the risk that she'd believe me instead of her sister.

"And the boring clothes." Pinkie's giggle grew louder, echoing throughout the library.

"Mistress Lita trusts me to get the job done." Jinx stood taller as she walked. "Once the ceremony is over and the mistress gets her way, she'll have more power and more control. And so will I."

CHAPTER NINETEEN

If I hadn't already made the decision to leave, the lies I'd been told sealed the deal. The potion had endangered my friends. My great grandmother had taken the banshee clan's magic. Maybe the banshee clan wouldn't have needed me so badly if a witch, who I now knew was Mistress Lita, hadn't cursed them.

I'd decided not to leave with Stone because the Dark Angel had taken Lavender and I'd believed it was my fault. Was it? Maybe it was another scheme to make me stay at the coven. To make me think my magic was uncontrollable. I wanted to learn how to use my powers, but not at the expense of my friends, my relationship with Stone, and my freedom.

Once I rescued Lavender, there'd be no staying to learn more and definitely no Ascending to become leader. My stomach churned. I couldn't even think of Mistress Lita as family.

I'd spent the night studying books in my room. Reading, practicing spells, wand movement. Getting dressed in the academy uniform, I was more confident. I'd learn the ways of a witch quickly. I had to.

Even though I was assigned to sit with Raven, Aster, and Arabella, I ignored their gossip. Instead, I focused on the day's readings and the instructions from the teacher. After being up all night, my guilt about Lavender doubled as I stared at her empty chair. The need to confront

Mistress Lita and tell her the reasons I would refuse to Ascend bubbled in my brain. My mind, body, and psyche were exhausted.

Raven tapped on my arm. "I can tell you're upset. What's wrong?" She genuinely seemed concerned.

Had I misjudged her the way I'd misjudged Jinx and my great grandmother?

I needed to talk to someone. I couldn't tell her about most of my problems. I couldn't tell anyone because my real friends were gone. "I miss my friends and haven't heard from any of them."

Stone said he would find a way to communicate with me. He hadn't. Or maybe he had and I'd just never gotten the message.

"This isn't the twentieth century." She twirled her wand through her black hair. "You can send the first message."

Her suggestion piqued my interest. "I know how to send a message magically inside the coven."

"Since we're going to be besties..." Raven reached into her bag and took out a device similar to the one Simon had used to bring Stone the king's message.

I jerked back, surprised by her statement about being besties. Cassia was my bestie, although she hadn't been around a lot lately. I hadn't gotten the chance to tell her about her sister and I wasn't sure I should.

"I can help you communicate outside the coven."

My gaze narrowed. "Why are you helping me? You didn't even like my friends."

"Which is why I'm helping." Raven gave a pouty frown. "I was mean to your friends and I want to make up for it."

Her pouty lips made me think she was kissing up to me. Did she know I was supposed to become the next leader of the coven? My mouth filled with bitterness. I couldn't say that I was declining the leadership position.

"I'll let you teach me how." I would learn how to send a message outside the coven and in the process, she wouldn't learn what I wanted to communicate.

Raven handed me the device. "Type who you're sending it to and a general location, you know, like the coven or the banshee encampment."

"Can I send it to the human palace?"

"Of course. They have these devices."

"Why do you have one?"

"My father is a warlock elder." She *pffted* as if it wasn't a big deal. "Then, type in your message."

Focusing on the note, I quickly typed my message to Stone telling him that I'd be leaving the coven in the next day or two. I kept my note short and to the point. I'd express my feelings for him in person when I arrived. If everything worked out, I'd leave tomorrow on my seventeenth birthday. "Okay. How do I send it?"

She mewed her lips. "You're not going to let me read the note?"

I shook my head. "It's private."

"Ooh. It's a love note," she spoke loudly.

Aster leaned toward us. "A love note to Damien?"

My cheeks heated. "No and no way."

"Fine." She hit a couple of buttons and the message was gone.

"And it will get through the coven perimeter wards and any other obstacles?" Like enchantments or curses.

"Yes, no problem." Raven waved her hand in a breezy fashion indicating that sending a message outside the coven was no big deal.

Except I'd learned that if it didn't go along with the customs and rules it was a big deal.

When I entered Spellcrafting, Cassia flapped her hand at me. Reluctant to sit by her, I trudged forward. I couldn't tell her about the Ascension, the plan with the warlocks, or possibly even her sister. I couldn't tell her I knew she'd lied.

"Destiny, I'm so sorry about Lavender and the Dark Angel." She clamped her hand around my arm and whispered urgently. "I really didn't know he actually existed. I thought he was a legend. I'd been told by my family that he was a fable concocted to keep young witches away from the dangerous river and waterfall. I can't believe he's real."

I wasn't sure if I believed her. But this was Cassia, why would she lie?

Taking a seat, I crossed my arms. "Well, he is real and he's evil."

"I know!" Her shrill squeal hurt my ears. "I can't believe it. Jinx told me everything that happened."

"Jinx?" My body stiffened.

"Yes, darling, my sister." Cassia bumped her shoulder against mine.

My brain debated. Her sister was my enemy. I had to warn her. "I over-heard Jinx talking to a friend about how the potion they were giving our non-witch friends didn't help them breathe. It persuaded them to change their minds about staying in the coven."

"Are you sure?" Cassia's doubt cut my confidence about confiding.

"I know what I heard." I wanted her to believe me. I'd expected her to believe me.

Cassia was my friend. She'd never doubted me in the dungeon or when we were both captives of the banshees. Why would she doubt me now?

"I understand that she's family, but she lied about how she felt about me and our friends. She knew the coven was trying to make them leave."

"I don't believe it." Cassia jerked her head. "Can you prove what you heard?"

Frustration and anger balled in my gut. I knew telling one sister that the other was bad would be difficult. The two had seemed close. What if Jinx had lied to Cassia too? "No, I can't prove it. I shouldn't have even been in the library."

"What were you doing in the library late at night? Meeting Damien?" Her suggestiveness made the frustrated ball in my stomach flip.

"No." Although maybe instead of sending a message to Stone, I should've sent one to Damien demanding to know the rescue plans.

"Damien's cute and his magic skills are good. He's an excellent flier." She bumped up against me again. "You already know, don't you?"

She referred to him taking me up on the broomstick.

"His family is wealthy and powerful, well, for a warlock family." She both praised and demeaned him in one sentence. "Don't you think Damien has the dreamiest eyes?" She fluttered her lashes.

"If you like him so much, why don't you date him?" I had more important things to talk about than a guy's eyes.

"He's better suited for you. I enjoy dating multiple warlocks, or at least I did. Now, there's just the werewolf." She added Lukas as an afterthought and didn't even call him by name.

I sighed. Cassia was different at home. Flirtatious and gossipy. A partier who actively encouraged me to date other guys when she knew my feelings for Stone. Had she always been this way and was only different in the dungeon and banshee clan? She must've reverted to her old self once she was back with family and friends.

Peering straight ahead, I tried to listen to the teacher as thoughts ran around in my mind. Could I confide in Cassia? Could I trust her with my plans and secrets?

"Let's hang out tonight," Cassia whispered in my ear. "There's a private warlock party we could attend."

Case in point proving how much she'd changed. "I can't tonight."

She stared at me, ignoring the teacher completely. "Why? Hot date?"

"No." My cheeks warmed. I wanted to meet with Damien. "I've got something I need to do."

She angled her head, squinting at me strangely. "Are you having dinner with Mistress Lita?"

"Yes." I grabbed at the excuse.

"We can go to the party afterward."

Shaking my head, I couldn't look at her. "I can't. I've got too much studying to do. I'm way behind."

I hated being unable to confide and hated lying even more. Although the need to study was truthful, I just wouldn't be doing it tonight.

She kept staring. My skin crawled with guilt. I ignored her, pretending to listen to the teacher. When class was dismissed, I scurried out. I couldn't wait for the day to end.

Lavender was supposed to be in my next class. Of course, she wasn't there. My lungs wheezed. I'd read the chapters assigned and more, and was ready to answer questions from the teacher. I wanted to answer correctly so I knew I was learning. It wasn't about the prizes. I'd learned my lesson the hard way about competing.

I studied through lunch and went the rest of the school day with my head down, learning, learning, learning. Time was running out.

Damien wasn't at flying training. He was the only reason I went. I didn't need to learn to fly with a broom or with weapons. I wouldn't be here for long. How long depended on Damien.

My bones hardened and I stood tall. I couldn't wait any longer for him to make a plan.

Ditching training, I went back to my room and sent a message to him.

Not a love note. A demand.

⤜⤜⤜ ⤛⤛⤛

I stopped dead in my tracks when Provost Morgane apparated into my room. There was no privacy in the coven.

"You're late for tutoring." Her white dress proved she was already in mourning.

My pulse raced faster. "Is there news about Lavender?"

"No." Her firm response wasn't really an answer.

Trepidation tripped in my pulse. "I thought you'd...I thought you'd be busy with...rescuing Lavender."

I worried about saying her name again to the provost. I couldn't believe Mistress Lita was doing nothing.

Provost Morgane's face flickered with sadness before she became stoic again. "We are working on your mistake."

Jerking back, I felt as if she'd slapped me. I couldn't deny this was my fault. But I couldn't cave either. I was angry that the witches had no rescue program. "Are you working on a plan? Because I heard differently."

"*Your* great grandmother has given up." The provost blamed me for that as well.

"I disagree with Mistress Lita."

"So happy to have your support." Provost Morgane's sarcasm sharpened like a knife. "Let's open to page one hundred and ninety-three in our magical history book."

The book materialized in my hand and I almost dropped the heavy volume.

"The Inferis Coven has been the most powerful coven for centuries. Everyone fears us because..." Provost Morgane's pause stretched with tension. "...your great grandmother had the foresight to mate with the Dark Angel."

Her words slugged into me and I stumbled a few steps backward. Mistress Lita was the Dark Angel's Death Mate. The realization was like a bolt of lightning lighting the sky. She'd die and travel with him to the Underworld. Of course, she'd never told me.

A million thoughts poked and prodded. One stood out. "Did they have children?"

"Yes." She plopped onto my bed and crossed her legs.

Of course, they did. I did the genealogy math in my head. My grandmother, who I'd never met, was half witch and half dark angel. So was my mother. And I...

"Your great grandmother is a very important witch for a reason." Provost Morgane picked her words carefully. "She's been a very good ruler for our coven for a long, long time."

The way the provost stretched the end of the sentence made me curious. Also afraid. Whenever I learned something about my family it was negative. I needed to be sure. "Am I related to the Dark Angel?"

"He's your great grandfather." She swung her foot up and down waiting for me to put the pieces together.

I let the thought sink into my psyche. Thoughts and truths formed. More family members. More bad family members. He was the Dark Angel. The keeper of the Underworld. The guardian of the River Styx. People were terrified of him. I was terrified of him. Yet, he was my great grandfather.

I'd believed I was a banshee for most of my life. Then, I'd learned I was half witch, or part witch I guess. And now I find out I'm also part Dark Angel. This must be the reason my powers were erratic and uncontrolled. Mistress Lita had told me his offspring had special powers.

How could I learn control if I didn't know what I was? "A...a...tribreed."

Jinx had used that word last night in the library, but I hadn't realized she was talking about me. I racked my brain trying to remember exactly what she'd said. Anger billowed starting in my belly and sailing up my throat, growing hotter and harder on the way.

"Is there anything else I don't know about? Anything else that I am?" I shot the words out like bullets. "Banshee, witch, and now Dark Angel. What else should I know?"

Provost Morgane softened. "That's it. Except..." Her tongue stuck out of her mouth and she licked her lips. She struggled with what she wanted to say.

I dangled on the edge waiting. "Except?"

She stuck out her tongue again. Her expression went bitter. "Nothing."

Pressing my foot into the carpet, I demanded. "There must be more. What aren't you telling me?"

She smiled, making the hard lines around her lips more pronounced. The smile wasn't real. "Mistress Lita searched for you since the death of your parents. You're very important to her."

My anger morphed to contempt. "Important to her schemes."

I couldn't say anymore. Even now bitterness flooded my mouth. But if Damien knew I was next in line, Provost Morgane must know too.

"By your silence, I can tell you disagree with your great grandmother." She studied me, watching for a reaction.

I couldn't even nod my head.

"Good." Satisfaction oozed. "No one as young as yourself should have to sacrifice her future for someone else's greed over power and control."

A dark shiver passed along my spine. The provost meant by becoming the coven leader I'd be giving up what I really wanted to do with my life. Didn't she? How would that give Mistress Lita more power and control? She'd die and go down the River Styx.

I peered into an abyss of unknown. "Why are you telling me this? You must hate me after what happened to your daughter."

Provost Morgane licked her lips a couple of times as if trying to decide what to say. "There's nothing I can do for my daughter and I'm tired of the direction the coven is heading."

Did she want me to become the leader or not? I opened my mouth to tell her I was going to say no tonight. I couldn't speak. But I had to say something, and since she'd been so forthcoming I wanted to inquire about one more thing involving family relations even if everyone on this side of my family was sinister.

"When your daughter was kidnapped by the Dark Angel, my great grandfather, he said he'd see me soon. Was that a threat?"

Provost Morgane raised her chin and continued to watch my reaction. "It was a warning."

CHAPTER TWENTY

"Tonight is the night." Mistress Lita rubbed her gnarled hands together when I arrived in her suite of rooms wearing leggings and a black shirt. Where I was going I didn't need nice clothes and I refused to dress up for her.

Tonight *was* the night. For me, it was the night Damien was going to help me meet the Dark Angel, my great grandfather, so I could persuade him to let Lavender go. Originally, I hadn't planned to come to dinner. Why should I, when I knew she'd be angry at my decision not to lead. But after learning all she'd refused to tell me, my blood boiled and I had to confront her.

Blowing out a breath, I relaxed trying to act casual. "Is it true I'm a tribreed?"

I knew it was fact. Would she tell the truth?

"What?" She struggled to stand. Wearing another black dress that hung on her frame, she pointed at me. "Where did you hear such a thing?"

"It doesn't matter." The boiling and roiling warmed my skin, imitating a witch's brew. "Am I?"

Her gaze narrowed, highlighting the deeper wrinkles, the sallow eyes, the deeply sagging skin. Her long hair straggled in coarse, uneven waves. "Yes."

"And the Dark Angel is my great grandfather."

"Yes."

"Which means you're the Dark Angel's Death Mate, you married him and had a child with him." If she was answering truthfully, I needed to confirm everything I'd learned from the provost. I wanted to hear it from my own great grandmother.

"Yes. You have to understand—"

"I understand." My skin was on fire. She'd told me nothing. Nothing about me or my heritage. Nothing about my great grandfather. "What I don't understand is why you didn't tell me."

"I have an obligation to the coven." She smiled sweetly trying to persuade. Her mouth flattened. "So do you."

"No." Shaking my head, I crossed my arms ready to argue my point. "I have no obligation to anyone except myself."

And Stone and my friends, who I'd always thought of as family.

"The Inferis Coven will cease—"

"Stop. I'm done with the lies." I swiped my hand, imagining cutting off her falsehoods. "The coven won't cease to exist. The warlocks would become the leaders and control the coven."

She scoffed with superiority. "Then everyone in the coven might as well die. The warlocks don't know how to lead. They haven't done it in centuries."

"Because you have." The statement erupted out of my mouth. I combined genealogy math and actual math. The provost had said she'd ruled for a long, long time. "How long have you led the coven? How old are you?"

Witches didn't live forever. I'd learned that in class. How was she still alive? Especially when the rest of her family died so young.

She appeared flustered, licking her dry lips and flickering her white eyelashes. "It's impolite to ask a woman's age."

My hands balled into fists. She'd never be straight with me. "You know how old I am. *Exactly* how old."

"Tonight is your last night as a sixteen year old." Her voice filled with anticipation. She crossed slowly to the couch. Her bones creaked as she sat down. "Do you want to know how old I was when I became the Death Mate of the Dark Angel?"

I un-balled and re-balled my fists. Now, she wants to tell me her life story. I didn't care. I didn't want her laying more lies on my lap. I already felt terrible for Lavender. I glanced at my grandfather's old watch on my wrist. I didn't have much time before I had to meet Damien.

Mistress Lita sneered. "Sixteen almost seventeen."

My stomach churned. She'd been so young. "Your parents allowed you to marry at such a young age?"

"It was my decision. My choice." Her strong tone revealed her inner determination. "He was an old man. I chose to do it for the good of the coven."

Just as she expected me to do.

Was the decision good for the coven or good for her? She didn't live with the scary Dark Angel and she remained powerful. And my decision? Would that help me, the coven, or just her? Provost Morgane's comment haunted me. *No one should have to sacrifice their future for someone else's power and control.* Did she mean Lita had sacrificed or I would be?

"I expect you to do the same." Mistress Lita crossed her hands and placed them in her lap. She believed this was a done deal.

It was as if her hands were around my neck instead of in her lap.

"No." I started to take a step back and stopped myself. I couldn't exhibit fear. "I refuse to take the leadership position."

"I see." Her fingers tapped together and her serene smile gave me the shivers. She sounded pleased with my response. "You'll have to renounce your Ascension at midnight."

My nerves skittered. "I have other plans."

"Nothing is as important as the Ascension Ceremony." Her mouth twisted into a smirk. "If you don't show, your answer will be yes."

Great. Now I had a deadline for the night. Meet with Damien, sneak into the Dark Angel's lair, rescue Lavender or convince him to let her go, and be back by midnight to declare that I was not going to become leader of the coven.

⟶⟫ ⟪⟵

"I have an early birthday present for you." Cassia grabbed my arm right after I left the mistress' suite of rooms. She wore tight jeans I'd never seen her wear before and a black shirt. I wondered if she was headed to the warlock party.

She knew I had dinner with my great grandmother. Tonight, I'd left early and she'd been waiting for me.

I hated the thought of arguing with my only living relative before denying her what she wanted and leaving forever. Maybe not only. I wasn't sure if the Dark Angel was considered a *living* relative. I'd have to ask him tonight.

"Come with me." She practically squealed.

My shoulders slumped and I hung my head. I wished my life was normal and I could celebrate my birthday. Instead, my great grandmother had turned my birthday into a deadline. "I can't. I've got to be somewhere."

She winked. "Oh, you're not going to want to miss this."

Dragging me down the hall, she kept insisting I *wanted* to see this. When we arrived at the door to my room, I was taken aback. I'd expected another secret passage or tunnel.

Flinging open the door, she announced, "Ta da!"

Stone stood in the middle of the room. My gaze devoured him. It had been one day since he left, still I missed him. He wore a formal suit from his closet at the palace and held his body rigid, uncomfortable being in my bedroom. He must've been running his fingers through his now short blond hair because it stuck up in places. No smile greeted me.

Even so my heart leapt. Stone was here. I couldn't believe it was him. "Are you real?"

"Of course, he's real." Cassia's tone bothered me as she stepped into my room. "How could he not be real? A witch can't create a person. Or a giant."

I shook off the trepidation. I couldn't worry about Cassia right now. Stone was here and she'd brought him to me. I rushed forward, jumped up, and wrapped my arms around his neck. His arms wound around me a bit slow, surprised by my greeting. I kissed him on the lips. He didn't respond.

My heart tumbled and I tilted back. I let my arms slip from around his neck and I lowered to the floor. "I can't believe you're here."

"He is." Cassia clapped her hands together.

I'd forgotten she was there, witnessing our reunion. It must be why Stone didn't react.

"Close the door." I didn't want anyone else seeing him.

She sauntered toward the door, closed it, and leaned back anticipating a scene.

"I got your note." Stone's same deep timbre sent chills across my skin, and not the good kind. Something was off. "I got here as soon as I could find a way to get inside the coven without your great grandmother knowing."

"That was a big risk."

"Can you believe it?" Cassia beamed as if she'd taken the risk herself. "He snuck in with the help of the fairy princess."

An odd way of referring to her, Cassia knew Princess Ellery's name. It was the same way Cassia had called Lukas the werewolf. But she didn't matter right now. Stone mattered. I glanced at my watch. So did the time. I was already late.

"I'm sorry, Stone. Stay hidden in my room and I'll be back soon." I hugged him again, needing to be close. The warlocks would never trust him and if I told him my plan he'd want to come and protect me. But I had to do this alone. "I need to be somewhere."

"Where?" Cassia's eyebrows arched.

I scrunched my nose in an annoyed snarl. Why was she suddenly interested in what I was doing? She'd left me alone most of the time when I could've used a confidant.

"It's dangerous for you in the coven, Stone." I remembered what Jinx had said about getting rid of my friends. "There's something I need to do. I'll be back," I hoped, "and then we can leave the coven together."

"No." Stone's harsh response had me pausing mid-exit.

"No?"

"I'm here to tell you to take the leadership position in the coven." His stilted speech set off a warning.

Maybe he didn't understand that if I took the position I couldn't leave the coven for any long period of time. "If I," my tongue tasted the bitterness, "do that I can't come with you to Reximus Palace."

He could talk about it, use the actual words. I couldn't.

"I know." His expression didn't change. No warmth or understanding. No softening of the blow I sensed coming.

I teetered on the edge of before and after.

"What're you saying?" My heart shattered remembering the agony of when he'd left me.

"I'm saying you should stay at the Inferis Coven and become the leader. We're too different and you're too powerful. We're over, Destiny."

Each of his cold words carved into my heart.

CHAPTER TWENTY-ONE

y heart should be breaking.

It wasn't. I must be numb. Stone was my rock. He was the person I turned to for comfort and advice. I must have so much pressure and worry that I couldn't react in a normal way. Our goodbye when he'd first left the coven had taken more of a toll on my emotions than him breaking up with me.

Stone didn't shift. He made no move to console or protect me from hurt.

Something was off but I couldn't figure out what.

I glanced at my grandfather's watch again. I was going to be late and I had an important deadline. "We'll talk about this when I get back. Stay here."

His brow furrowed and he squinted, appearing confused.

"Stay here," Cassia repeated, treating Stone like her pet. She followed me out and closed the door.

"Are you okay? Stone broke up with you." She hurried next to me.

"I'm fine." I wasn't fine. But I didn't know what to think.

I kept walking.

Something ticked in my center telling me this wasn't right. Stone's posture was wrong. Or was it me? Mistress Lita, Provost Morgane, and even Cassia had counseled that Stone would hate my power and position. He'd feel useless at the coven and maybe what they said had come to fruition.

"If you're fine, he clearly didn't mean as much to you as you thought." Cassia gripped my arm and squeezed, sympathizing while speaking wisdom.

Stone meant everything to me. I couldn't deal with this right now. "Can you stay with him?"

"Where are you going?" She yanked my arm, forcing me to stop.

I couldn't tell her. Damien didn't want anyone to know he was helping me. "I've got something I have to do, for Mistress Lita."

She released my arm. "You should listen to Stone and take the leadership position."

Ignoring her suggestion, I looked her in the eye. "Keep him safe."

Pivoting, I darted down the hallway. I hoped Damien was waiting and I'd still have enough time to go to the banks of the River Styx and save Lavender. I had to believe Stone would wait until I got back so we could have a complete conversation. Not just him telling me our relationship had ended without saying why. Not him ordering me to take the coven leadership position.

I tripped on the thought and my feet followed.

Putting my hands out for balance, I replayed the conversation in my head. I'd never told Stone about the leadership position. I hadn't been allowed to speak of it because of the Secretum Bond. I hadn't told Cassia either, although she might know because she'd studied coven history and has lived here most of her life. Had she told him about what my great grandmother expected?

Cassia had said she had a birthday present. Had she known he planned to break up with me on my birthday eve? Negative thoughts about my friend jabbed at my brain as I jogged down one corridor after another. At one point, I thought I heard hissing. When I scanned the area, I saw nothing.

Coming to the secret tunnel Cassia had shown me, I understood going through would take me past the breaking point. There'd be no going back once I went against Mistress Lita's wishes. My chest constricted, slowing my pace. I was angering one of the two family members I had left and I'd abandoned Stone with someone I didn't fully trust.

Had I lost another friend?

No way could I have brought Stone with me on this mission. He never would've been able to sneak through the coven. I paused. How had he snuck past the wards and enchantments? Non-witches weren't allowed inside the academy.

Was it another trick?

Like the potion supposedly letting my friends stay but actually causing them to lose their willpower and making them sick.

Exiting the tunnel, I scampered toward the waterfall. The roaring pounded in my head with my many thoughts. Who to believe? Who to trust?

I hadn't trusted my grandfather and I should have because he was trying to protect me. I hadn't trusted my friends at first and they hadn't trusted me. They didn't even like me. But eventually, we'd believed in each other.

Now, I wasn't so sure about Cassia. She acted different in the coven. Or was I the one with the problem?

I hadn't trusted Stone at first. And now I trusted him implicitly even though he'd broken my heart.

I'd trusted Mistress Lita after the shock of learning she was my great grandmother. Until I'd discovered too many secrets and she'd been ruthless about Lavender.

Weighing each relationship, I needed to find a happy medium. I needed to trust and believe in myself to make the right decisions.

"You're late." Damien half hid behind a large boulder, his dark curly hair sticking above the top.

"Sorry, I..." Sliding to a halt, I rubbed my hands on my leggings. I didn't know what to say.

That I was hiding a giant in my room. That I'd discovered the Dark Angel was my great grandfather. That I knew tonight was the night I had to declare my intentions. I couldn't physically talk about the last item.

"We only have two hours to get you in, convince the Dark Angel to give you Lavender, and get you out." Xenos held out a black blindfold.

Nerves twinged in my midsection. "What's that for?"

"We're not showing you the secret entrance." Ulrich flexed the muscles on his arms, ready for a physical fight. "It's too close to the site of the Ascension Ceremony."

They didn't trust me and yet I was supposed to have faith in them. I hated the doubt sweeping me at this moment.

"Knock it off, guys." Damien hit Xenos' hand with the blindfold. The black material fluttered to the ground. "She'll be brought to Subterrane Abyss for the Ascension Ceremony. This is a shortcut."

"This is the warlock entrance." Xenos' long frame snatched the blindfold from the ground.

"For warlocks only." Ulrich's chin thrust up and down in an emphatic nod.

The nerves in my gut kicked and pulled in an internal battle. Nothing was going as planned tonight. I glanced at my watch. I didn't have much time until I had to declare my intentions.

"We agreed to help Destiny." Damien's rushed and impatient tone didn't soothe my nerves. "We don't have time to argue. Let's get going."

He put his arm around my shoulders and led me behind the waterfall on a rain-slicked narrow path made of rocks filled with puddles. The roar of the water hammered in my ears. Darkness fell once we slipped behind the curtain of water. Pitch darkness. The dampness went straight to my bones.

I shivered. If I lost my guide, I'd never find my way out.

"Lux." Damien's wand lit at the tip.

The small blip of light comforted.

"Duck your head." He let his arm slip to my waist and led me into a narrow tunnel.

I shivered again. Most legends say the Underworld is scorching. This area wasn't. Stalactites and stalagmites grew both up and down, crowding the cavern and making navigation difficult. The rough texture of the formations reminded me of tree bark. A damp, musty smell clogged my sinuses.

We were near water. Which water was the question? The Helvete River, the Dark Angel's Veil waterfall, or the underground River Styx.

"We're cutting it close." Xenos came up behind us. He flicked his wand at three torches and lit up the cavern.

The torches brought light into the nooks and crannies. The cave was larger than I thought and had dark tunnels going off in various directions. The ground was hard and covered in black sand. The thick stalagmites growing up from the floor could hold a horse and the floor was pockmarked with holes.

I knew I had a deadline. Why did they? "Why?"

"We've been watching the barrier between our world and the underworld to figure out how to help you." Ulrich picked up a thick rope. "It's been thinning."

That can't be good.

Damien swiveled around to face me. "When do you turn seventeen?"

Jerking back, I gaped at him. "Tomorrow."

"The Ascension Ceremony is tonight at midnight." His dark eyes went wide. making an important realization.

"It's when...I announce...decision." Bitterness flooded my mouth and I felt queasy. I might not be able to speak about the position but I could spit out random words. "No."

Since we were talking about Ascension they'd understand what I meant.

Damien nodded and his expression became concerned. I'd thought the news would make him happy. Warlocks would control the coven. "You have to be out before midnight, Destiny."

He made it a life or death deadline.

My lungs shrunk imagining being imprisoned in the coven, even if I was leader. "If I miss...ceremony..." More bitterness gushed into my mouth.

"Your answer is an automatic yes." He finished my sentence because I couldn't.

Since the warlocks didn't want me to become leader they wouldn't leave me down for any length of time. They needed me to say no. Even though Damien and his friends were helping me, they weren't on my side. They assisted for their own purposes.

I had no one to truly count on anymore. Not Stone. And possibly not Cassia. Definitely not Mistress Lita. Each name was a slash to my soul. I was alone.

Which was okay for now. I'd rescue Lavender, decline the leadership position, and find out from Stone whether it really was the end for us.

"If you're on the banks of the River Styx at midnight, Mistress Lita will get exactly what she wants." Xenos helped pull the rope.

My head hurt. If I got stuck, I'd miss the ceremony and become leader whether willing or not. Unless I got stuck down there forever.

The three warlocks exchanged glances. Their silence tensed in my spine.

Hisssss.

"What's that?" Ulrich pointed to the ground.

My head whipped around and I scanned the perimeter of the cavern thinking Mistress Lita might've found us.

"A snake." Xenos picked up the green reptile. "What's a snake doing here?"

Damien stopped playing with the rope to stare at the reptile. "It's a witch's familiar."

I frowned. Cassia had a snake for a familiar. Even though she'd professed to hating snakes when we'd first met. She'd changed so much since we'd arrived at the coven and I didn't know her anymore. And I'd left Stone with her. Worry ratcheted up. Even if he really wanted to break up with me, I hated leaving him in danger. I couldn't go back now. He was strong and cunning. And Lavender's life was at stake.

"Get rid of it." Damien continued pulling a long rope from his bag.

Xenos left the cavern with the snake.

Would Cassia betray me? "Do you think the snake will report back to its witch?"

"Doesn't matter." Damien took one end of the rope and tied it around my waist leaving a long tail. "You'll already be down the rope."

I pulled my chin in. "Excuse me? The what?"

He held a portion of the thick braided rope higher. "The rope. You'll be rappelling through one of the holes in the spot where the barrier is weakest."

This made no sense. I was a witch. A tribreed. "Why don't I use a broomstick or fly?"

Damien shook his head while continuing to stare.

My muscles tightened because I didn't appreciate what he wasn't saying. "Why don't you use magic to send me down?"

Simple.

"No can do." Xenos came back into the cavern wiping his hands on his black pants. "Witch and warlock magic doesn't work on the banks of the River Styx."

My stomach braided, imitating the rope. I'd have no magic to defend myself against the Dark Angel.

"What about banshee magic?" I could finally figure out which magic was which.

"Nope." Ulrich shook his head.

Great. I'd have no magic to escape. No magic to defend myself. Just my scintillating conversation and convincing arguments.

"We're wasting time." Xenos tied the other end of the rope around a stalagmite.

Apprehension skittered across my skin. I tugged at the rope testing its durability. "What if the plan doesn't work? What if I can't convince the Dark Angel to let Lavender go or it takes too much time and I go past midnight?"

Damien patted my arm and led me to one of the larger holes in the ground. "You won't. You'll do fine."

He acted like Stone, believed in me. My eyes stung. Stone had broken up with me. Was it because of the power thing? Doubts swarmed, clogging my throat. I couldn't think about my broken relationship now.

I peered down the dark hole, letting my end of the long rope dangle down. "You're telling me the warlock elders climb down a rope for their meetings with the Dark Angel?" There must be a better way.

"The Dark Angel opens a single portal. I don't know how it works." Xenos tied a thick knot to keep the rope from slipping off the stalagmite. "Right now, right before the Ascension ceremony—"

"When the chosen successor is about to turn seventeen," Damien gentled, making me leery. It had to be bad news. "The entire barrier between the coven and the banks of the River Styx becomes permeable. Holes form. That's why I guess you were turning seventeen soon. I just hadn't realized it was tonight."

"We've read in history books that warlocks have accessed the banks of the River Styx to search for recently deceased loved ones by going through temporary access points." Xenos curled part of the rope around his forearm.

Damien squinted away. "The points close up when the old leader—"

"Or the future supposed successor goes through." Ulrich stood tall and put his hands on his hips, daring anyone to contradict him.

Blinking, I tried to wrap my mind around what they were saying. The barrier between the coven and the banks of the River Styx loosened, disappeared, or became transparent enough for the old leader of the coven to pass through and be with her Death Mate. Mistress Lita and the current Dark Angel. What had Ulrich meant by the future supposed successor?

"That's...that's..." Bitterness flooded my mouth and I couldn't say anymore.

I'd just determined that I needed to believe in myself and my decisions. This was my decision. To trust Damien and his friends. To save Lavender. To go down to the River Styx no matter the risk.

I glanced at my watch. It was now or never. I had less than two hours to rappel down, find Lavender, and either sneak her out or convince the Dark Angel to let us both go. I checked the rope around my waist. My pulse raced, but I stilled my heart. I had to be composed and capable. If something went wrong, I'd never get out. I'd never see any of my old or new friends again. I wouldn't get to tell Stone I loved him.

Shaking myself out of my funk, I sat at the edge of the hole. My legs dangled into the dark.

I could do this. I had to do this. I'd been in tighter spots before. Stone and I would patch things up and we'd leave together. And Cassia... I jerked. I didn't know what to do about her.

"We'll lower you down." Xenos used magic to hold the rope.

"It's a narrow gap." Damien warned and reassured. "You can do this."

I appreciated his cheerleading. Tugging on the rope, I tested the strength. "And you're going to use magic to lower me slowly and pull me back up."

"We can use magic on the rope from up here." Ulrich nodded. "Don't become untethered."

I scampered to the edge of my seat.

"Ready?" Xenos asked.

I jerked my head down. "Ready."

Scooting off the edge, I had a moment of weightlessness before I free fell.

My stomach vaulted up while my body catapulted down. Pitch blackness surrounded me in a fog. Then the rope jerked taught and I exhaled in relief. I was going to be okay. The rope was a long, magical leash that would pull me to safety.

Sulfur burned my nostrils and the background thundering of the waterfall was replaced by the roaring of the river below. The dampness from above warmed and perspiration formed on my back.

I gripped the rope with white knuckles. If I fell, I had no powers to fly down. I'd end up floating down the River Styx or hitting the ground or falling at the feet of the Dark Angel. He scared me more than dying. I had to stay calm and quiet.

The sensation of going lower conflicted with being unable to see the changing movement. I peered down and couldn't spot the bottom. I didn't know how far I'd gone or how far I had to go. The temperature rose to a baking level. Sweat coated my fingers gripping the rope. Taking a soothing breath, I knew I was doing the right thing. I couldn't live with myself if I abandoned Lavender and left the coven forever.

What would Stone think if he saw me taking this gamble? He finally believed I could fight on my own yet he still wanted to protect me. He'd be angry if he thought I was in danger. Or would he? He'd broken up with me.

My heart wailed. After this was over, I'd tell him how much he meant to me, and hopefully he'd respond in kind because our break up seemed off kilter. Stone didn't act like himself and he shouldn't have known about many of the things he'd used as reasons for the break up. So how did he find out?

A flash of light blazed. Heat, hot as an inferno, stroked me with the fingers of the devil.

I stared down. The light metamorphosized into a bright flame in the darkness. Not a single flame, a blazing fire.

My gaze widened and terror shrieked through me. "The rope's on fire."

Damien couldn't hear me. He'd explained that magic didn't work down here, yet the flame hadn't been natural. It had been a form of magic. A protection ward or an attack.

My lungs constricted and I couldn't breathe.

The fire climbed the rope faster. Smoke billowed, filling the darkness. The rope frayed.

The flames crept up the rope like a wick on a bomb. I'd catch on fire and explode.

"Damien!" My muscles went taut and I started climbing back up. "Damien, pull me up!"

Had he heard and was ignoring me? Was I too far away? Did my voice not carry?

My foot slipped on the rope, I slid back down, and I screamed.

Flames licked at my feet.

I tucked my feet higher and grimaced in fear. I was going to burn to death. The heat attacked as much as the fire. Perspiration poured off my back. Sweat and tears dripped down my face. I couldn't hold on much longer.

Unwrapping my feet from the smoking rope, my entire body dangled. I couldn't hold myself in this position much longer. The fire crept up the rope faster. The rope tied around my waist began to smoke.

I inhaled sharply and patted the rope trying to suffocate the flame before it suffocated me.

Coughing, I pushed the rope away from my midsection trying not to get burned. The smell of the charring line filled my nostrils. The braided rope holding me started to fray.

My eyes rounded. I knew what would happen next.

The threads unwound. Weakened. Snapped.

And I fell.

CHAPTER TWENTY-TWO

I was alive.

With blackness surrounding me, I used my senses to confirm. I heard the roaring of the underground river. I smelled the awful sulfer. I felt the hard ground beneath me and rocks behind me. Pain ricocheted around my body.

I was definitely alive and injured.

Agonized needles shot up my arm. My ankle throbbed. Blood dripped down onto my cheek from a searing cut on my head. At least I think it was blood. I shuddered even though it wasn't cold. It was hot. Boiling hot. Sweat formed on my upper lip and brow, pooling on my lower back. This was more torrid than any banshee steam vent.

This was purgatory.

Or close to it. I must be on the banks of the River Styx, close to the Gates of the Underworld. If I didn't get out before the barrier closed, would I be stuck here forever? I'd lost the rope tether and it wasn't just black. It was pitch black again, like it was before the fire. The magical spark igniting the rope was gone. I could see nothing.

A shiver zigzagged across my skin. I could die here. Die of injury or thirst. I'd never get to tell Stone that I loved him. He'd leave believing I didn't care enough to come back and say goodbye. Maybe he didn't even care. If he truly wanted to break up with me, maybe he'd leave before I returned.

A spasm rocked my chest and I heaved. I couldn't think that way. I had to survive.

"Damien!" My shout echoed around me.

A low growling was the only response.

My pulse stopped. Not Damien. Not human. Not majik.

Surveying, I tried to pinpoint the location of the growl. It came from three different directions.

The guttural discord grew louder. Closer.

I tried to scoot back. A sharp pain jabbed my leg. It must be broken. Magic could fix the bone, but magic didn't work on the banks of the River Styx.

A flash of fire caught my attention. A growl accompanied the flash.

My muscles tensed. That's how the rope fire had started and now it was coming to burn me to death. Terror sizzled down my spine. I wouldn't die of starvation. I'd die at the hands of whatever thing bounded toward me.

A glimmer of white shown in three different places. The white shapes were triangles ending in points. Many, many points. Teeth.

Sharp, canine teeth.

A wet hair smell assaulted my nose. Three dark round shapes with peaked ears lumbered forward. Three heads.

I swallowed.

And one body. A three-headed dog.

Slobber dripped from its open mouths and it appeared hungry.

For me.

Horror chewed through my innards the way the dog's teeth might do to me soon.

The three-headed dog paused on big, thick paws. His rotund muscular body was on high alert.

My ribs constricted poking imaginary holes. A wheeze whistled out of my mouth.

Three heads cocked. Listening.

I froze, trying to make myself as still as possible. My heart refused to listen, pounding so loud Damien could probably hear it high above.

Three large noses pressed to the ground and sniffed. The suction tugged at my hair. My body slid forward and I gasped. I held onto the edge of a crevice in the rock wall, stopping myself from being sucked in.

The dog growled again. He, or they, must smell me.

The dog sniffed again.

I gripped the crevice in the wall tighter.

Biting down on the agonized pain, I curled into a ball hoping the dog wouldn't spot me in the dark.

An orange light flashed in the distance like the fire from the dog's mouths. But it was more of a glow than a fire. The glow grew bigger and flew higher.

Fairy or foe? Why would a fairy be down on the banks of the River Styx?

The glow grew in size. Was it getting larger or closer?

A ball about the same size as the glow stuck in my throat. Either way I was in trouble.

A flying shape emerged in the glow. It was him. The Dark Angel.

He appeared different in the low light. Not as big or as scary. Maybe it was the angle. He wasn't high above the churning waterfall.

A tunic hung loosely on his frame and he looked like a regular old man except for the horns sticking out the sides of his head. His gray hair flitted with an imaginary breeze. His wide nostrils flared, smelling an intruder. Smelling me.

The ball in my throat dropped into my gut and landed with a thud.

When he spotted me on the ground, he landed and examined me, saying nothing.

I wanted to squirm. But if I did he'd see my injuries and know I was vulnerable. After several moments, I couldn't take the silence anymore. "You said we'd see each other soon. Well, here I am."

His many wrinkles deepened. His dry, cracked lips lifted...lifted into a grin. He chuckled.

The noise was coarse and rough. Different from the taunting chuckle he'd used when he took Lavender.

Sympathy swarmed inside me. Leaning back, I hadn't expected laughter at my stupid joke from the wicked monster. The movement shot a sharp pang up my leg and I tried to hide a wince.

"Maybe I'm a better prophecy writer than Lita." His gravelly tone reflected internally.

I sucked in a sharp breath. "You wrote the Wicked End Prophecy?"

My question came out louder than expected causing the dog and it's three heads to growl.

"Lay down, Cerb," the Dark Angel commanded.

The dog laid down and yawned. All three mouths.

"No, I said that we would meet, which we have." The Dark Angel raised his skeletal hands with long, dark nails. Sparks projected out. "Lita wrote the prophecy."

Torment teased me. My great grandmother had lied and betrayed me once again.

"She wrote the prophecy so you'd feel obligated to return to the coven believing that she could save you from a wicked end."

I firmed my lips. "I'll save myself."

"I hope you will. First, let's get rid of that pesky Secretum Bond." He flicked one long dark finger and sparks shot out, wrapping around my torso. "There will be no secrets between us."

A tugging sensation replaced the bitter taste that was always in my mouth.

"And now to heal." His entire body swayed as he waved his arms in a circular pattern.

More sparks shot out from his fingers, arced forward, and wrapped around my leg. I braced for more torture. The pain in my body tingled and drew away from me. More sparks shot out and wrapped around my head. I stopped bleeding. The Dark Angel had healed me the same way Mistress Lita had healed scratches on my face.

Tentatively, I flexed my leg and arm. "I thought magic didn't work down here."

"Witch magic doesn't. Only dark magic. I'm not a warlock anymore. Being Dark Angel gave me stronger powers, but also takes away so much." He sounded pompous and sad at the same time. He held out his hand. "Stand. Let me get a better look at you."

Getting to my feet, I grasped his long fingers lightly afraid they might break. And I thought my great grandmother was looking older with each day. He appeared ancient.

"You resemble your grandmother." He had barely whispered the thought.

"Lita?" She was my great grandmother and his Death Mate. I didn't resemble her. He was old and probably confused.

"Angelita." The name was spoken loud and clear and angry. "Your grandmother. My daughter who died."

Sympathy centered. "I'm sorry for your loss."

"Lita will sacrifice whatever and whoever she wants." His words whipped up and settled in a forlorn foam.

My ears seared with his anguish. Taking a step on my newly healed leg, I sidled closer to him. He didn't seem so evil.

"I'm shocked Lita allowed you to come early." His words jolted me.

"She doesn't know." My voice edged with smarminess. "I came on my own."

A soft smile lit his countenance. He must be pleased with my rebellion.

I straightened my shoulders. Time was running out. "I came to ask you to release Lavender," I added a plea. "It was my fault. I was the one picking the plants. She warned me not to pick near your waterfall."

As I rambled his eyes changed. It went from acceptance to surprise.

If he didn't agree to free Lavender I didn't know what I'd do. At this point, she was the most important thing. If he'd release her, he must have a way to send her back and I hoped he would send me too.

Shredding inside, I knew the right thing to do. "If you want, I'll take Lavender's place."

The Dark Angel laughed. It was more incredulous than rusty with big billows.

This wasn't funny. I was willing to sacrifice myself and he made fun of the exchange.

"You both can go." He scowled at the sleeping dog. "You must hurry."

Surprise zonked. followed by a celebratory thrum. "Really? Thank you so much."

"You can hold onto her and use your flying ability to rise." His voice lowered.

"My magic doesn't work here." I snapped my fingers and nothing happened.

"The magic I gave you works." He snapped his fingers and a ball of light blazed.

"Dark magic." The words buzzed.

"Let me get your friend." Pivoting away, his back bowed in despair. His head was down and his shoulders defeated.

His loneliness emptied my earlier celebration. He'd been down here for centuries.

"Great grandfather," the title sounded strange on my tongue. "I'll find a way to visit you."

He stopped and trundled around slowly. A world of hurt and knowledge suspended on his expression. He stared at me trying to see my deepest, darkest thoughts. He licked his dry lips as if afraid to say what he wanted. "I'm sure I'll see you after the ceremony in an hour."

"You won't." The only reason I'd regret declining the leadership position was because I wouldn't be able to communicate with him. "I'm not accepting the leadership position."

"Do you know what happens at the ceremony, child?" By the softening of his voice, he definitely didn't want to be the one to tell me, yet he wanted me to know.

Discomfort inched inside of me. I wasn't a child and I'd proved that by coming to rescue Lavender. Nothing he said could scare me.

"At the ceremony, I announce whether or not I will Ascend into leadership of the coven." Pursing my lips, I realized he really had removed the Secretum Bond. "I'm not going to accept the leadership position."

"Then you will Descend." He thundered.

My brow furrowed. "I don't understand."

"The choice isn't whether you will Ascend into the leadership of the coven. It's whether you will Ascend or Descend. Ascend to leadership or Descend down to me. To the River Styx. To the Underworld forever. Like my beautiful daughter, Angelita." His raw voice sent jagged chills through me. "And if I know Lita, which I do, she won't give you a choice."

CHAPTER TWENTY-THREE

A scend or Descend?

Ascend to leadership or Descend into the bowels on the banks of the River Styx.

The Dark Angel's accusation against my great grandmother made me dizzy. The chills stabbing me inside made me weak. "That's not how Mistress Lita described the Ascension Ceremony to me."

"Of course, she didn't." His resigned tone laid the truth bare. "She forced my poor Angelita to stay down here until she died. Her own mother used the sacrifice to strengthen her powers."

Stunned into silence, I grappled with the information. It wasn't the Dark Angel who was a monster. It was my great grandmother. A tickling in my brain brought back what Provost Morgane had said, that I was important to the mistress.

"Lita sent her daughter, your grandmother, down here after she gave birth to a child. Lita raised the child, your mother, as her own and when your mother ran away to marry a banshee it probably saved her life." He watched me with intensity. "And yours."

My lungs heaved at the thought of my mother running away from home. It must be the reason she'd marked herself as a banshee and why she'd kept me away from my witch family. She must've known how dangerous Mistress Lita was to both of us.

"Until now." His cry mimicked a death knell.

The death bell rang in my head. I sank down onto the hard ground. "I don't understand. Lita, my great grandmother, plans to sacrifice me as she sacrificed her own daughter?"

"Yes." A sheen glimmered in his eyes. "Lita was such a strong, intelligent witch. We fell in love and married when she was young. I'd believed she'd be happy guarding the River Styx and the Gates of the Underworld at my side. Now, I wonder if she'd used me all along." His sadness showed that he loved her even after everything she'd done. "When she became pregnant, she convinced me that she had to leave so our baby could be born healthy. My lovely little Angelita."

My chest constricted pinching at my heart. The witches believed he was malicious. He was only lonely.

"If we'd had a male child, I believe Lita would've stayed like Desmerelda." He frowned, trying to convince himself. "She doesn't matter. Because the baby was female, Lita refused to leave the coven. Her family was very powerful and when she became leader I knew she'd never return. I admit I acted out. I kidnapped witch after witch hoping to discover one of them was my child."

That's why he had a bad reputation. He'd kidnapped witches trying to find his own child. It was understandable, but wrong, especially if those witches died.

"Lita kept our child away from me until she discovered there was a way to enhance her own powers by sacrificing Angelita." His voice cracked. "She forced our teenage child into a marriage with a warlock. When Angelita had a baby, she sent our daughter down to me on her seventeenth birthday eve. To enhance her own powers and live longer."

I wheezed.

"She kept the new baby. Lita knew in order to continue to grow stronger, to magnify her powers, she'd need another sacrifice."

Horror scraped through my lungs. I jumped to my feet to pace. "How long did she think she could get away with this?"

"She still is." He held his head while his entire body trembled. "My daughter lived with me. But she was never happy. She could never leave or have a life of her own." He sniffled. "Angelita never met her own daughter except for the moment she was born."

"My mother." Tears pricked and I sniffled.

"Yes." The single word sighed out of him. "Lita planned to raise her, have her get pregnant, and then send her down to me after the baby was born so she could continue her autocratic leadership."

My horror deepened, convulsing to the depths of my soul. My great grandmother was a monster.

"I don't know if your mother knew Lita's plans or if she simply fell in love and ran away. Either way, she escaped this terrible tragedy of Lita's making. When your mother died, your grandfather Anvers Snow had the sense to hide you away. Lita was furious."

"I thought Grandfather was hiding me from the banshees." I'd always miss him.

"Maybe he was hiding you from them, too." The Dark Angel sounded tired. "But it seems she's won again."

Determination straightened my spine. I faced my great grandfather. "No. She hasn't."

"You're here, aren't you?" His entire body slumped against the wall. "I'm ready to head down the River Styx with my Death Mate. I have been for decades."

His defeated position collided with my will to survive. Even though he wanted the cycle to end, he didn't have the strength to fight. He'd accept whatever Mistress Lita demanded.

Not me.

I needed a plan. He'd confided in me and healed me. I now knew the truth. Working up my nerve, I wrapped my arms around his thin body. His bones poked through his thin and wrinkled skin. It was icy to the touch but a fever smoldered inside him.

His arms creaked around me. He hadn't hugged anyone in a long time. His body shuddered with a sigh or an internal cry.

The hug felt right. He felt like family to me.

He dropped his arms not having the stamina. Swiping at his eyes, he took a step back. "I hope you succeed."

I needed information more than anything. "How can we stop this cycle?"

"Instead of her sending you down, which gives her more power, she needs to be sent down. Then, we'll head down the river. A new Dark Angel will take my place, and you will become leader of the coven."

I shook my head. "I don't want to be leader of the coven. But I do know someone who wants to become the Dark Angel."

I told him my current predicament. I wasn't ready to lead and believed it was time for a change at the coven. Mistress Lita had caused enough harm. The Dark Angel nodded along, his expression becoming more interested and more intense as I spoke. At the end of our discussion, he beamed. "Don't forget, you have Obsidian's Fire, a powerful weapon."

I held out my hand and he placed his in mine. It was the opposite of our initial meeting. "I need your help to defeat her."

CHAPTER TWENTY-FOUR

"I'm sorry the Dark Angel took you," I apologized for the thousandth time to Lavender as I hugged her close. Together, we stood on a flat rock where the Dark Angel said I'd gather the most power.

He stood by shouting instructions. "Seek the darkest part of your soul. Ignite your dominant energy."

Finally, I was learning the basics of control. From my great grandfather, a man I didn't even know existed a week ago. A man I pitied and respected and loved.

Below my feet, the rock heated. I focused down and concentrated. Flames sparked and snuck out around the rock.

"Eep." Lavender's scream pierced the air.

I peered down. "I love you."

"Excuse me?" Lavender dug her nails into me.

I ignored her. Even though we'd just met, I loved my great grandfather.

"Goodbye Destiny. Thank you. I know you'll succeed." His statement lifted me on a pedestal.

I'd succeed for him and myself. I'd sooth his spirit and send his forever love to him. Even if Lita didn't want to go.

The flame, my flame, grew higher and higher. The rock lifted and Lavender and I were carried up. It was akin to riding an exploding volcano except I controlled the fire.

Lavender clung to me. "I...," hiccup, "I warned...," hiccup, "warned you." Her head was buried into my side.

She had warned me to stay away from the Dark Angel and his waterfall. But I was glad I hadn't listened. I never would've learned the truth or met my great grandfather.

Had he acted differently toward Lavender?

I held her firm, wanting to comfort as best I could while concentrating on our exit. "Did the Dark Angel do anything to you?"

"He...he..." Her entire body shook. She raised her head and a smile broke out. She was laughing. "He talked my ear off."

I cleared my head with a shake. She'd gone from upset to laughing in seconds. She must be in shock. "Is that a form of torture?"

She giggled again. "He talked about his love and how much he missed her, how she betrayed him." Lavender loosened her hold on me. "Love. Can you believe it? A beast like him."

My lips firmed. "He's not a beast. He's a lonely old man."

"Thank you for facing him." She grew solemn and gratefulness displayed in her gaze. "For saving me."

Satisfaction streamed through my veins. I'd saved her and gained another friend. And a great grandfather, although I hoped after our planning both the Dark Angel and Mistress Lita would rejoin as Death Mates and pass on.

Lavender clung to me and I was glad for her comfort. I wasn't sure where we were headed. Except up. That was what mattered. The stone rose higher and went through a hole like the one I'd gone down.

After passing through, I let the rock hover for a few seconds. Surrounded by stalagmites and stalactites, it was a cavern similar to the one I'd lowered from. I stepped off the stone and tugged Lavender down to the ground with me.

I released my hold on the fire and the stone dropped.

Exhaling, I was glad I hadn't gone back down with the rock. I glanced at my watch. Only twenty minutes until midnight. My stomach twinged. What if after all this we get lost in these dark passages?

"Damien!" My voice echoed through the caverns and tunnels. "Damien!" I yelled louder. "Xenos! Ulrich!"

"Xenos?" Lavender's pale cheeks brightened. "Why is Xenos here?"

"He helped me get down to the riverbank." I studied her. Was she crushing on him?

"Destiny." Damien rounded a corner and ducked under a shiny rock. "You're back. You're okay."

He sounded surprised. I'm thinking his plan wasn't as thought out as he'd claimed. "When the rope caught fire…"

"Lavender." Xenos pushed Damien out of the way and ran to hug my friend.

My brow arched. Maybe there was more between them than a simple crush.

"You did it!" Damien grabbed my arms and jumped up and down. He brought me in for a hug.

"I can't believe you saved her." Ulrich hugged Lavender and me.

A big smile bloomed. "Ye of little faith."

I'd succeeded in the rescue but there was so much more to do. I glanced at my watch. And about fifteen minutes to do it. To succeed.

Damien became earnest. His puppy dog eyes begged. "Did you ask the Dark Angel about his replacement?"

"There will be no replacement." Mistress Lita's raging shriek echoed into the cavern. She hobbled in from the same tunnel through which the warlocks had entered. A black hat sat on her head covering long, brittle, gray hair. Deep wrinkles covered her face and her pointy nose was topped by an ugly green wart. "What are you up to?"

She'd gone full fairytale evil witch.

Dread deadened the nerves inside me. We were in trouble but I didn't care. My great grandmother didn't scare me anymore. And I'd saved Lavender when everyone else had given up.

I pushed her forward. "I saved Lavender."

Mistress Lita stared down her nose at my friend proving she never cared about the girl's life.

Cassia peeked out from behind the mistress. Our gazes connected and she looked away.

My heart hardened against her. She *had* sent her familiar to spy on me. She must've told my great grandmother what we were doing. She wasn't my friend.

I remembered how much she'd changed. Maybe too much. Cassia didn't enjoy snakes or parties or hooking up with a lot of different guys. Jinx, on the other hand, had talked about a pretense and wearing ugly clothes in the library that night when she'd talked about a tribreed. She must be using an enchantment to mirror her sister. Realization slapped me awake.

I'd read about the spell in one of my classes and if the witches were in the same family, it was even easier to execute. Where was the real Cassia?

Someone pushed in from behind. He had to crouch way down to get below the low hanging rock of the cavern. Chains rattled around his hands and feet. "*Hvitspyd.*"

"Stone." My voice wavered.

He was pale and his gaze shifted in confusion. I glared at fake Cassia again. Why would she expose him to Mistress Lita?

"Destiny." Stone spotted me and rushed forward, chains rattling. "I—"

He'd almost reached me when he stopped. Stopped walking. Stopped talking. Stopped trying to get to me.

Mistress Lita had flicked one finger. Her lips pursed in an annoying position as if he was a small insect. She'd made him stop. She'd put a spell on him similar to when the provost had blocked his ability to speak.

I firmed my lips and anger spewed in my bloodstream. Mistress Lita didn't care that she'd broken the rules because she'd been committing atrocious acts for decades. I sized up Cassia again.

Or should I say fake Cassia? It was the only explanation.

If Jinx could pretend to be her sister, she also could've put a spell on Stone to break up with me. Why? I glanced between her and Mistress Lita. They must've schemed together. Stone had told me that he wanted me to take the leadership position which was supposedly what Mistress Lita wanted.

Hah. The Dark Angel had told me differently.

"Release Stone from the spell." Stepping in front of him, I balled my hands into fists and tilted forward.

Her dark chuckle etched in my skin. She pointed her wand at me.

Everyone leaned away. They were shocked I'd spoken back to her. The warlocks stiffened, afraid to move. Xenos grabbed Lavender and pulled her behind him.

I refused to be cowed. I'd seen too much, knew too much.

Damien stepped to my side. "Destiny made a daring rescue of Lavender. Why are you angry?"

Mistress Lita's lips twisted into a malevolent smirk. "Working with you. Working against coven leadership. Working with warlocks to take over the coven."

She grew angrier with each sentence. The words bulleted, a verbal attack, and I experienced each with stinging agony. This was the death of any relationship we might've had as a family.

"You will be punished." She howled, offended by my insolence. She pointed with her wand. "Going against me and rescuing one little witch."

Lavender squawked.

Mistress Lita swung her wand and jabbed at the three guys. "Aiding the warlock enemies."

Damien gaped. "We're not—"

"Bringing those monstrosities into the coven." She whipped her wand at Stone. "And back again."

Stone's mouth tightened with anger and his gaze shot fury. Even frozen, he expressed care for me. No way did he want to break up.

"I didn't..." I trailed off.

Guilt flashed on Fake Cassia's expression. She must be working with my great grandmother and they both understood that I wouldn't believe a break up message. They'd brought Stone to the coven and forced him to break up with me in person. Crossing my arms, I didn't really believe him even in person. Not now.

"Take your pick of what crime you committed." Mistress Lita fluttered her hand. She'd already decided I was guilty which would make sacrificing me easier in her mind. "Punishment for your crimes will be severe."

"Oh, like spending the rest of my life on the banks of the River Styx?" I jutted my hip trying to act casual. Underneath rage spiked. I hated her threats and her lies. My rage exploded into confidence. Stepping into her space, I needed to be close for the scheme I cooked up with the Dark Angel to work. "I spoke with the Dark Angel and I know *everything.*"

Her brows arched high on her head. Confusion shimmered and her eyes went wide. She scoffed. "You're a sixteen-year-old girl, not even a full witch. And a witch who doesn't even know how to control her powers at that. You don't know everything."

Her demeaning tone rubbed into my wounds. New and old wounds. I couldn't control my powers because I'd just learned what I truly was. A witch, a banshee, a dark angel. "I know I've finally met a family member who actually cares about me."

Lavender *oohed*. She hadn't known the Dark Angel was my great grand-father. Jinx, twinning Cassia, didn't react. Neither did the warlocks.

"Did you ever love him? Or did you use him to have a child with dark angel blood?" I thought about the sad old man and my pulse sped. Mistress Lita had sacrificed her own child and wanted to do the same thing to my mother. To me. My racing pulse blitzed ready to attack and defend. The ground beneath my feet shook. "And then you used your child, Angelita."

Mistress Lita flinched.

The others sucked in. If I told them every one of her crimes, they'd be even more shocked.

"Now you want to sacrifice me." My instincts lit into fury and blasted.

The ground shook again. Small rocks fell.

Dark magic. *My* magic.

"Oh moons! Are you pregnant?" Fake Cassia ogled me and Damien. She must know the mistress' schemes because she knew I needed to have a child for the atrocity to continue in perpetuity.

Stone's eyes widened. Even in his enchanted state his countenance spoke volumes.

"No!" Disgust carried in my tone. I liked Damien as a friend. He'd helped me when Fake Cassia hadn't. But I would never be with him. I loved Stone.

"Destiny, let's not air our family grievances in front of everyone." Mistress Lita's sternness told me that she thought she was in charge of the situation. Of me. "It's almost midnight and your seventeenth birthday."

The simpering smile at the end of her statement set me off. She didn't care about my birthday. Only what my turning seventeen meant to her. "I'm turning seventeen. How old are you turning, a million years old? Because that's how you look."

"How dare you!" She shrieked.

Criticizing her age had been immature. The Dark Angel had explained as the barrier between worlds became weaker, she couldn't hide her true age. "You wrote the Wicked End Prophecy so I'd return to the coven."

"I foretold the prophecy." Her quick denial showed she lied.

"A lie!" I gritted my teeth and balled my fists. The ground rocked.

The prophecy had been hanging on me like a weight since I'd learned about it. I thought it meant I'd help the banshees and the regent destroy the new king's government. Now, I understood what it was supposed to mean. "You wrote the prophecy. You wanted me to have a wicked end. Why? So you could justify sacrificing me for your own greed to increase your powers and your life?"

"Sacrifice? What sacrifice?" Lavender piped up. She must be too shocked to be afraid.

"Tell them *Great Grandmother*." I sneered at her title. "Tell them I never had to decide whether to become leader of the coven or not."

Mistress Lita's eyebrows arched higher this time.

I emphasized a sneer trying to act completely in control. "The Dark Angel relieved me of the bonding enchantment. I can talk about anything I want, including my decision." My fingers sparked in my clenched hands. I still didn't have complete control of my magic. But I knew it would come. The ground quaked more violently. Glancing at my watch, I needed to decide how far to push her into action. "Except I never had a choice, did I? You're going to sacrifice me to extend your life, your leadership, and your power."

The warlocks and Lavender crouched by the nearest cavern wall behind me. Fake Cassia hunched her shoulders trying to protect herself. Stone couldn't move, couldn't defend himself or me. Determination steeled my spine. I'd shield him and everyone else.

Mistress Lita's laughter curled around me. Something wicked simmered in her gaze. Something deadly. "Why would I allow you, a part banshee, non loyal witch, to become leader? I'm the best leader for the coven and always will be. You never had a choice."

She raised her wand and screamed, "*Descendere ire ad Gehenna magna nepotem*. Bring me her life source and her strength. *Descendere ire ad Gehenna magna nepotem*. Bring me her life source and her strength."

She kept yelling the spell. An orange glowing ball leapt from her wand, whirling and spinning. Ripples streamed out in waves, destroying stalagmites and stalactites in their path. Sand from the ground tore around the cavern hitting everyone. A tunnel arch collapsed. She didn't care what or who she harmed as long as she got her way.

The fiery, glowing ball came at me. Came for me.

My fury doused. Old doubts skittered causing panic and horror.

My watch struck midnight and I knew this was the sacrificial curse.

The curse that would send me to the banks of the River Styx forever.

Chapter Twenty-Five

Could I counterbalance the spell?

I sucked in a breath and gathered my strength. My mind went to what the Dark Angel had said. This was my moment. I refused to stand here and accept this fate.

This destiny.

Pulling out my wand, I focused on what the Dark Angel had told me to do. I matched my voice with hers. "*Descendere ire ad Gehenna magna avia.* Bring me her life source and her strength."

Mistress Lita hesitated. "Where did you get that wand?"

"Provost Morgane gave it to me and the Dark Angel taught me how to connect to Obsidian's Fire. Hades' fire." He'd taught me many things.

"He's not as good a teacher as I." Mistress Lita sliced with her wand and pointed it at me. "*Descendere ire ad Gehenna magna nepotem.* Bring me her life source and her strength."

Every time she said *nepotem*, meaning grandchild, I screamed *avia*, meaning grandmother, and accessed my dark magic threading it through my tone. I used the wand connected to my great grandfather and the power I'd received from him. The power I never understood how to control because I didn't realize where the magic came from. "*...magna avia!*"

The orange glow reeled forward, twisting and rotating, licking at my skin with an intense heat.

"*Descendere ire ad Gehenna magna avia*. Bring me her life source and her strength." My voice rose to a high pitch, the highest pitch I'd ever spoken.

My pulse battered my veins and pounded in my head. My fingers perspired on the wand, getting slippery in my grip. I had to hold on. I teetered on the edge. If I failed, I'd spend the rest of my life in darkness.

"*Descendere ire ad Gehenna magna avia*. Bring me her life source and her strength."

The orange glow coming for me stopped inches away. It sizzled for a moment in place resembling a fiery tornado. It stalled. Then the orange glow tornado unwound in the other direction, going back the other way.

Going toward Mistress Lita and wrapping around her. She emitted a bloodcurdling scream.

Raising my shoulders, I tried to cover my ears.

Her screams diminished as the fire took control, blazing brighter and brighter, and exploding in a flash.

And then Mistress Lita was gone.

"Ahhhhhhhhhhhhhhhhhhhhhhh!" My wail released the pressure inside my head and my soul. The banshee wail wasn't scary anymore. It was a proclamation. The wicked witch was dead and the Wicked End Prophecy was gone.

My heart didn't hurt for her. My heart ached for the relationship I'd wanted with my grandmother, Angelita. And great grandfather, the Dark Angel. After this, he would be gone too. At least I was giving him what he wanted, to be reunited with Mistress Lita in death and travel down the River Styx together. She was definitely going to the Underworld.

Triumph didn't roar inside me. Sadness and relief that it was done filtered through my bloodstream. She'd done terrible things to me, my family, the coven, everyone.

I double-checked my friends behind me. They were alright.

Weakness invaded my limbs and I staggered back. "She's gone." I needed to say it out loud.

"What happened?" Lavender braced my back to help me stay standing.

"The Dark Angel told me how to counteract the sacrificial spell." Numbness encased my chest. "I turned it around on Mistress Lita."

Damien rushed to the spot where she'd stood. "You sent Mistress Lita to the River Styx?"

"Yes." My eyes stung. Melancholy, mourning, and plain exhaustion combined inside me creating a strange physical reaction. This was finished.

Stone stumbled as he started walking again. The chains around his wrists and ankles clanked.

I heaved. The magical hold on him was broken. I used magic to take off the chains and they clashed to the ground. "Stone?"

"Are you okay?" Reaching me, he wrapped his arms around my waist.

I felt safe. Whole. Loved. I finally knew who I was, what I was. A banshee who was proud to wear the mark. A witch who would help the warlocks rebuild the coven. A dark angel who'd never guard the River Styx. I took a deep breath and my lungs filled with freedom. I finally knew what I wanted for my life.

To be myself, my whole self.

To guard the kingdom from insurrectionists.

To be with Stone.

I looked at him, really saw him. "I'm fine. Are you okay?"

"Yes." He gazed around appearing lost. "Where am I? One minute I was at Reximus Palace and then Cassia showed up and brought me to the academy which I didn't think I could enter." He clutched his head. "Things are foggy."

From a spell.

Smiling at him, I pivoted. "Cassia! Or should I say Jinx?"

Counting the remaining majiks in the cavern, I realized Fake Cassia was gone. She must've been caught in the blast.

"Where did Cassia go?" Stone swiveled around, always the protector.

"I'm right here." Cassia, or Jinx pretending to be Cassia, emerged from behind a large stalagmite near a tunnel opening, doing a finger wave. "Oh my stars! Everyone's okay."

I pointed my wand. *"Funiculs ligare."*

A portion of the rope I'd used earlier sprang up and wound itself around Fake Cassia. She'd brought Stone into the academy and this cavern. She'd been working with the mistress all along. She'd wanted me to be sacrificed.

"What're you doing?" Damien pushed away from the wall and moved toward her.

"That's not the real Cassia." My chest tangled with anguish. The real Cassia had missed so much. I had to find out where they'd hidden her. "It's Jinx pretending to be Cassia."

Her eyes widened and she tried to hold up her hands. "No. I'm really Cassia." The girl sniffed. "Jinx, my evil sister has been pretending to be me. She held me captive and I escaped. Tell her Stone."

Stone's mouth gaped. "I don't...know."

I kept my wand pointed at her. My hand didn't shake. She was trying to lie her way out of the situation.

"Look at my clothes." She tugged on the shula skirt. "These are my clothes from the day I arrived. Jinx wouldn't let me change."

"You dressed like Cassia when you were pretending to be her. Still are." I knew Jinx had hated wearing modest clothes.

"I'm Cassia." Desperation clung to her tone. "When I escaped from the basement of our home, I came to the academy. I saw you and my sister, who looked exactly like me, talking about the break up in the hall. I couldn't believe Stone would break up with you."

She spoke as if she was on my side. Doubts trembled in my hand holding the wand.

"You dashed off and I went to your room to get help from Stone. I over-heard Jinx talking to him pretending to be me. She told him her familiar had followed you to this cavern and she'd reported the information to Mistress Lita. Jinx's plan was to bring Stone and kiss him right before Mistress Lita sacrificed you." The girl telling the tale panted. "Jinx wanted the image of me kissing him to be the last thing you saw. She's villainous."

The doubt wormed up my arm and through my center. I crossed my arms. "Jinx is a good actor."

"I swear it's me Cassia!" She sounded scared, resembling the old Cassia. "I followed her and Stone. That's why I came from over there. I was hiding, waiting to alert you." She pointed at an area away from where Mistress Lita and Fake Cassia had entered.

My mind ticked. Fake Cassia had been standing beside Mistress Lita. This Cassia wasn't bold and had hidden until she found an opportunity to show herself after the action ended.

Stone stared at her trying to discern the truth. Damien's gaze swung between me and the girl. Lavender clung to Xenos' hand, afraid to act. She'd been through so much already and I hated seeing her in distress. Ulrich took a warrior stance, awaiting an order.

An order from me.

Why? I'd denounced becoming the leader and this was one of the rea-sons. I didn't know the answers. "What do you think, Stone?"

He knew her as well as I did. I trusted his judgment.

"I don't remember anything from before I arrived at this spot in chains." He shook his head clearly frustrated. "Is there something only Cassia would know?"

I studied her again. When we'd first arrived in the coven, Cassia had said she'd been communicating with her sister and told her about us. Now, I knew why Jinx was so interested. The question had to be from the time after Cassia's capture by the banshees because she hadn't been able to communicate while she'd been captive.

A test question might be in order. "What did you do to Regent Theobald?"

The cavern filled with silence. Tension radiated between everyone.

"I stole his clothes and he wobbled out of the tent naked." She smirked at the memory.

The group behind me laughed.

"Real Cassia might've told her what happened." Stone's narrowed gaze told me he watched every move Cassia made. "What color were Destiny's sheets at the banshee encampment?"

"How am I supposed to remember something so insignificant?" Cassia's wild eyes and open mouth exhibited outrage. She jutted out her hip. "I was in her room when the bed was made. What about you?"

"Oooh!" The group behind us playfully mocked.

Did Stone remember the color of my sheets? We'd innocently laid in the bed together.

"I'm not the one under questioning." Red flagged his cheeks. He was embarrassed too.

Needing to distract the others from what they might be thinking about Stone and me, I asked another question. "What happened to our friend Violet? Why is she in a frozen state?"

"She sacrificed herself in the human dungeon to save us. She flew toward the guards to freeze them and they shot her." Cassia sniffed. "Violet got caught in her own magic and froze. The hibernation probably saved her life."

Lavender and the warlocks murmured, recognizing Violet was a hero.

"True." I veered to the group behind us. "Is there a spell that allows you to steal someone's memories?"

"Not that I'm aware of." Lavender shook her head. Damien, Xenos, and Ulrich shook their heads in agreement.

"Come on, Lavender," Cassia pleaded. "You've known me since we were kids. You must realize I'm me."

"Jinx did a convincing job of acting like you." Lavender stayed back clinging to Xenos' hand.

Jinx slipped up a couple of times. She'd said *Oh moons* instead of *Oh my stars*. She'd flirted with warlocks and pushed the limits on the more modest clothes Cassia wore.

"Where is Lukas?" Stone threw out a question similar to my thoughts.

"My sister probably scared him away." Cassia snorted and then she became serious. "He took Violet to the fairies."

"Did you ever kiss Lukas?" I hated to ask such a personal question, but she'd already hinted at intimacy with her sheet question.

Cassia sniffled. "*I* never kissed Lukas. My sister did while pretending to be me, and she told me every intimate detail." Distress scraped through her explanation.

Her hurt pinged in my chest. Cassia had really liked Lukas and would never have a true first kiss with him now. Jinx had stolen the experience from her and scared him away. I didn't want to continue questioning Cassia causing her more pain. She'd answered everything correctly and I was almost positive this was really her.

"What do you think Stone?" I might be strong and confident, but I'd still ask for advice.

His brow furrowed. "If you're the real Cassia, what happened to your sister?"

"I don't know." Cassia's lip quivered. "She was devoted to Mistress Lita. When I was locked up, Jinx had bragged about how the mistress told her that if she went along with the plan she'd become second in charge of the coven."

I inhaled sharply remembering that night in the library how she'd bragged about having more power. "She knew I'd be sacrificed."

Cassia nodded. "I'm sorry."

"This Cassia has a banshee mark. Jinx would never wear the demeaning symbol on her forehead." Damien was right. "Jinx—pretending to be Cassia—was standing right by the mistress." He stepped toward Cassia. "Either Jinx was hit by the blast or she decided to follow Mistress Lita."

It did make sense. This Cassia had come from a different place. Fake Cassia had been standing by the mistress. Had I sent her or had she chosen to go? Jinx might be evil but I wouldn't send her to the banks of the River Styx on purpose. "What're we going to do?"

"The warlocks will find a way to rescue Jinx." Damien stood tall, confident in himself. "We'll work with the elders. And when she's safe, we'll make sure she gets punished for what she's done to you."

"I'll work with you to rescue her." Cassia's selflessness took my doubts away. "She is my sister after all."

This was the real Cassia. Because even though her sister had wronged her, she wanted to help. I removed the rope from around her. "Sorry, Cassia. I had to be sure."

She hugged me tight. The real Cassia.

"If you become the next Dark Angel, you could make Jinx your Death Mate," Xenos joked.

Damien arched a brow at him. He was actually considering the suggestion. Did he think he could change her or did he realize the extent of her wickedness?

"Why haven't you gone down if you're the next Dark Angel?" Switching gears, Ulrich brought up an important point.

"Maybe it doesn't happen immediately."

Damien's answer faded when Stone grabbed my hand and tugged me into a small passage.

"Before something or someone else interrupts us, I want you to know I never would've broken up with you. I love you, Destiny."

The deep timbre of his voice echoed in my heart. I took a tremulous breath and tears sprang to my eyes. Happy tears. We'd waited so long to express our feelings for each other, I didn't want to wait any longer.

I jumped into his arms and kissed him on his left cheek. "I." I kissed him on the other cheek. "Love." I kissed him on his left cheek again. "You."

My lips finally pressed on his sealing the deal. We loved each other and were an official couple. From this point forward, we'd decide everything together.

He plucked my lips one more time, not really wanting to stop. "I felt helpless, standing there unable to do anything, watching you be attacked by your great grandmother." His agony came through in his tone.

I understood, but I also needed him to understand we were partners. Equal partners. "I'm not helpless. I vowed to protect you like you vowed to protect me."

"Like we vowed to love each other. It's why we make a great team." He gave me a quick kiss. "Because we're both protectors. Of each other, of our friends, of our kingdom."

"Agreed." I kissed him back and stayed comfortable in his strong arms, reflecting over my most recent adventure. "I've learned a lot during my days in the coven and I know I need to learn more."

"What does that mean? Are you staying?" His nostrils flared. "Even though the message from King Zacharye was phony, while I was there he formally invited you to sit on the counsel. I told him I'd ask you. With your knowledge of both banshees and witches, you'll be an asset. And we'll be together."

"The message was phony?" Another way the mistress had tried to get rid of my friends. Then my head heard the rest of Stone's statement and my insides melted. I wanted nothing more. I'd be helping the king and be beside Stone. And finally be home. Home with Stone and home to where I'd lived with my parents, home where I truly belonged. "I—"

A commotion coming from deeper in the tunnel stopped our discussion. Provost Morgane stalked through the passage. Her hard expression changed to relief upon seeing us. "There were several disturbances to the barrier. You're near the ceremonial cavern. Has the ceremony taken place?"

I detached from Stone, keeping hold of his hand. This was too important to wait. "I've got a surprise for you, Provost Morgane."

She placed her hand on her bosom. "Destiny, you survived."

"I did more than survive." Indicating that she should follow me, we exited the passage into the cavern.

"Mom!" Lavender ran into her mother's arms.

The sincerity of their love warmed. A mother-daughter bond never broken. My smile faltered. I wished I could still hug my mom. Dad and Grandfather were gone too. And Lita, she'd never been real family.

Stone put his arm around my waist sensing my upset. I smiled again. I might not have a familial bond, but I had Stone and Cassia and my other friends, new and old.

"I'm so glad you're alive." Provost Morgane leaned back examining her daughter.

"Destiny saved me." Lavender's pronouncement filled me with happiness and satisfaction.

The provost hugged her daughter again and kept her arm around her shoulders. "Thank you so much, Destiny." The provost's gaze widened and she crossed her wrists. "I guess I should be calling you Mistress Destiny."

"No." I shook my head. "I'm not accepting the position. I'm going to live at Reximus Palace. I'm not a full witch and don't know witch customs or rules. I'm sorry. The warlocks will be leading the coven."

"With your help, Provost Morgane." Damien gave her the sign of respect. "The warlocks want to make the Inferis Coven equal for everyone."

My spirits raised. The coven was in good hands, just like the banshee clan. And the entire Kingdom of Alandaska with King Zacharye in charge.

"I'll be more than willing to help." Provost Morgane's tension relaxed. She skimmed the area. "What are your plans, Cassia? Are you leaving with your friends?"

Provost Morgane didn't question her identity. She must not have known the pretense.

Cassia stared at the ground showing the shy girl I loved. "I'm going to stay at the coven. There are family bonds I need to repair."

She didn't want to tell the provost what had happened, how her sister had fooled everyone, proving her loyalty again.

Provost Morgane frowned. "What will you do at the palace, Destiny?"

I squeezed Stone's hand. "Stone and I are going to be counselors to King Zacharye. And if you'll allow it, I'll use a portal to come back to the coven for school."

She grinned as if I'd passed a test. "That's a great idea because your tribreed magic is untamed."

"Your what?" Stone's mouth gaped.

A trickle of fear speared through me but I quickly squashed it. He loved me no matter who or what I was. I knew that now. "I'm part dark angel. The previous Dark Angel was my great grandfather."

I hoped he was less lonely now that he had my great grandmother with him. Even if she was sinister.

"I love you no matter what you are." Stone beamed and he glanced at the provost and back at me. "That's all you are, right?"

Laughter bubbled with my joy. "That's all I am. I'm the banshee-witch-dark angel who's in love with you."

Chapter Twenty-Six
EPILOGUE

A guttural growling caught my attention.

I crouched low and plastered myself against the wall made of hot rock. I didn't know where I was. It was a cavern, similar to the one I'd been hiding in. And yet this was different. A dark pall hung over the area and the stink of sulfer burned my nose. I choked down on a cry.

It growled again, and this time the noise came from three different directions.

Or was that just my terror causing me to hallucinate?

"Hello? Destiny?" I swallowed, trying to hold down the panic rushing from my chest. "It's Cassia."

My friend wouldn't be growling. She'd be cursing her great grandmother.

I tried to stay calm. After escaping from my parents' house, I'd snuck to Destiny's room in the academy to find *myself* with Stone. Except it wasn't me. My sister Jinx had used a spell to pretend to be me. Secretly, I followed Jinx and Stone to a passage near the Dark Angel's Veil waterfall where they'd met Mistress Lita. I'd hidden, unsure how to help my friends. Mistress Lita sent the sacrificial spell at Destiny and I'd been about to jump to her defense when she'd turned the spell around on Mistress Lita and my sister.

Mistress Lita had deserved to Descend. But my sister, even though she'd been bad, didn't deserve to die.

Without thought, I'd apparated by Jinx and pushed her out of the way. There'd been a flash of light and then darkness. I'd been caught in the blast. My heart cracked knowing she wouldn't have done the same for me.

"Jinx? Are you here?" My voice trembled. Had I pushed her far enough away so she hadn't been affected? If so, she'd better try to find me here.

Where exactly was here?

It was hot. Steaming hot. And dark. Too dark to see very far. The hard stone beneath me was jagged and warm. A river roared nearby. The upper Helvete River or the River Styx?

All the air evacuated my lungs, whooshing out of my mouth and becoming a surprised and fearful squeak. My pulse spiked. It couldn't be. But where else was possible? "I'm trapped on the banks of the River Styx."

With my gaze darting around, I searched for an escape. All I saw were rocks above and rocks below. The only exit was down the River Styx and I wasn't ready to die.

What would Destiny do? She'd rescued Lavender and gotten out. How?

"Destiny." My tone weakened. She'd talked to the Dark Angel and if she wasn't here, it meant Mistress Lita Descended. If I pretended to be her favorite sister, she'd help me. "Mistress Lita!"

I snapped my fingers to do the twinning spell to make me resemble Jinx. Nothing happened.

Of course. Witch magic doesn't work on the banks of the River Styx. Only magic from the Dark Angel, dark magic. Magic I didn't possess.

The growling grew louder, closer, and came from three different directions.

I curled my legs up and pressed myself against the wall. How many terrifying animals were down here? Only an animal or a monster could make that noise. My brain jolted. My near-perfect memory came up with the answer.

A Cerberus.

According to history books, the three-headed dog helped guard the Gates to the Underworld.

The animal plodded into the open. Three heads. One body. I was more terrified of the heads. Three fang filled mouths with slobber dripping. When the slobber hit the ground it steamed. Three noses with wide, flaring nostrils. Surely, it could smell me. Six glowing eyes.

Horror shrieked through me and my muscles tensed. I'd be eaten alive before Destiny or Mistress Lita saved me. If Mistress Lita *would* save me. I wasn't sure considering she and Jinx had cooked up the scheme to kidnap and replace me.

Tension wired through my nerves. I picked up a thick stick, needing to defend myself.

The white stick felt light and hollow. A bone.

"Ick!" I dropped the stick.

The monster dog huffed and pounced closer.

I grabbed the bone again. "Ew." I needed something to defend myself. Had it belonged to one of the kidnapped witches? One who was now dead. My mind filled in the scenario and I shuddered.

The dog stretched his head and sniffed. He bent low, flexing his big, black paws with sharp nails. His rotund muscular body went into a crouched position. He was about to spring an attack.

I scrambled back against the wall. "Stay away." I held out the bone like a sword.

The dog angled his head, or should I say heads, watching me and the bone. More slobber came out of his mouths and he huffed. He'd tear me apart with his three mouths and feast on my body.

"Mistress Lita!" Hopelessness invaded and swirled around my soul. I'd heard tales of the Dark Angel kidnapping young witches. Lavender had been taken right in front of Destiny. But she'd come down to save the witch. "Destiny!"

I knew she couldn't hear me either. Surely, she'd realize I was missing. Jinx would explain how I'd saved her from the spell and Destiny and Stone would rescue me.

My chest contracted. Where was Lukas? He hadn't been in the cavern. Jinx better not have harmed him.

The dog must've gotten tired of watching. He leapt toward me.

I pushed myself against the wall and ripped my sister's jeans. The dog growled and slobber dripped from his mouths onto my cheek. I clutched the bone, my singular defense.

Suddenly, a teenage guy loomed above me, flying. His dark, wavy hair flopped in front of his face. Thick, dark eyebrows emphasized his bronzed skin and black eyes that stared above a straight-edged nose. His sculpted cheekbones and square jaw gave him an angular, yet manly appearance.

Before dying I thought you were supposed to see your past, not a handsome hallucination.

His mouth descended and touched my lips. He kissed me.

An electric zing went through my body and zapped my nerve endings. Shocked, my gaze went wider. "What do you think you're doing?"

"Saving you." His thick lips twitched.

Wooziness filled my head. Not from his kiss. "You don't save someone from a Cerberus with a kiss."

"Cerb just wants to play." He took the bone from my limp fingers and threw it.

The dog ran after the bone.

My shoulders relaxed. The Cerberus behaved like a regular dog. I should've thought to throw it instead of hanging on to the bone. One threat was gone.

The guy held out his hand to help me. Or hurt me.

I skirted backwards, my pulse continued pounding remembering his lips on mine. My first kiss and from a perfect stranger. I only wanted a kiss from a certain werewolf. "Don't kiss me again."

"My mom was able to stay on the banks of the River Styx with the Dark Angel because of the kiss."

My brow furrowed. "Your mom was the Dark Angel's Death Mate?"

"No." Sourness filled the single word. The guy slapped his hand on black leather pants and I jerked back. "The Dark Angel, my father, had already committed to someone. My mom was a witch he'd kidnapped. She died when I was seven."

"You kissed your mom?" I twisted my lips in a gross expression.

"The Dark Angel gave her the Kiss of Afterlife. Unlike Mistress Lita, my mom wanted to stay with me and him."

"I'm not staying." Determination straightened my spine. "My sister will tell everyone what happened and my friends, Destiny and Stone, will rescue me."

And Lukas. Where was Lukas?

"There's no way out." The guy smiled again displaying devastating dimples. "Mistress Lita and the Dark Angel have traveled through the Gates to the Underworld. I'm the new Dark Angel. The barrier between worlds has closed. You're stuck here forever, Cassia."

I hope you enjoyed Snow Witching White! If so, I'd love if you left a review at your favorite retailer.

Just because Destiny's story is over doesn't mean A Glass Slipper Adventure series will end. Stay tuned for news on Cassia's and Violet's stories by joining my newsletter at www.allieburton.com

CINDERELLA ASSASSIN

Did you miss the first book in the series, Cinderella Assassin?

Cinderella Assassin

A Glass Slipper Adventure Book 1

She wishes she could fit in. But if humans discover her secret, her life will be no fairytale.

Ellery "Elle" Milford needs to keep her fairy heritage undercover. But after her wicked stepmother refuses to let her go to the royal ball with the fully human kids, the sixteen-year-old half-breed defiantly parties with her smoke sprite bestie... who promptly gets arrested. And the only way to rescue her is for Elle to cut a deal with her fairy godmother: All the magic necessary to infiltrate the palace in exchange for assassinating the prince.

Determined not to harm a hair on the heir's noble head, the reluctant hitwoman's mission goes sideways when she falls for the very guy she's supposed to kill. And after uncovering a plot to destroy every single supernatural creature, Elle is torn between the desires of her heart and the needs of her magical friends.

Can the headstrong half-fairy juggle a budding romance with a daring prison break before it all vanishes in a puff of smoke?

Cinderella Assassin is the first book in the charming Glass Slipper Adventure YA fantasy series. If you like spirited heroines, clever takes on classics, and unique blends of tech and wizardry, then you'll love Allie Burton's spellbinding story.

Buy Cinderella Assassin to dance into danger today!

"What a great story - super unique retelling! Characters were so dynamic and interesting. I loved it!" – Reviewer

Excerpt:

My stomach jiggled. "How will I ever get past the detectors at the palace with these magical items?"

The clutch, the dress, and my very own fairy blood would betray me.

"That's what the shoes are for." Gardenia, my fairy godmother, held out her hands and two glass-heeled shoes appeared.

The clear shoes sparkled in the light. Two-inch heels led to a slender sloping arch. A decorative green jewel topped off near the toes.

"I enjoy shoes as much as the next girl but how are high heels going to help?" I'd decided on the dress based on practicality. I couldn't run in high heels.

"These shoes are made with Elfin glass and they aren't only high heels." She pinched the gemstone and the heels lowered. The shoes became flats.

"The shoes will be acceptable at the ball, and when you go to find Arbor you can make them more comfortable."

I'd known this would be a dangerous quest. Getting past the sensors at the palace, searching for Arbor. If I got caught, I'd be arrested or worse. I might need to run, but Arbor was worth it. "Clever."

Gardenia's arched eyebrows asked what else would be expected. Wearing no make-up from what I could tell, she had a natural beauty. Rosy cheeks, pink lips, white-flawless skin smelling of flowers and cut grass. "The shoes also have deflection technology. Magic and majik."

"So, the SCUM won't detect I'm half-majik." Nodding, I let confidence seep into my skin. This deal was definitely in my favor.

"Or the magical items in your possession." She snapped her fingers and another item appeared in the palm of her hand.

A knife.

I flinched and my skin prickled.

"This is the Dagger of Justice. It weighs the guilt of the intended target." She reached up toward my head. "You will wear it as a hair ornament."

The sharp steel point glinted. The ruby-encrusted handle reminded me of blood. Blood I might make flow.

"W-what do I need a dagger for?"

"To complete your end of the *Binding Promise*." Her pupils flashed with a winning gleam, yet her expression stayed deadly serious.

The words *Binding Promise* sizzled between us having a life of its own.

My muscles tensed and the hairs at the back of my neck stuck up. This wasn't like the bet we'd made earlier today. How bad could my end of the promise be if it didn't include fairy academy? But if it wasn't bad, why would I need a dagger? I should've asked before I'd agreed, except I hadn't been thinking because of my guilt about Arbor.

My throat tightened. "What do you want me to do with the dagger?"

Gardenia's lips lifted in a slight smile. "Assassinate Prince Zacharye."

A Note from Allie

I hope you enjoyed Destiny and Stone's adventure. As you can tell by the exciting epilogue, there are more A Glass Slipper Adventures to come. To get information about the rest of the series join my newsletter and receive a free book. You can join at www.allieburton.com/contact.html.

If you enjoyed SNOW WITCHING WHITE, please leave a rating or review at your place of purchase. Reviews help other readers find books they may love, and help authors gain traction and be able to write more books.

I love to hear from my readers! If you have any questions or comments, or just want to say "hi," please feel free to email me at allie@allieburton.com or connect with me on www.twitter.com/@allie_burton and www.faceboo k.com/AllieBurtonAuthor and www.instagram.com/allieburtonauthor .

If you're interested in my other young adult series, below is additional information. Thanks for reading SNOW WITCHING WHITE!

Allie

ATLANTIS RIPTIDE

Atlantis Riptide

Lost Daughters of Atlantis Book 1

When a girl runs away from the circus...

For all her sixteen years, Pearl Poseidon has been a fish out of water. A freak on display for her adoptive parents' profit. Running away from her horrible life, she craves one thing—anonymity. But when she saves a small boy from drowning, she exposes herself and her mutant abilities to Chase, a budding investigative reporter.

Now, he has questions. And so do the police.

Once Pearl discovers her secret identity, she learns she's part of a larger war between battling Atlanteans. A battle that will decide who rules the oceans. A battle raging between evil and her true family. Will she find a way to use her powers in time to save a kingdom she never knew existed?

This is the start of a young adult fantasy action-adventure novel series. "Sweet summer young adult paranormal with death-defying underwater rescues." Reviewer

Other books in the Atlantis series: Atlantis Red Tide, Atlantis Rising Tide, Atlantis Tide Breaker, Atlantis Dark Tides, Atlantis Twisting Tides, Atlantis Glacial Tides.

ALSO BY

<u>A Glass Slipper Adventure-Young Adult</u>

Cinderella Assassin

Cinderella Soldier

Cinderella Spy

Snow Wicked White

Snow Warrior White

Snow Witching White

<u>Lost Daughters of Atlantis Series-Young Adult</u>

Atlantis Riptide

Atlantis Red Tide

Atlantis Rising Tide

Atlantis Tide Breaker

Atlantis Dark Tides

Atlantis Twisting Tides

Atlantis Glacial Tides

<u>Warrior Academy Series-Young Adult</u>

Warrior's Destiny

Warrior's Chaos

Warrior's Prophecy

Warrior's Curse

<u>Castle Ridge Series-Contemporary Romance</u>

The Romance Dance

The Christmas Match

The Flirtation Game

The Playboy Switch

The Billionaire's Ploy

The Heartbreak Contract

Find all of Allie's books on her website https://www.allieburton.com

About Author

Allie Burton has always been a reader and writer. She wrote her first novel at the age of twelve when she was stranded at a hospital by a snowstorm. Receiving her first romance from her grandmother, she fell in love with the genre. As an adult, she read young adult books with her own teens and was excited to find something fresh and new. Now, she writes both.

Having so many jobs became great research material for the stories she writes. She has been everything from a bike police officer to a mascot escort to an advertising executive. She has lived on three continents and in four states and has studied art, fashion design, and marine biology.

Allie is a member of several writing organizations. She loves to ski, golf, and run. Currently, she lives in Colorado with her husband and two children.